Praise for

THE BOOKISH LIFE OF NINA HILL

"Move over on the settee, Jane Austen. You've met your modern-day match in Abbi Waxman. Bitingly funny, relatable, and intelligent, *The Bookish Life of Nina Hill* is a must for anyone who loves to read."

—Kristan Higgins, *New York Times* bestselling author of
Always the Last to Know

"Meet our bookish millennial heroine—a modern-day Elizabeth Bennet, if you will. . . . Waxman's wit and wry humor stand out."

—*The Washington Post*

"Abbi Waxman offers up a quirky, eccentric romance that will charm any bookworm. . . . For anyone who's ever wondered if their greatest romance might come between the pages of books they read, Waxman offers a heartwarming tribute to that possibility."

—*Entertainment Weekly*

"It's a shame *The Bookish Life of Nina Hill* only lasts 350 pages, because I wanted to be friends with Nina for far longer." —Refinery29

"I hope you're in the mood to be downright delighted, because that's the state you'll find yourself in after reading *The Bookish Life of Nina Hill*."

—PopSugar

"*The Bookish Life of Nina Hill* will put a smile on your face the entire time you're reading it. It's a light, fun summer read with a cast of colorful and lovable characters that you wish were real and that you had on your trivia team. This book is the perfect beach read or pick-me-up for a cloudy day." —Hypable

"[A] quirky, sweet story." —*Woman's World*

"In this love letter to book nerds, Waxman introduces the extraordinary introvert Nina Hill. . . . With witty dialogue and a running sarcastic inner monologue, Waxman brings Nina to vibrant life as she upends her introverted routine and becomes part of the family. Fans of Jojo Moyes will love this."
　　　　　　　　　　　　　　　　　　　　　　　　　—*Publishers Weekly*

"Waxman has created a thoroughly engaging character in this bookish, contemplative, set-in-her-ways woman. Be prepared to chuckle."
　　　　　　　　　　　　　　　　　　　　　　　　　　—*Kirkus Reviews*

"Book nerds will feel strong kinship with the engaging, introverted Nina Hill, who works in a bookstore, plays pub trivia, and loves office supplies. . . . Readers will be captivated by Nina's droll sense of humor."
　　　　　　　　　　　　　　　　　　　　　—*Booklist* (starred review)

"Charming and relatable for any introvert who would rather pass time with fictional characters than people, but will rise to the occasion with the right support."
　　　　　　　　　　　　　　　　　　　　　　　　　—BookTrib

"Book lovers will absolutely relate to the central character in Abbi Waxman's third novel."
　　　　　　　　　　　　　　　　　　　—*O, The Oprah Magazine*

"If you relate to staying in and JOMO (joy of missing out), you'll relate to Nina."
　　　　　　　　　　　　　　　　　　　　　　　　　—Betches

"Fast, light, and fun."
　　　　　　　　　　　　　　　　　　　—Modern Mrs. Darcy

I WAS TOLD IT WOULD GET EASIER

Abbi Waxman

Berkley
New York

BERKLEY
An imprint of Penguin Random House LLC
penguinrandomhouse.com

Copyright © 2020 by Dorset Square, LLC
Readers Guide copyright © 2020 by Dorset Square, LLC
Penguin Random House supports copyright. Copyright fuels creativity, encourages diverse voices,
promotes free speech, and creates a vibrant culture. Thank you for buying an authorized edition of this
book and for complying with copyright laws by not reproducing, scanning, or distributing any part of it
in any form without permission. You are supporting writers and allowing Penguin Random House
to continue to publish books for every reader.

BERKLEY and the BERKLEY & B colophon are registered trademarks of
Penguin Random House LLC.

Library of Congress Cataloging-in-Publication Data

Names: Waxman, Abbi, author.
Title: I was told it would get easier / Abbi Waxman.
Description: First edition. | New York: Berkley, 2020.
Identifiers: LCCN 2019056858 | ISBN 9780451491893 (trade paperback) | ISBN 9780451491909 (ebook)
Subjects: LCSH: Domestic fiction. | GSAFD: Humorous fiction. | Road fiction.
Classification: LCC PS3623.A8936 I23 2020 | DDC 813/.6—dc23
LC record available at https://lccn.loc.gov/2019056858

First Edition: June 2020

Printed in the United States of America
1   3   5   7   9   10   8   6   4   2

Cover art and design by Vikki Chu
Book design by Alison Cnockaert
Map by Julia Waxman

This novel is dedicated to the memory of the wise, warm, and wonderful John Melissinos, and to his wife, Candice, and daughters, Chesney and Logan. I love you all very much and always will.

All journeys have secret destinations of which the traveler is unaware.

—Martin Buber

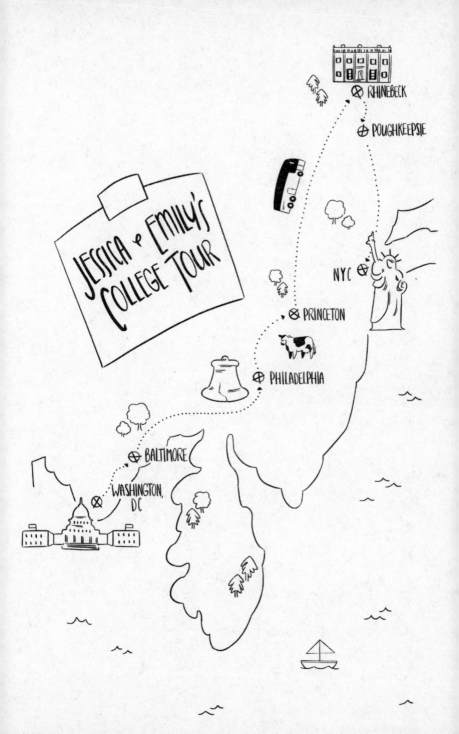

1

JESSICA BURNSTEIN, 45, FULL OF OPTIMISM

I left the house this morning, determined to take the day by the horns and throw it over my shoulder like a scarf, if necessary. I'd had two cups of coffee, I'd remembered to floss, and I was going to tell my boss the crap with Valentina simply wasn't going to fly anymore.

Forty minutes later, because this is Los Angeles and it takes forty minutes to go anywhere, at any time, I walked into the office slightly less full of beans and with "TiK ToK" by Kesha stuck in my head. I wasn't entirely sure how I felt about that, but it was the last thing playing when I turned off the car. *The party don't start till I walk in . . .* If only I had half her confidence.

I could hear John before I could see him, which was par for the course. Classic iron hand in the velvet glove, my boss, and if occasionally the gloves are fingerless and the fingers a little bit stabby, so much the better. Southern to the core, with all the civility and elegance that implies, but with a Yankee carpetbagger's eye for profitable misery. Our law firm doesn't openly chase ambulances, but John does love a tearful plaintiff. He can smell salt water before it steps off the elevator.

I spotted his head over a carpeted cubicle wall. It was angled in such a way that I knew he was with a client. Maybe even a potential client; there was an especially unguent quality to the way his hair fell over his forehead, his eyes hooded with concern. He's handsome, in the way any large predator is handsome—best appreciated from a safe distance. Up close the extra rows of teeth tend to be a distraction.

As if feeling my disapproval, John looked up and spotted me.

"Ah, Jessica!" he said as if his whole pitch had been waiting for this moment. "You must meet our newest client."

As there were nearly half a dozen legal assistants in cubicles between the two of us, we both charted an intersecting course and met up—as if by magic—by the impressive double doors to the office suite.

"Mrs. Falconer, this is Jessica Burnstein, a partner and one of our most brilliant attorneys."

The woman, who was older than I had suspected from John's level of intensity, gazed tremulously up at me. "Will she be on my case?"

"No," said John firmly. "I will be handling your case myself."

Older *and* richer, then.

The lady and I shook hands, and I applied the carefully calibrated smile lawyers use when they're meeting someone who has probably been wronged in some way but whose opportunity for vengeance/justice has arrived. The smile says, *You're fine now, but I'm sorry for your loss/accident/partial dismemberment/inability to compete interna-*

tionally in your chosen sport. After nearly twenty years of practice, it comes pretty easily.

John ushered Mrs. Falconer to the elevators, and I headed to my office. As I passed Laurel, my assistant, I told her to ask Valentina to come and see me.

Valentina is younger than me, hungrier than me, and after my job. I'm her mentor, so that's fine with me. It's been eight or nine years since I took her under my wing; she's ready to leave the nest, and I'm ready to make room. However, John was using Valentina's future as a stick to prod me with, and I was tired of it.

Valentina came in and shut the door behind her. She slinked— there is no other word, unless it's *slunk*—across the carpet and flowed into a chair. It's not her fault she's a partial liquid; she was born that way. Natural beauty is no more of an achievement than deformity is a punishment—it just is. Valentina is incredibly smart, and one of the hardest-working lawyers I've ever met. In a business where appearance contributes to success, she makes sure the first impression of beauty is quickly overwhelmed by the second and more lasting impression of competence. Beauty always fades, but it lasts so much longer if you lay a thick layer of intelligence and integrity underneath it.

"Good morning, Jess," said Valentina. "How goes it?"

"It goes," I replied evenly. "I have a feeling John is going to talk to me today about making you a partner."

"Excellent."

"Yes, except I think he's going to be a sneaky bugger about it."

Her delicately arched eyebrows rose a little. "In what way?"

I shrugged. "In some way I haven't anticipated yet, because he likes to keep me on my toes. Has he said anything to you?"

She shook her head. "Nope. Not a word."

I looked at her. Was it possible she was lying? A momentary flicker of doubt . . . but she saw it in my eyes and leaned forward.

"Jessica, he's not the only one with a plan, remember? Don't underestimate me. I want to make partner, and I want you to be head of litigation so I can slipstream you all the way to the Supreme Court." She sat back. "A wise woman once pointed out to me that men have dominated the legal profession for decades and used their collective power to improve things for other men, both inside and outside of the law. It's our turn now."

"Who told you that? Me?"

"No, my grandmother."

"The one that's a judge?"

"No, the one that's a hairdresser."

"Right." I paused. "So . . . you're ready?"

"I'm ready, and so are you. Go on your trip and don't let him ruin it by coming along inside your head."

"That's a horrible thought."

She stood up, again appearing to defy the laws of physics. "You're welcome." She turned and walked to the door, pausing once more. "Plus, if you can handle a sixteen-year-old girl, you can handle a fifty-five-year-old guy."

"You would think."

She left, and I swung my chair around and gazed out the window. Across the canyons of downtown Los Angeles was a skyscraper that featured a glass slide on the outside of the seventieth floor. My daughter Emily and I had gone down it once, and I'd been much less scared than I'd expected. The thought of the lawsuit that would arise from dropping a tourist a thousand feet onto a busy stretch of downtown LA told me they'd probably made the slide strong enough to drive a truck down. Emily had stopped halfway down the slide to examine the construction and post pictures to Instagram, and afterwards we'd had one of the few conversations in recent memory that hadn't devolved into an argument about her future. I thought about our upcoming trip to visit colleges, and wondered if we could work something life-threatening into the itinerary every day in order to maintain the peace.

Laurel buzzed me. "Jessica, John wants to see you in his office when you have a minute."

"Alright, let him know I'm on my way."

But I waited ten minutes, because, you know, power move.

John was sharpening his scythe as I came in—wait, did I say *scythe*? I meant *pencil*.

"Ah, Jessica."

I wondered if he always said *ah* before he said my name, and I'd somehow failed to notice it. Maybe he thought my name was Ahjessica?

"John," I replied, proving that we were at least each talking to the right person. I started to sit down, whereupon he told me to take a seat, as if I'd been waiting for permission. That BS might work on a junior lawyer, but I'd been at this game too long.

"Already taken, thanks," I said. "How can I help you?" By phrasing it that way, I put him on the back foot, because he'd actually requested my presence, not my help. Pay attention, folks, it's a master class in here.

"You can't," he laughed, which is why he's the boss. "But I wanted to talk to you about Valentina."

I nodded and waited.

He leaned forward. "Look, you and I are similar people. We know how things work, right?"

Forced teaming. Google it. It's what manipulators do to make you feel a connection they can then exploit. I've read *The Gift of Fear* (which everyone should), so I said, "I don't think we're all that similar, John, and you wanted to talk about Valentina?"

Sidenote: I actually like John, despite the fact he often behaves like a jerk. He's an incredible lawyer who thinks better on his feet than most people do sitting down, and he's taught me everything I know. But I trust him only because I know how he lies.

John smiled. "I like Valentina, she's extremely capable."

"Yes."

He regarded me narrowly for a moment, then relaxed his face. It's his way of miming, *I'm not sure I understand you . . . Wait, now I get it because, damn, I'm smart*. He must practice in a mirror. "I know you think she should make partner this year."

"I thought she should have made partner last year." My face betrayed nothing, which I'm long past practicing in a mirror.

"But there is the issue of the board."

My breathing was steady. "In what sense?"

"Well, you know . . ."

"No, I don't."

"The board wouldn't want it to look like we were, you know, reacting to current events."

"Which current events, John? Please speak plainly." (Again, side-note: When buying time, phrase your delaying tactics as mild criticism—*I'm sorry, that didn't make sense/Please restate that, it wasn't clear/Your language is garbled, please remove that scorpion from your mouth.* It makes your conversational opponent scramble a little. Side sidenote: If your questioner has a scorpion in her mouth, deal with that first.)

He appeared to be mildly uncomfortable, which is one of his tells. John has never been mildly uncomfortable in his life; he was about to lay on a thick layer of BS.

"Well, the #MeToo thing, the harassment thing . . ."

I raised my eyebrows, waiting for him to continue.

"The board is concerned if we promote too many women at once, it will look like we're reacting to social pressure."

"Social pressure to promote capable people?"

"Women."

"Which other women are up for partnership?"

"Janet Manolo. Just Janet."

I took a breath. "And the board thinks making two women partner in one year is too many? Last year you made three men partners and no one wondered about that." I suddenly thought of the RBG quote about enough women on the Supreme Court being nine.

He capped and uncapped a pen. "Well, there was the thing with Jackson . . ."

Jackson was a dirty word around the office. He was a partner who'd been fired earlier that year, much to the satisfaction of every other lawyer in Los Angeles, most of whom had hated him for years. I frowned at John and angled my head slightly. "The 'thing' being the way he offered an assistant a gram of coke to show him her breasts? Are we calling that a 'thing' now? It was illegal, it was repulsive, and it was why he got fired and sued in civil court. What on earth does Jackson's inability to do his job have anything to do with Valentina's brilliance at hers?"

"It's not me, Jessica, it's the board. They're worried about how it looks."

I frowned, and bounced my foot. "John, you're forgetting who you're talking to. Please spell out what you mean, because I'm going out of town in two days and I don't have time to parse and reparse what you're saying, looking for clues."

John pretended to consider whether to speak plainly or not, when obviously he'd been working up to this moment the whole time. He'd manipulated me into asking him to do it so he could make me responsible. I think I'm pretty good at directing testimony, but John really is a master.

He turned up his palms. "Look, if you really want me to spell it out . . ."

I said nothing. Fool me once.

John hesitated, which he only ever does on purpose. "Valentina is a woman. She's . . ." Again, pretending to be uncomfortable, John continued, "A very attractive woman. The board is concerned if we promote her to partner this year, this soon after the Jackson thing . . ."

I uncrossed my legs and leaned forward. "Stop calling it a 'thing,' John, like it was an adorable eccentricity. He didn't wear cowboy hats in the office or collect Disney miniatures. He broke several laws, state and federal, traumatized another human being, and cost the firm millions of dollars and untold reputation points."

"Precisely. The board is worried if we make Valentina a partner this year, people will think it's payback for Jackson. That he did something to her, and we're making her a partner to keep her quiet."

I considered this for a moment. It was perfect in its evil, sexist subtlety.

"Let me see if I understand you, John."

He raised his eyebrows at me, and for a split second I saw that he was actually unsure what I was going to say. He doesn't like to be in that position. I put him out of his misery.

"You're saying that a brilliant lawyer, a woman who has worked for the firm for over a decade, brought in major clients and extensive revenue, who regularly speaks on international panels and authors articles in journals, in two languages—"

"I know Valentina is qualified, Jessica."

I raised my hand. "You're saying this person cannot be promoted as she deserves because another lawyer—a male lawyer—behaved like a total pig."

"Well, people might assume . . ."

"That she only got promoted because she had dirt on Jackson? The implication being that he assaulted her, too, but rather than cold-cock him into next week and have him arrested, she would use it to further her own career?"

For the first time in my experience, John genuinely looked un-comfortable.

"You know how people talk, Jessica."

I shook my head. "No, John, I know how male lawyers talk, and how they assume other people think. Valentina deserves to make partner because of her work. That should be the only criterion, John, and would be the only criterion if she were a man." I was steamed. "Let me be very clear. If you don't promote Valentina—and Janet, who also deserves it—I will resign in protest."

John looked at me calmly, and I suddenly wondered if he'd wanted to force me into this position all along. "If you do that, people will think it's because of Jackson, too."

I took a breath. "John, not everyone looks at the actions of women and assumes that somewhere a man is responsible for them. That's you."

He sat back in his chair and steepled his fingers. "My hands are tied on this one, Jess. The board . . ."

"That's bullshit, John"—I pointed at him—"and you know it."

"I promise I'll make them partners next year. We're pretty partner-heavy right now anyway."

I looked at him. "So you won't be making any partners this year, then?"

Long pause.

"Well, no, we'll be making Maier and Mako partners. They're excellent lawyers."

"And have penises."

"Irrelevant."

"How are their penises irrelevant but Valentina and Janet's ovaries are a total deal breaker?" My voice trembled, and I suddenly felt myself wanting to cry with anger, which is so not my favorite feeling.

I'd love to become enraged without getting emotional, but that's just not how I work. If I'm not emotional, I don't lose my temper. You see the problem? Unfortunately, as I said earlier, John can smell salt water a mile away.

He got up and came around the desk. "Jess, don't get all upset." He patted me on the shoulder, as if I were a horse. A short horse sitting in a chair, but it was that kind of reassuring touch he was going for.

"I'm not upset, John, I'm furious."

"Well, you look upset." He got up to go back to his chair. "Why don't you take the rest of the day off? We'll be telling Valentina and Janet the news later, and I know it would be hard for you to be here."

I swear to you I felt my tears getting sucked back into my tear ducts. "You're telling them last thing on a Friday? That's kind of a dick move."

He shrugged. "It's just business, Jess."

"No, John, it's blatant sexism and total bullshit."

"You're entitled to your opinion."

I stood up. "It's more than an opinion, it's the truth. You had Jackson working here for months after rumors started, and it was only when there were male witnesses that you started paying attention. Now you're literally not promoting someone because of their gender, *which is illegal*." I could feel my heart pounding.

John laughed, "What, you're going to sue me now? You're a partner, too, Jessica, you have a responsibility to the firm. And to yourself— your share of the corporate profits this year will pay for several years of college." He smiled at me and said, "Aren't you going on a college tour with Emma next week? Just wait till those tuition bills start rolling in, you'll soon stop worrying about anyone else's salary."

I stared at him, and while I hate to use a cliché, the blood was literally rushing in my ears. Tears were pricking my eyes again—traitors—but I knew what I wanted to say.

"John, it's not about salary. It's about equity."

"Jessica, their time will come. I promise."

"Their time is now, John, or I walk."

He shook his head at me. "Don't be silly, Jessica. Don't let your emotions get the better of you, you're too good for that."

"Are you going to make them partners?"

"No."

"Then I quit." I turned and walked to the door.

"Jessica, don't be so childish."

I paused and turned on my heel like a boss. "Why don't you go and say that to the board, John, then give me a call. I'm out next week, as you say, and I won't announce my resignation until I'm back. Fix it, John."

I opened the door. "And by the way, my daughter's name is Emily, not Emma." I walked out, closing the door behind me.

Fuck, fuck, fuckity fuck. Now what was I going to do?

I got into my car and did what women have done since the dawn of time: I called another woman. Presumably, an ancient woman had to actually run over to her friend's cave, but thanks to technology, our best friends are now carried around in our pockets, conveniently nestled close at hand.

Frances and I became friends when our kids were toddlers, meeting at a "mommy and me" music class that made overenthusiastic use of the cowbell. I'd been dutifully chiming along to "Baby Beluga" for the eighteenth time when I happened to catch Frances's eye across the circle, whereupon she'd swiftly mimed cutting her own throat, and the rest is history.

The phone rang a couple of times, and then she picked up. *"Frances's Home for Unloved Mothers. We appreciate you when no one else does."*

"I just threatened to quit my job."

"Empty threat or actual plan?" This is one of Frances's greatest strengths: She always hits the ground running. She could open her front door to find the entire neighborhood on fire and she'd simply turn around and fetch a bucket of water. She's got the filthiest mouth of anyone I've ever met, but she's rock solid.

"Unclear."

She sighed. "Tell me."

"John . . ."

"Your dickish boss John, or the John who works at the dry cleaner's?"

"My boss. Why would I have threatened the dry cleaner that I was going to quit?"

"Good point."

"Besides, the dry cleaner guy isn't John."

"He is."

"He's not. He's Johnson."

"He introduced himself to me as John."

"Probably because his parents named him after a slang term for 'penis,' but I know the truth."

"You're drifting, get back to the story."

"So, John wasn't going to promote Val and another woman to partner because of the scandal."

"The coke-for-tits scandal?"

I frowned. "Yes, has there been another scandal I missed?"

"I don't fucking know, I don't work there, do I?" There was a scuffling sound in the background. "Hang on, Jess, the puppy is stuck in the duvet cover." She put the phone down on something, and I could hear her untangling the dog. "I'm back."

"Yes, the coke-for-tits guy. How did the puppy get in the duvet?"

"Accidentally, obviously. You think he was helping me fold the laundry?"

"No, although that would be helpful."

"Right? Fuck catching Frisbees, folding sheets is definitely Best in Show."

"Anyway, John said the board didn't want to seem to be appeasing the '#MeToo-ers' . . . "

"Whoever they are . . ."

"Precisely, so I said if he didn't promote them, I would walk."

"And he said?"

"He said that would be foolish."

"And you said?"

"I repeated my threat and walked out."

There was a pause while she considered this. Then: "Do you think I was stupid to get a puppy?"

"A hundred percent, but the kids were very persuasive."

She sighed. "I think you did the right thing. He doesn't want to lose you, and if you end up leaving, you can take the other two women with you and start your own firm. It'll be fun, you can name it after yourselves and order new letterhead."

I sighed. "And I'm leaving day after tomorrow for the college tour."

She laughed. "There you go, that'll be a total freaking disaster and therefore a great distraction from the impending end of your career."

"Wow, that's super supportive."

"I scare because I care."

"Thanks."

"In other news, this morning Sasha told me I make her want to jump off a cliff."

"What prompted that?"

"I said her uniform skirt was too short."

"And that gave rise to suicidal ideation?"

"Teenagers. They're all about balance and reason."

"Good point." I pulled up in front of the house. "I'm home. Talk to you later."

"We never close," she said, and hung up.

My god, I'm grateful for the friendship of women. A strong female friendship is like a romance that kept its mystery and never beached itself on the shores of exhausted intimacy. It was the first six weeks of a new relationship, except, you know, forever. Friends listen carefully. They poke fun at each other, keep favorite cookies on hand, and can tell the difference between hormonal and genuinely pissed off. They're Team You when you're arguing with your partner, Team

Both of You against the children, and Team All of You against the world.

Plus, you love their children. Not like you love your own, but close. Sasha and Emily are only a few months apart in age and have been tight as ticks their entire lives. They take each other for granted, unlike their mothers.

Frances likes silver more than gold, won't eat eggplant, and thinks prostitution should be legalized. She knows I disagree with her about the eggplant and the jewelry but agree on the hookers. I knew she was The Friend for Me when one day she showed up at my door with toilet paper because she'd seen it written on the back of my hand and knew I hadn't made it to the store that day, and she had. Name me one husband who would do that. That's right. None.

2

EMILY BURNSTEIN, 16, STRESSED BEYOND BELIEF

This week cannot end soon enough.

I got off the bus and walked through the school gate. *Deep breath, Emily. Keep your head down and push through. Straight to the library through the side door, hide in European History till first bell, front of the class and eyes forward until lunch, back in the library, Comparative Religion this time, no one's ever there. Two classes after lunch, take the side gate and home by four. Out of town by lunch on Sunday and gone for a week. Plenty long enough for the dust to settle.*

Skidding between two classes, I had no option but to take the upstairs hallway, and—because God hates me—the principal, Mrs. Bandin, was coming out of her office. I had literally just crossed the point in the hallway where all other avenues of escape were closed— I would have walked into the janitor's closet if I could have—so I panicked internally and glided along like nothing was wrong.

She watched me come, smiled at me as I passed, and I'm pretty sure watched me the whole way down the corridor.

I swear to you . . . *she knows.*

Seven days with my mom, away from here—any other time it could feel like a punishment, but right now it's the perfect escape.

JESSICA

I walked into the house. It was quiet, unless you count the distant sound of a badly loaded plate gonging in the dishwasher. Emily was still at school, where she'd much rather be than at home with me, and the live-in nanny, Anna, lives a daytime life I know nothing about. I used to think I couldn't wait for the house to be all mine again, when every surface wouldn't be covered with crusty baby plates or plastic dogs with impossibly long eyelashes or packs of Costco baby wipes. But of course, silence comes in many flavors.

Let me be clear: I love being a mom, and when Emily was little it was wonderful. She was a fat, round, good-humored baby, like sunshine dipped in butter. When she said her first word, and it was *Mom*, I felt like I won the lottery. Of course, the word soon became a jabbing spear in my side every time it was uttered, because it was uttered about forty thousand times a day.

"*Mom, why . . .*"

"*Mom, what . . .*"

"*Mom, who . . .*"

And of course, just *Mom* . . . said in a tone of voice or frequency of repetition that, were it weaponized in some formal way, would probably end all human conflict. One afternoon of solid, endless requests for things that are immediately thrown on the ground or for food that is "made wrong" or for toys that are "not right" would make anyone agree to anything. But you get the hang of it, and the soft hand resting on your arm while you read, the snuffly kisses in the middle of the night, and the running jump when you get home from work are sweet rewards.

Not to mention the development of new, albeit nontransferable skills: the ability to pause like a hare and hear the sound of crayons moving over wallpaper three rooms away. The mastery of pea balancing on a shallow plate so none of them roll into the string cheese (thereby rendering themselves inedible and possibly deadly). And, of course, changing diapers in complete darkness, without waking the baby, while tears of exhaustion drip from your chin. I nailed them all. It's the world's most wonderful and most terrible job, and if you do it well enough, you get fired.

After the toddler wars were fought and won, I moved into what was, for me, *Peak Kid*. Six to twelve. The golden years. Emily loved me, she listened to me, she thought I knew everything. She ate well, she slept well, she laughed at fart jokes, she told fart jokes . . . it was great. When she said *Mom* it was with love, or with a specific request that could usually be responded to with a sandwich, a tissue, or a firm *not in a million years*.

As a single parent I didn't really have the option of staying home, not that it would have worked for me, to be honest, and I'd returned to work once Emily was old enough. I had my mom to help at first, and then I moved to Los Angeles and hired a nanny. I worked long hours, I got promoted, I felt fulfilled personally and professionally, and I managed to balance motherhood and career flawlessly.

No, of course I'm joking. It was occasional sparkling moments of triumph dotted over long stretches of uncertainty and failure. There were days when I felt I'd managed, and days where I knew if I hadn't had the help of several other women, both at home and at work, I would have dug my own grave and climbed in.

Just when I thought I was finally getting a little better at the balancing act, when Emily was happy at school and work was going well, and I was senior enough to be able to leave at a reasonable hour to eat dinner with my kid, and have weekends free to spend with her, everything changed. She woke up a teenager, and all the skills I'd learned were useless, and all the time I'd fought to have with her was spent waiting for her to come home from hanging out with friends she'd much rather talk to than me.

If I said it was awesome, you'd know I was being sarcastic, right?

That's what I thought.

I went to the grocery store to pick up dinner, and to ponder whether or not to tell Emily I'd just potentially torpedoed her tuition money.

When I came back, there was a different quality to the silence.

"Em?"

Still nothing, but I noticed her sneakers by the door. She was home, presumably lurking in her dank, bone-strewn lair upstairs. Hopefully packing for the trip.

If my life were a Choose Your Own Adventure book, I'd have two options at this point. One, walk into the kitchen and not check on Emily. Have a cup of coffee and unload the dishwasher. Stare into the middle distance and adjust my underwire. Or two, go upstairs and speak directly to my daughter, because she's probably got headphones in and can't hear me calling. That would lead to another fork in the road: She could nod pleasantly, we might exchange a smile, maybe even a hug, and she'd reassure me her packing was all done. Or—and this had a high probability—she'd frown at me as I appeared in her doorway, tug out a single earbud, raise her eyebrows at me, and say, *What?* in a tone of voice that implied I was interrupting her solving the problem of clean, limitless energy. I'd feel a tiny pang of pain, tempered with irritation at being talked to like that, and ask her about the packing. She'd shrug and say, *Of course*, as if being unprepared is something alien to her, and implying my lack of trust is hobbling her ability to grow as an individual. Then, two days into the trip, we'd discover she'd forgotten to pack even a single pair of socks and the rest of the week would be spent with *I told you so* hanging over us like an unacknowledged fart.

My mother didn't raise no fool. I walked into the kitchen and turned on the kettle.

EMILY

I checked my list again: seven days of underwear, extra shoes, soap, socks, and sanitary protection . . . check, check, check. Dude, I am so on it.

I paused. Was that Mom? Silence, then distant noises from the kitchen. Guess she didn't even want to say hello to me. Charming.

I checked my list a second time and threw in another pair of socks. My mom might not have been interested in my life, but she definitely taught me how to pack.

Sunday

Los Angeles to Washington

Fly to Washington, DC

Check into hotel

3

JESSICA

Emily, who up until that moment had been silently gazing at her phone as if frozen to a stump, suddenly said, "Mother, the Lyft is here and he's only going to wait three minutes." She shifted her feet in my old Converse high-tops. I love that she wears them, not that I could ever tell her that. I have to pretend to be vaguely irritated, to make the theft more fun.

"Why?" I was hunting through my purse for something, but I've now completely forgotten what. I'm telling you, I've got a brain tumor the size of a clementine.

"Because that's what it says on the app." The ancient Greeks had the oracle of Delphi; we have an app for that.

I gave up my hunt for whatever it was. "Well, go start putting your bags in the trunk, then, and see what the actual driver says. He's probably more flexible than an app."

Emily huffed her way to the door and slammed it. Door slamming—if I may digress for a moment—is a matter of art for my daughter. If Emily wants to express herself, she's adept at threading the needle between firm closing and actual slamming. Then, when I yell, "Stop slamming the goddamned door," she achieves plausible deniability with an injured tone. Of course, if she's leaving the house, she has more options. Emily would probably say she shut the door firmly. I felt a slam. Maybe the slam is in the ear of the beholder. Or be-hearer?

Anna, our live-in nanny, was standing there, patiently waiting for this part to be over so she could go back to bed. I'd told her she didn't need to get up, but she thinks I'm incompetent (probably based on extensive observation). We don't really need a full-time nanny anymore, but I frequently have to work late, or on the weekends, and get little to no warning. Part of me knows Emily, at sixteen, is totally capable of taking care of herself, but a bigger part of me thinks it's a good idea not to leave her alone too much. If you think about it, it's like having an old-fashioned wife waiting for me at home, fallbacking my career so I can excel in that arena, and plastering over any cracks my kid might fall into. I'm not 100 percent confident it's working all that well, but Anna has been part of our family for a long time, and you can't fire family.

"Good luck," Anna said. I'm sure she did wish me luck, but I had a sneaking suspicion she also enjoyed the prospect of me spending seven days alone with my teenage daughter. Anna is from El Salvador, raised her own three kids, and then moved to the States to help Americans raise theirs. She's an intelligent woman, and I'm confident she appreciates the irony of my situation: I work incredibly hard to make enough money to pay her to do the work that would prevent me from working hard enough to make the money I need to pay her to do the work . . . and so the circle of capitalism goes. Hakuna that matata, ladies.

Anyway, Anna and I get along pretty well, although we're basically shift workers sharing the same job. Both of us know the job's coming to an end, because this trip is about looking at colleges, and then, in another year, Emily will leave home and we'll both be unemployed. The difference being Anna was going to retire to El Salvador and play with her grandkids, living in a house her kids had built for her in the village they'd all grown up in, and I was going to be alone, rattling around in my pod like the world's biggest loser pea. I'd go to work, forget everything except what was in front of me, and then come home and call Emily's name before remembering she wasn't there anymore.

"Mother!!" Emily was shouting from outside. Two full syllables, both exasperated. I won't miss that part.

I wheeled my bag to the street. "Aren't you going to say goodbye to Anna?" I swear to you my tone was neutral, but Emily frowned. You'd need a micrometer to measure her hair trigger these days. Maybe that was what I was hunting for in my bag.

"Of course!" she snapped. She ran to Anna, giving her the kind of full-on, 100 percent hug she hasn't given me in about three years. Anna looked at me over my daughter's head, and her eyes held apology tempered with a very light sprinkling of pride. We both know Emily loves me, we both know it's age-appropriate for her to separate hard from her mother, but I suspect Anna enjoys those moments when Emily is nicer to her than she is to me.

I hadn't told Emily about quitting yet. I didn't want to freak her out, and I was kind of hoping my power move would work and John would sort things out before I got back. Besides, this trip is about reconnection and bonding. Em and I are going to be alone together, we're going to talk, we're going to laugh and cry, we're going to salvage the shreds of our relationship and weave them into a beautiful blanket that will keep us warm for the rest of our lives. Something like that, anyway. Some thought that can be typeset against a sunrise and shared online.

No pressure.

EMILY

This trip is going to be a total yawn, but I am so glad to dip I wouldn't care if we were silently touring monasteries in rural Wisconsin. (No, I'm not sure why that popped into my head. I think I saw something online about millennial nuns, don't judge me.) When Mom originally suggested this organized college tour, I kind of raised my eyebrows, especially once I realized it was a load of kids and parents, and therefore enforced socialization, which I hate. But nothing said I had to talk to anyone, right? Besides, at the rate Mom is going, we're going to miss the plane anyway.

My mother is one of the smartest people I've ever met. She's a lawyer and can see a hole in an argument from a mile away, which makes life a little challenging. However, for some reason, it takes her approximately forever to get out of the house if she's not going to work. On a workday she clacks around in the kitchen, her wireless earbuds and vacant expression the only clues to the conference call she's attending, grabbing coffee and unsalted almonds and taking whatever weird supplement she's trying out that week. She always wears her hair in one of those low knot things at the back of her head, like a ballerina, but I think she's prettier when she wears it down. If I walk in she points at her ears so I won't speak to her, and then—if I'm lucky—she'll throw me a smile before leaving, clicking the car keys in her pocket. On a non-workday, like today, she only has to put her phone in her purse and walk out, but she's always forgetting something, or going back to turn something off, whatever. Let it burn, I say.

Generally, she's been a lot spacier lately. I'm not going to drop the *M* word, but in Health we learned it gives you brain fog to go with your dry vagina and night sweats. I'll be brutal; they didn't really sell it, though it was still better than that childbirth video. It's amazing there's anything left of your vagina to dry out.

My phone pinged and I told Mom the Lyft guy was waiting. She snapped at me to stall the driver, no pressure, that's fine. Then when she finally dragged her butt outside, she sarcastically reminded me to hug Anna as if I'd forgotten. Which I had, not the point. Anna is awesome; she takes care of me and leaves me alone, which is the very definition of good parenting, in my opinion. She doesn't expect all that much from me, unlike my mother. I'm doing my best here, but for Mom that's never going to be enough.

The Lyft driver was on top of his game. No four-star ratings to lower his average, no sir. He had water bottles. He had hand sanitizer. He had cool jazz playing, and the car smelled of coconut and mango. A mini-vacation on the way to vacation.

I asked my mom if we were sitting together on the plane, but she didn't know. I'm not scared of flying, but I don't love it, and Mom said the flight was over five hours long and longer on the way back. Kill me now.

I love my mom, don't misunderstand me, she's just a bit up in my beak. She thinks about me too much, it's creepy. My friends think she's cool, but that's because she's not going to remind them to clean their room or ask about their homework. She waits till they're gone and then leans in my doorway, like she's, you know, dropping by, and asks forty thousand questions. If she cares so much about my homework, she should do it herself.

JESSICA

"Mom?"

I smiled at Emily. "Yes?"

"Are we sitting together on the plane?"

"Actually, no. I have to fix it at the airport." When I'd checked us in the night before, I'd seen the mistake but hadn't been able to fix it online. Emily shook her head.

"It's fine." She paused. "We don't have to, I just wondered." In her lap her hands made a half gesture that disowned interest in the outcome.

"Okay," I said, letting it go, which is my latest parenting strategy. Apparently, I have a tendency to overanalyze everything and then dare to ask follow-up questions, and she gets pissy and I get pissy and we're off. We're only ever three sentences away from a fight.

My sister, Lizzy, had gently pointed out this habit, and after wasting forty minutes defending myself, I accepted that anxiety about

Emily was making me treat her like an unfriendly witness. But not on this trip, baby. On this trip I was going to take some sage advice and talk to my daughter as if she were a visiting cousin from another state.

"How long is the flight?" asked Emily.

"Around five hours, give or take."

"That's nuts, it's quicker than driving to San Francisco."

I bit down on the explanation of time as a relationship between speed and distance. This was something else Lizzy told me not to do.

"You're mom-splaining," she'd said carefully. "It makes Emily feel like a child and she doesn't want to feel that way. It's better intentioned than mansplaining, but equally as irritating." Lizzy is a completely disorganized part-time teacher and mom of three whose husband is barely contributing enough money as an actor to keep them in ramen noodles, and who is inexplicably happier than I am. Her kids are all at Peak Kid age, so she doesn't know about teenagers yet.

So I said nothing. Both then, to Lizzy, and now, to Emily.

EMILY

In eighth grade I did a project on Los Angeles International Airport for Social Studies. I had to read about the history of air travel, traffic patterns, architects; it was like 10 percent of the grade. I was a total suck-up. I worked on that thing for *weeks*. I made one of those tri-fold boards and a freaking diorama with little bushes my mom found somewhere, and tiny cars and planes. I really got into model making

31

and origami and that kind of thing, and I got an A, not to flex or anything. However, the only fact I remember is that LAX gets over eighty-four million passengers a year, and as we came up on the terminal, it looked like every one of them had decided to travel today. The driver squeaked past two buses and defied the laws of physics to fit into a space much smaller than the car. Five-star review for you, sir.

I followed my mom into the terminal. She knew where she was going, because she always does. She's very certain, my mom. I snapped a pic of the terminal while we were checking the bags, then captioned it *Gateway to hell* and posted it. The terminal smelled of coffee and printer ink, like always. I got that feeling I get in airports: DEFCON 3, slightly on edge, ready for delay or confusion. Then I noticed a cute guy walking towards the security line, and I start moving in that direction, one of my rolly wheels clicking loudly. Awkward.

JESSICA

Emily was ahead of me at the scanners, and I watched as she easily removed her shoes, dropped her laptop and phone in one tray and her jacket in another, and turned to go through the metal detectors. This is what air travel is to her; this is what it's always been.

I remember September 11 clearly; we all do. I'd been filled with joy, walking my dog in Riverside Park and enjoying what was, even for New York in early fall, an exceptionally beautiful morning. I was a young lawyer, working hard but having a lot of fun, and my life rolled ahead of me like the yellow-brick road. Of course, that had been 8:00 a.m., and by 9:15, things would never be the same again, but for Emily, who at that point was an unsuspected and rapidly dividing clump of cells in my body, this level of airport scrutiny and anxiety was normal. If they'd waved her through with a smile and let her run up to the gate, she'd refuse to get on the plane.

Somehow an entire family had gotten ahead of me at the line for trays, so I was able to watch Emily go through the metal detector and wait for her stuff. A cute guy smiled at her, but I don't think she even noticed. She's very pretty, but in a way that apparently isn't fashionable right now: She has her own eyebrows, her own hair color, her own cheekbones and freckles, and in general she's more Hepburn than Kardashian. It's all very well that I know Audrey's a better choice than Kim (no offense, Kim). Emily needs to know it, and it doesn't seem like she does.

When I got to the gate, I headed to the desk to try to change our seats. I'd thought Emily was right behind me, but when I looked around, she was nowhere to be seen. I remembered she'd muttered something about Starbucks. The check-in agent didn't look thrilled to see me, but then again, I was probably either the first of many or the last of many, and I would pace myself, too.

"Yes, hi," I said, with what I hoped was the right blend of friendliness and efficiency. "I was wondering if it was possible to change seats? My daughter and I aren't sitting together, not really sure why, my assistant made the reservation"—*assistants, seriously, what can you do?*—"and we'd really like to be together on the flight . . ." I trailed off and showed the agent the little square code thing on my phone screen.

The agent, who looked like she didn't care if a walrus made the reservation, scanned the phone and gazed at her invisible screen.

"Oh, I'm sorry, we're fully booked. Your best bet is to wait until you're on the flight and ask the attendant if he or she can help you swap with someone."

"Has everyone checked in?"

"No, not yet."

"So there may be empty seats anyway?"

The woman looked at me and then at something to my left.

"We're not together?" It was Emily, who had arrived holding an enormous cup colored pink and blue in stripes. Honestly, does she know nothing about glycemic load or bladder capacity? I'd be willing to bet she'd spend longer photographing that than she would drinking it.

"No," I said, hoping she'd back me up and guilt the gate agent into pulling strings.

"It's not a problem," she said instead, the little traitor. "It's not like we're never going to see each other again, we're going to be constantly together for seven days." She smiled at the gate agent and added, "It's probably a good thing."

Instead of being cool, I said, "Don't you want to sit with me?" and even I could hear the telltale inflection of hurt feelings.

Emily couldn't, apparently, because she shrugged. "It doesn't matter."

"Oh."

Emily started to turn away. "Mom, it's not a big deal, I'll see you at the other end." Then she walked away and slid down a wall to sit on the carpet, putting in her earbuds and pulling out her phone. Already sitting separately.

I turned back and saw the gate agent looking at me properly for the first time. *Fantastic, now she thinks I'm one of those mothers who helicopters even while on an actual airplane.*

Instead the woman handed me a fistful of drink vouchers, and said, "I have a teenager, it's delightful. Have a drink on me."

I smiled uncertainly, worried she was about to offer me some advice from her secure spot in the future of my life. Sometimes this advice is the best (*Oh, yes, my four-year-old did that all the time, you don't need to book a therapist, shampoo the rug*) and sometimes it's useless (*Oh, you should never bribe your kids with M&M's, they'll get addicted to sugar and die an early death*).

However, the woman merely lowered her voice and said, "Good luck. Have a nice trip!"

EMILY

I was waiting in line at Starbucks when my phone started blowing up. Texts from Ruby, Sienna, Francesca . . . "Call me."

"What's up?" I called Sienna first.

"Dude," she said, sounding stressed, which is so not her vibe. "Mrs. Bandin called Lucy's parents and now her dad is flipping out."

Lucy is a junior, but she's in a different friend group. "On a Sunday? What for? Why?"

"No one knows. Lucy's not saying. And I heard Bandin called Rosalie Sumner's parents, too. What the actual frick?" She paused. "You know those girls, right?"

I swallowed. "I'll call you back." I hung up and smiled at the

Starbucks woman, despite the fact that I felt like throwing up. "I'll have the Unicorn Frappuccino, please."

"What size?"

I was on autopilot. "Venti, please."

I called Sienna back, trying to keep it together. "Hey. Yeah, I know them, we do stats together."

"What do you think happened?"

"No idea. Did she call anyone else?"

"Ruby said she called Becca's mom." This was more serious. Becca was in an adjacent friend group. I knew Becca pretty well.

"Wow," I said, the sounds of the airport bending and stretching around me as I walked mechanically back to the gate. I could see my mom standing at the desk and headed towards her. *Don't say anything* . . .

"I gotta go, plane's leaving soon. Text me."

"Cool." Sienna hung up, and I reached the gate.

Mom was pissed that we weren't sitting together, but I was relieved. I needed time to think. I could only guess at what was going on, but my guess was pretty educated. I slid down the wall and sat there on the carpet, then distracted myself by getting a great pic of my drink superimposed on a plane so it looked like it had wings. I didn't actually drink very much of it, but the picture was sharp.

When we landed I had like three hundred snaps, forty-two texts, and even a Facebook message, which could only be my grandfather. I scanned the texts and took a deep breath. I put my phone away and waited to get off the plane.

This is the bit of flying I hate the most. The plane lands and even though everyone's flown before, half the passengers get to their feet and stand awkwardly waiting for the doors to open. It's like repeatedly pressing the elevator button, totally pointless. I remember when I was younger, my mom whispered to me, *People who punch elevator buttons over and over think they control the universe*, and I bet land-and-stand people are button punchers all the way. They freak me out; they're big and tall and standing between me and the door. Until this point we've all been civilized travelers, but now we're revealed to be several hundred people in a highly flammable metal tube.

I pretended my seatmate wasn't looming over me, holding his carry-on six inches above my actual head, and took a picture through the window of the plane. I captioned it, added a cute location tag, and sent it. *Here's where I am, people, in case you were wondering.* We're like spacewalking astronauts, re-tethering ourselves to the mother ship by phone. Nobody wants to be that guy floating away with the reflection of the moon in his visor, right? Or the lone wildebeest on the nature documentary, stupidly eating grass while a lion creeps up on it. Our phones keep us safe in the herd, although right now I'm trying to ignore the vibrating coming from inside my bag. My English teacher Mr. Libicki would say I'm overdoing the metaphors, but he still talks about Myspace, so, you know, consider the source.

JESSICA

When I turned off airplane mode, a whole series of texts came buzzing in. For a moment I felt anxious, then remembered my kid was sitting somewhere on the same plane and was therefore unlikely to have been in a car accident. One was from Valentina, one from Laurel my assistant, and four were from Frances. Despite Frances's many wonderful qualities, she is a terrible texter. She never sends one text if four are possible. She types, she hits send, she thinks of something else and sends that, and then she thinks of yet another thing and sends that. I'd asked her why she didn't simply wait to hit send until all her thinking was done, and she was genuinely surprised and said her brain didn't move on to the next thought until the first one had been sent. But as I've already noted, she makes up for it elsewhere.

"I've been thinking about your new law firm . . ." read the first text.

Then: "You can have those billboards you see all over LA, with a giant picture of you wearing a power suit in a dubious shade of blue . . .

"And it can say: Wronged? Make those bastards feel the Burn!

"Because your name is Burnstein, get it?"

I grinned, then realized I was the only one still sitting in my section of the plane and scrambled to my feet. I checked the seat-back pocket, because that's how I've lost several phones, then I spotted it hiding in my own hand. I need coffee.

Emily was waiting for me, more or less patiently, inside the gate. She was staring at her phone, of course, but looked up and smiled as I came off the Jetway.

"How was your flight?"

I smiled back and said, "It was fine, how was yours?" like two normal people greeting each other. This was going to be easy. I cannot believe I thought that; had I learned nothing?

"I watched movies, it was alright." She turned and headed off, slinging her backpack on her shoulder. "We have to get the bags, right?"

"Yeah." I followed her, slipping my phone in my purse. Emily was walking and texting at the same time, which always makes me wonder if humans will develop some kind of crown-of-the-head sonar, like dolphins or bats. Maybe she already has it, because I've never seen her run into anyone. Bit of a disappointment, I won't lie.

The hotel was a standard chain hotel, but they'd added a lot more eagle-themed decor than would normally be advised. By focusing on eagles and flags, they'd managed to emphasize their location at the heart of American government without appearing to take sides. There were also a lot of state flags decorating the walls of the lobby, and, as always, I felt jealous of Michigan. I mean, yes, California has a bear, and that's cool, but Michigan has a moose, an elk, an eagle, and what appears to be Sasquatch, at least in the version hanging in the lobby. There's a lot going on, for a state flag.

Up in the room, Emily immediately flipped open her laptop and connected to the Wi-Fi.

"There's an actual TV, you know," I said. "Maybe we could watch a movie?"

She looked up, surprised. "Wow, I haven't watched an actual TV in ages." She regarded the big box for a second, then shrugged and went back to watching the smaller screen in front of her. "I'm okay, thanks."

I frowned. "Okay you don't want to watch a movie, okay you don't want to watch TV, or okay something else?"

She frowned at me. "Uh . . . I don't feel like a movie. But go ahead."

"Won't that bother you?"

She waved her earbuds at me, then popped them in her ears.

I hesitated for a second, then said, "Don't you think it would be nice to do something together for once?"

She didn't hear me.

"Em? Emily?"

"What?" She pulled out a single earbud and glared at me. "Why do you talk to me when you can see I'm not listening?" The human voice is capable of many subtleties, but she wasn't employing any of them.

I shot back, "Why don't you listen when you can see I'm talking to you?"

She sat up a bit. "Alright, what is it?"

I sighed. "It doesn't matter."

"Clearly it does. What? Is it about the trip?"

"No, I was saying it might be nice to do something together."

She waved her hand around at the room. "We are doing something together. We're spending a week looking at colleges and stressing out about my lack of future. Isn't that enough?" She paused. "It sure is for me."

That hurt a bit. I knew I should let it go, but I don't know . . . I was tired, I had expectations I shouldn't have had, and I was hungry.

"Well, I'm sorry being around me is so exhausting." I knew as soon as the words were out that I had just put myself in the wrong, which is an incredibly galling realization. It's one thing to be irritated, it's another to express it, and it's a third to relinquish the high ground with your first salvo.

I know Emily so well I could literally read her thought process. A minute widening of the eyes—she wanted to fire back. A breath—she knew she shouldn't, because right now I was the one who owed an apology. And then her mouth opened and clearly her hormones had come crashing around the corner of her mind and told her to fire on all cylinders.

"It's not exhausting, being with you. It's . . . stressful." Her tone was calm. Then she stuck in the knife. "It's not like I get to do it all that much so, you know . . ."

Somewhere she has a list of my buttons, I swear. There's probably an app for it. "Well, you have me all to yourself for a week now."

"Do I?" She sounded scornful. "Did you leave your phone at home?" She didn't wait for an answer. "Did you even put a vacation bounce on your email?"

I said nothing, because I hadn't. This is the problem with being able to work from anywhere . . . you end up working from everywhere.

She regarded me coolly for another moment, then sighed and turned back to her screen, putting her earbuds back in so she didn't hear my sigh.

I went to take a shower. When I stepped in I felt like crying, but managed to wash that away with everything else.

When I came out of the bathroom, she was asleep. Or pretending to be asleep. It's a funny thing; at home she never goes to sleep before I do, but right now she was sacked out at 9:00 p.m. Which wasn't even 9:00 p.m. for us, seeing as we had just arrived from the other coast. At home she wouldn't even have started her homework.

But I climbed into bed and turned out my light, too. Two can play at that game.

Monday

Washington, DC

8:00 a.m.: Warm-up breakfast

10:00 a.m.: Georgetown University

12:00 p.m.: Lunch near the White House

2:00 p.m.: George Washington University

3:00–6:00 p.m.: Optional Ford's Theatre visit or tour of the Mall
(*included in your package*)

7:00 p.m.: Dinner and dancing at El Presidente—
wear comfortable shoes!
(*three-course meal included, drinks extra*)

Overnight in Washington

4

JESSICA

In the $2 billion industry that is college admissions consulting, Excelsior Educational Excursions—or E3, as they've recently rebranded themselves—is a pretty big player. They certainly rule the Los Angeles market and when parents say, about college tours, "Oh, we're E3-ing the whole thing," it's a quick way to identify themselves as the kind of parent I like to call Private Helicopter Parent. They aren't bad people, necessarily—I mean, here I am, doing it myself—but they enjoy ostentatiously subcontracting their parenting, whereas I'm mildly anxious about it. They love to drop phrases like *our Latin tutor, our tennis coach, our college admissions professional*. I would like to think it's because they're as freaked out as I am by the responsibility of successfully launching a brand-new boat into a perilous ocean, but I think it's because they're dicks who like spending money and showing off about it.

E3 offers a *highly personalized, custom tour itinerary*, and yet manages to book ten kids with accompanying parents on every tour. I guess they're all individual in exactly the same way. The woman in charge had set up a "meet and greet breakfast and information session" in a small conference room at the hotel. Our arrival was not auspicious.

"Crap," said Emily, pausing as soon as we stepped into the room. "It's Alice."

Alice Ackerman was a girl in her grade, and her mother was supposedly a friend of mine.

Damn it.

EMILY

I was severely non-stoked to see Alice Ackerman and her crazy mother. Usually my friend group knows everything about everyone all the time, so how did this actually useful information get missed? I wonder if they knew and didn't tell me. Great, now I'm anxious-er than ever. More anxious. Whatever.

Alice is the kind of girl we're all supposed to be, but I don't even want to *want* to be her, if you get me. Just seeing her gives me a level of cognitive dissonance my teenage prefrontal cortex can't even handle (AP Psychology, just saying). I get a jumping nerve in my eye and a pain in my butt. Here's the thing I do envy about Alice: She doesn't give a shit. She didn't go to middle school with any of us; she arrived on the first day of ninth grade and assumed control ten days later. Even seniors talk to her. Perhaps instead of middle school she'd gone to some kind of underground training facility, where alpha girls are hatched from pods. Her father is something important at a studio; she goes to a lot of premieres, and shops all the time. She got her license recently—I heard her parents hired a driving teacher who taught her two hours a day and took the written for her—and then received an adorable little electric car and it was, you know, perfect. The car has its own hashtag.

She and I were friends at the beginning. I guess she saw I was mildly popular and kind of funny (I'm not saying that, my friends say that), so she hung out with my friend group for a while. But after a few golden weeks of total focus, she shut down on me like an eclipse, and for the last two years she's left me alone, out here in the penumbra (see, I did pay attention in Physics).

But that's what she's like. She spins at the center of the high school universe and her gravity pulls people in, but she spins so fast that most of them get flung back into the outer rings. (Dude, I am killing this outer space metaphor; Mr. Libicki would be stoked.) Now she has a core group of ~~sycophants~~ friends she likes to tease, torment, and favor, plus a long tail of lesser kids who watch out for crumbs, like those little fish that follow sharks.

Of all the kids at school who could have been on this tour, she's the one. FML, right?

And her mother is a total freaking nightmare. My mom is never mean about other people, and she once said that Mrs. Ackerman was not a nice person. That's strong stuff, for Mom.

JESSICA

Daniella—*Call me Dani*—Ackerman is not the kind of mother I want to be, but I think she's the kind of mother I'm supposed to want to be. Back at the beginning of ninth grade, her kid and mine were friendly for a bit, so I invited her for coffee. It made me want to blow my brains out, not even joking, and I hang out with lawyers all day. She's one of those women who are on top of their own game, their daughter's game, the school's game, and anyone else's game that was available for topping. She knew where the school stood in relation to every other school in Los Angeles, she knew where the students matriculated, she knew what subjects her kid was going to take for the next four years and what her SAT and AP scores were going to be, more or less (this was years in advance, don't forget). She knew which extracurriculars Alice was going to take, what sports she was going to do—nothing too common, something useful at application time . . . javelin? Something where the college would have a team but not enough players.

As Dani had laid out her four-year plan for Alice, I stirred my coffee into coldness and tried not to burst into hysterical tears. Honestly, at that point I was pleased Em seemed happy at school and ate her lunch and did her homework before midnight. I had started thinking maybe I could work from home Friday afternoons so I could see a bit more of my kid (not that Emily is ever home on a Friday night, but this was before all that started), and hadn't realized I was supposed to be marshaling my forces for college already. Thank GOD the girls drifted apart so I hadn't ever had to hang out with Dani again. We smiled and cheek-kissed at school events and made empty promises to have coffee or lunch or take an exercise class together, but we both knew these were social-grooming promises and were never actually going to happen. Like I have time to take an exercise class.

But now here we were, trapped with a small group of people and a rapidly drying tray of pastries. It was too late to go back up to the room and disguise myself as a plant or something, and now Dani had spotted us.

"Oh, my goodness, is that Jessica Burnstein?" she said loudly. "Look, Alice, it's Emily!"

Alice looked up from her phone. "So it is." She returned to her phone and started working her thumbs. *At least her kid is as antisocial as mine. Teenagers are the great leveler.*

I sighed inwardly, plastered a smile on my face, and went over to hug Dani with every apparent enthusiasm. *FML, right?*

EMILY

Mom's handling this; she fakes it for a living. I've seen her get ready for big work events, all flying hair and cursing, hopping to put on a high heel, slippery straps that need tightening, *Can you do this necklace up for me, baby?* But then she sails out the door like a freaking movie star playing a high-powered lawyer, all glide and polish. She's two different people: Stressed-Out Mom and All-Powerful Lawyer. Nothing in between. Nothing she shows me, anyway.

I waved vaguely at Alice and then headed straight to the breakfast buffet. I was hungry, it was too freaking early in the morning, and if I didn't get my blood sugar up soon, I'd pass out. The biggest question I could handle right now was, jelly or cheese? My phone buzzed. It was a snap from Alice.

"Ten bucks my mother suggests we 'hang out' in the next thirty seconds." Alice still has my number, of course, and this is the thing with her: Her power lies in making you feel like the most amusing, important person in the room. She's also capable of being a total and utter bitch, of course, but she's a born politician: If she thinks you might be useful later, she'll only shoot to wound.

"I'll take that bet," I say.

"Oh my goodness, the girls should definitely hang out on this trip!" her mom said loudly. "And then we can escape and have some catching-up time!"

"See?" texted Alice. "Ten bucks."

"Double or nothing," I wrote. "My mom is about to lie and say she's been meaning to reach out."

"That's a great idea," my mom said. "I've been meaning to reach out, but I didn't realize you were going to be on this trip. We should have flown together!"

"Damn," texted Alice.

"We were in business class," Alice's mom said casually. "My husband flies so much for work we had miles for miles, if you know what I mean."

I could tell from Mom's face she was remembering why she didn't hang out with Alice's mom. Mom hates it when people show off. However, she's pretty good at politics herself, so she said, "How lovely," which is her way of saying, *You're an asshole.*

Then she looked at me and I pointed at the pastries, giving her an out. She got it and said, "I'm going to run and get something to eat, can I bring you anything?" And Alice's mom said she'd had a green smoothie after her workout, and my mom said, "That's fantastic," which is another phrase she uses when she lies. Then she turned and headed in my direction, and I hunted around for a muffin with lots of chocolate, because Mom might be annoying at times, but she's still my mom, and out in the world we're a team.

JESSICA

A young woman with the kind of complicated reverse fish-tail braid that I could probably learn to do on YouTube, if I had three hours to spare and fourteen extra fingers, stepped to the front of the room and smiled around brightly.

"Welcome, Los Angeles Tour Group," she said, with a surprising level of barely suppressed joy. "Please find a seat, and can I have everyone's attention?" She was maybe twenty-four, and I guessed this was her first job out of college, and she was determined to nail it. I examined her carefully made-up face, her bright eyes, her pantsuit and coordinated blouse and thought how proud her mother must be. That long blond hair must have been a delight to brush out and braid when this girl was ten, but one day she'd stopped letting her mother do it, and started bringing home Cs and uninspiring boyfriends, and her mother lay awake like I do. But it all worked out, and now this young woman gets up in the morning and brushes her teeth and combs her hair all on her own and sets out in the cold morning to do her work. I was suddenly filled with sympathy for her, as I am for all young people. It's a little bit hideous, that first part of adulthood.

The tour group stopped milling about and sat on the half-upholstered seats, which made exasperated puffing sounds as we sat down. I looked around and realized the whole room was essentially padded, with thick carpet and walls that appeared to have been covered with linen. Earth tones predominated. We could have been there to discuss literally anything, the room was so neutral: world peace, necrophilia, the splitting of the atom . . . I could faintly smell chlorine from the pool on the floor below, and the occasional distant sound that could have been playing or drowning, it was hard to tell. It was enough to distract me, like when a group of parents are sitting near a pool where kids are swimming and every so often your heads all turn at once to make sure the screaming is good screaming and not the kind of screaming that requires one of you to jump in fully clothed. Anyway, I wasn't feeling 100 percent relaxed, let's say that.

"I'm Cassidy," said the young woman, turning and writing her name on a large pad propped on an easel. She put a heart above the *i*, which I thought was a nice retro touch.

"I'm the coordinator for this tour, so remember my name and reach out to me for anything you need." She turned again and added her number to the board, and we all dutifully entered it into our phones, even though I knew I would forget to take it out once the tour was over and would occasionally go through my phone and wonder who the hell Cassidy was and why I had her number. I could feel Emily fidgeting next to me, presumably dying to be on her phone, and pulled some origami paper from my purse. She's a whiz at origami.

Cassidy beamed around and said, "Really, text me for anything. That's what I'm here for. You're all familiar with the itinerary, of course, but I'm going to go over some details and fill in some gaps." I decided Cassidy had probably had too much caffeine. "We're starting today at Georgetown." She began handing out large envelopes. "Here's your Georgetown packet. You'll receive a packet for each school, to help with your evaluation process." She smiled around again, and for a moment I imagined her up until 1:00 a.m. the night before, exhaustedly putting pieces of paper into envelopes until the sharp sting of paper cuts made tears roll down her photogenic young cheeks. I did the math: ten families on the trip, eleven schools, one hundred and ten individual packets. I opened my phone again and put *dauntless tour guide* next to her name. Never forget.

Cassidy took a breath. "There will be a twenty-minute presentation by the admissions department, then we'll break into two groups, parents and students, and tour the campus. That should take around forty minutes. Then we will reconvene for an early lunch and take the Metro to George Washington University. There we will have another twenty-minute presentation from their admissions folks, and another campus tour. After that you'll be free to explore DC as you wish or join either the Ford's Theatre tour or visit the Mall. Tonight we're all going for dinner and dancing at El Presidente!" She seemed thrilled at the prospect, which made one of us.

"Is the cost of dinner included in the tour?" asked a mom from the back of the room, while her son tried to disappear into the floor.

"Yes, it is." Cassidy nodded. "While each of you has your own goals for the trip, one of our goals is for you all to get to know each other, and hopefully continue to support each other through the application process."

I admired her enthusiasm, but she must realize that, unless we were already friends, we would barely speak to each other again. In fact, all of us would spend the tour evaluating everyone else's kids purely in terms of their competitive standing with our own children. This was the diplomatic meeting where individual countries agree on the terms of engagement and then go home and prepare to bomb the crap out of each other.

I'm sure Cassidy knows that. She must.

"And one note, before we move on: Please do not attempt to talk to the admissions people about your specific child. They are not going to remember anything, and it is their job to remain impartial and let the admissions process take its course. E3 has excellent access to the top schools, and we don't want to get a bad reputation." She took a deep breath. "Besides, you have to trust in the process . . . the schools work very hard to identify the right kids for their schools, and in the end everybody ends up where they're supposed to be. I truly believe that." She looked at us and—I'm not kidding—I think she teared up a little. I personally thought she was glossing over decades of institutional prejudice and societal privilege, but hey, I hadn't had enough coffee to argue.

Then, as if she hadn't just warned us not to attempt to subvert the course of true love as expressed through college admissions, Cassidy clapped her hands and told us to put our chairs in a circle.

EMILY

Listen, I'm in school, so I am a freaking expert on boredom, and this was at least an 8 on the scale. It was not a 9, because different kids and free pastries, but it was not a 7 because this chick was talking about crap I couldn't care less about. I could be asleep, and instead I was in this weird windowless place that smelled like a locker room and my hands were sticky. I was DYING to pull out my phone—several other kids were on theirs—but Mom would not go for that. She'll slap the phone right out of my hand if she catches me on it when someone else is talking. Mom had given me origami to do, thank god. I was going to fold a pistol and shoot myself.

I was hoping this trip would make me excited about going to college, but so far, bubkes. I wanted that November feeling, you know, when you suddenly remember the holidays are coming and your tummy gets all excited and it's like being seven again. Sienna and Ruby already know what schools they want to go to, what they want to study, what the entrance requirements are and how they're getting them. I don't even know what I want for lunch.

I wonder if putting a little heart above the *i* in my name would be cute or not. Maybe a star. Or maybe a dagger dripping blood because, honestly, kill me now. How much longer could this possibly go on?

The girl was still smiling, but then she said we need to put the chairs in a circle and go around and introduce ourselves. This was slightly less boring but infinitely more stressful. Fan. Tastic.

JESSICA

We moved our chairs into a circle. It was like an HR training on sexism in the workplace. I bet Cassidy has a communications degree.

"Alright then," said Cassidy, standing in the middle and turning to make sure her smile spackled us all evenly. "Let's go around the circle, and you guys can tell me who you are and one interesting fact about yourselves." She pointed at a random parent, across the circle from me. He was one of only two men in the group, and the better looking. He had sleepy green eyes, which was either sexy or indicative of sleepiness. Not that I was judging by appearances. The man frowned at her.

"Uh," he said, "what sort of fact?"

Cassidy made a charming shrugging gesture and said, "Whatever you think is interesting."

"What if there's nothing interesting?" The parent was clearly perplexed. He was wearing jeans and a hoodie, which is what I wished I were wearing. I was wearing the approved Mom uniform: nice slacks, a vaguely ethnic blouse, and a coordinating cardigan with at least 20 percent cashmere. I had the regulation small earrings, a wrist full of bangles, and a mildly interesting necklace in case someone needed a conversational gambit.

Cassidy was firm. "There must be. Or you can tell me where you went to college, if that's easier."

The parent made a face but nodded. "Uh, my name is Chris Berman, and this is my son, Will. I didn't go to college, so that was an unlucky backup choice for me."

Another pause, this time more awkward. His son sighed.

"My name is Will, and I would be the first in my family to go to college, so that will have to be my interesting fact." He was also wearing jeans and a hoodie, but his were cooler than his dad's. His eyes were less sleepy than his dad's, sharper. I felt Emily shift next to me, but when I looked over, she was just folding paper.

"That *is* interesting," said Cassidy overenthusiastically. "How exciting."

"I'm not there yet," said Will calmly. "Don't jinx me."

Cassidy laughed uncertainly and moved on. I could feel Emily looking at the boy, who was definitely her type, not that I would ever dare mention that to her. He was the kind of boy who looks like he prefers indie music to sports. She loves a tortured poet, my daughter, bless her inexperienced little heart.

Then it was my turn. I blanked for a moment and then pulled something at random from my dusty brain.

"Hi, my name is Jessica Burnstein, I went to Columbia, which is the last stop on this trip, I think. My interesting fact is that I nearly qualified for the Olympics in 1996. The Atlanta Games."

"Ooh," said Cassidy. "The one with the bomb! Which event?"

"Archery," I said, suddenly wondering if this had been a wise admission. I was sharing a non-fact, a thing that hadn't actually happened. I might as well have said I nearly got nominated for best original screenplay, but, you know, didn't (in that case it would have been because I'd never written a screenplay in my life). There were murmurings around the room as everyone made those noises you make when you're mildly impressed but have no idea what to do with the information you've been given. Sort of like a herd of wildebeests muttering about Tupperware. Embarrassed, I quickly added, "But I didn't make the team at the last minute, so, you know."

"Well, never mind," said Cassidy very sympathetically, which made me want to clarify I was totally over it, it hadn't blighted my life, it's not like I sat in the dark at night clutching a scotch in one hand and a quiver of arrows in the other, brooding. But it was too late, and now they all thought I was a brokenhearted Katniss Everdeen. I gazed at my lap and hoped Emily would come up with something distracting.

EMILY

Mom had just told everyone she failed to go to the Olympics, which wasn't weird *at all*, and then it was my turn. I had literally nothing to say, so I went with that.

"Uh, I'm Emily. I can't think of anything interesting . . ."

"I can think of something for you," said Alice, who was sitting a few people down. She smiled her snakiest smile. "She won the good penmanship award at school, three years in a row." She looked at the really hot boy, the one whose dad didn't go to college. "She has excellent fine motor skills." It's amazing how insulting that can sound.

"Uh . . . neat," he said, and I heard a hint of mockery in his voice. *Please let it be for Alice.*

I died. No, literally, my brain shut down and my body started degrading at the cellular level. Why was Alice exposing me in front of these strangers? What the hell did I do to her? And how did she know about the stupid penmanship thing? That happened before she was even at the school, which meant someone told her, which meant she was talking about me behind my back, which of course she was, but it still sucked. I looked at Cassidy, the girl running the thing, praying she would move on.

"Oh, you two know each other from school, of course! How lovely." She smiled patronizingly at me and said, "Penmanship is such a lost art." As this is because the need to write by hand is becoming obsolete, I had no response, and thankfully she moved on. Mom leaned over and squeezed my hand.

"I love your handwriting," she whispered, because occasionally she's extra like that. I squeezed back but didn't hold on very long.

Sometimes she has so much faith in me it freaks me out. Unconditional love is cool and everything, but not when you suspect you're unworthy of it.

After pretending to be invisible for a few agonizing minutes, I risked a look across the circle, and the hot boy was totally looking at me. He smiled and raised his hand in his lap to make a peace sign. Maybe I didn't have to shoot myself after all.

JESSICA

It's amazing how much I can hate a child. Alice purposely embarrassed Emily, and I would happily reach along the row of chairs and punch her in the throat. If Em came home from school and told me that story, I would have told her to shrug and rise above it, but it's very hard to rise above an intense desire to protect your cub in the moment. I wouldn't actually do anything, of course, because that would make Emily go ballistic and also possibly die of mortification, but if I get a chance to trip that little bitch later, I'm simply saying I might.

Oh good, Cassidy's reached Dani and Alice. Let's hope they make fools of themselves.

I'm a bad person.

Daniella shook back her hair. She's the same age as me, maybe even a couple of years older, but she's much better preserved and professionally tended. She is the wife of a studio magnate, after all.

"My name is Dani. I didn't go to college, either, because I was working as a model in Europe, so we have that in common!" She was looking at Will's dad, whose face suggested he thought that would pretty much be it as far as shared experience went, but Dani didn't seem to notice. She laughed and added, "Maybe I should go now. Alice and I could be roomies!"

Yes, I thought, Alice is going to totally embrace that idea.

Alice ignored her mother completely, showing more restraint than I would have given her credit for, and said, "My name is Alice, and an interesting fact about me is that I hold a patent."

We were all silent.

"A patent for what?" asked Will.

Alice smiled. "I can't tell you, it's still in development."

"Well, that's going to look good on your application, isn't it?" said Cassidy brightly. "Last week one of our tour members had started an international charity, but a patent is even better!" She nodded. "Who hasn't started a charity, right?"

Great, now I hate Alice even more. But then I caught Emily's eye and realized we both wanted to giggle. The whole idea of Alice holding a patent was ridiculous, the whole idea of doing it to look good on an application was even worse, and the particular agony of this whole breakfast suddenly threatened to overwhelm us both.

But we're tough. We bit our lips and kept it together until we got back to the room.

I'm proud of us.

5

EMILY

As I sat there listening to the admissions woman at Georgetown give a speech that encouraged us to be fearless and bold, but also underscored the need for quality applications and good grades, I wondered how we're supposed to be everything at once. How can you be a studious visionary who understands the secret language of employability but still be ready to cut ties with the ruling class and change the world while being a fearless artist and successful athlete? They do realize we're only sixteen years old, right? Mind you, Alice holds a patent, so I'm the slacker. I pulled out my pad and zoned out, glad I picked a chair at the edge of the room. Mom looked over, so I pretended to be taking notes, when actually I was doodling the admissions woman.

I was near the window, which was a strategic call, and I could see dozens of students hanging out, laughing and flirting and reading actual books and looking like they're legit enjoying themselves. I remember looking at high schoolers and feeling they had it together, only to get there myself and discover they totally didn't. When does that stop? (Asking for a friend.)

My mom was listening with total concentration, of course, to the admissions director. She was probably making a mental list of the pros and cons of every college we visit, and she'll present me with her findings and that will be that. She's pretending to care about my opinion—in fact, she's asking me what I think about forty times a day, even though the only answer I can ever give her is "I don't know"—but actually she'll tell me what I should do and be 100 percent certain of it. It'll be high school all over again. I wanted to do Shop, and Technical Drawing, but she said I had to do AP US History and freaking Bio, which I HATE, because it was *better for college*. My friend Leah did Shop and they freaking *welded*. Just saying.

JESSICA

I hoped this wouldn't go on much longer because I really needed to pee. I looked over at Emily and thank god she was paying attention. She was even taking notes. My phone buzzed with a new text. It was Frances. I hate it when people are on their phones when someone else is talking, it's so rude, but I was going to break my own rules because I'm an adult. Sorry, and also not sorry.

Frances texted, "How's it going?"

"Fine."

"Huh . . . that good?"

"You'll never guess who's here."

"Angelina Jolie."

"Her kids are too young for college."

"Maddox is already in college."

"How do you know these things?"

"I waste a lot of time online, ignoring my children."

"Fine, but no, not her. Daniella and Alice."

"No way."

"Way."

A pause, then: "How's Emily? Doesn't she hate Alice?"

I frowned, and looked at Emily, who was now gazing out the window and hopefully imagining herself crossing the very lovely quad. "Unclear. She seems blasé."

"She always seems blasé. That's her superpower."

Suddenly, Emily poked me and I realized everyone was getting up. I typed a quick *ttyl* and stood.

"It's the walking part," said Emily, looking like she'd rather be doing the sleeping part. I pulled on the coat everyone told me was overkill when I bought it; I'm not too proud to say living in LA has made me soft. I offered to buy Emily one, along with gloves and a scarf, but she said she'd rather die than dress like the Stay Puft man, so let's hope the tour is mostly inside.

EMILY

Oh my god we've been walking around campus for twenty minutes and I am going to freeze to death. I can't even text for help; my fingers are useless little icicles.

JESSICA

As the other parents and I were touring the campus, the guide kept stressing how employable the graduates of his college were. I was suddenly overcome with anxiety that I was going to quit my job and be totally unable to find a new one. John won't even notice I'm gone; he'll just hire a few of these spry, youthful graduates and call it a day. We happened to be passing the cafeteria, and I saw—across the crowded room—one of those muffins with the streusel topping, and before I knew it I had ditched the tour and was peeling off the paper wrapper. I am a very bad person.

The cafeteria made me feel like the oldest person in the world. I was surrounded by college students, all of whom seemed to be digging into giant salads and green juices, and were probably going to work out later. Where was the pizza? Where were the hangovers? I flipped through the brochure they'd given us, pausing at the "Tuition and Financial Aid" section. Let's see . . . $50K a year tuition (I'm rounding down), let's say $5K a year for housing, let's add another $5K for books, clothes, and soft drugs . . . Let's be friendly and call it a quarter of a million dollars. No problem (insert sound of choking, body falling to the ground).

I texted Frances again.

"Hey, I'm back." I waited a moment, then her answer popped up.

"Hey, back."

"I'm freaking out. I left the guided tour and I'm hiding in the cafeteria."

"Good choice. Get a muffin."

"I'm never going to get another job."

"You haven't actually quit this one yet."

"John's probably interviewing replacements."

"Doubtful. Did you get a muffin? How's Emily?"

"Yes, I got a muffin. She's okay. She's not actively hating me, anyway."

"Well, that's good. Sasha already told me I'm ruining her life, I don't understand anything, and she hates me. I haven't even had my third cup of coffee."

I grinned at the phone. "The holy trinity! Congrats on hitting your goals for the day already." I added a trophy emoji.

"Thanks. I'm pretty proud. At least Theo still loves me."

"Hah. His time will come."

I looked up from the phone and saw Emily, standing near the doorway with the rest of the kids, frowning at me. Well, *they* weren't frowning at me; it was only her.

"Gotta go," I texted Frances. "Emily just spotted me playing hooky."

"Busted," she replied. "Enjoy!"

EMILY

Mom's got a uterus of steel, I have to give her that. We met up after the tour was done and she greeted me like nothing happened.

"Well?" She smiled as she asked, and for a moment I didn't want to be angry with her about anything, and have a hug, but that never feels like an option anymore. And what if she'd been talking to school on the phone? It couldn't be, because she definitely wouldn't have been smiling.

"Well what?" I replied wittily.

"Did you enjoy the tour?"

I nodded. "Did you enjoy the cafeteria?"

"Yeah, although I have to tell you, the coffee wasn't that great."

I said, "You ditched the tour? After all that crap this morning about taking this trip seriously and paying attention?"

"Yes," she said, and leaned closer. "I was freezing to death, despite my coat, and I thought if I died you'd be really embarrassed, so I was honestly doing it to save your reputation."

For a moment I wanted to laugh, and she was obviously trying to be forgiven, but instead I frowned at her and turned away. This happens a lot. I get angry and I can't back down because if I back down it feels like losing, even though I know she's not trying to win. I guess I'm in the clear with school though, thank god, because she would definitely have led with that.

JESSICA

Emily was mad at me for ditching the tour, but what can you do? I tried to make a joke of it but she wasn't buying it. Teenagers can smell hypocrisy like blood in the water, and I was annoyed at myself for undermining my own credibility for a cup of coffee. But, dude, I was cold and I needed to check my email and I'm forty-five years old and if I want to get a cup of coffee I'm going to. See how mature I sound? I'd love to blame Emily for making me childish, but I think it's all on me.

Once the group was all there, we headed off campus to a nearby restaurant that Cassidy apparently picked simply because it had big enough tables. It smelled strongly of coffee and vaguely of shrimp, which was weird. I decided to risk further contact with my own child.

"Did you like anything about the college? Did anything stand out?"

Emily shrugged at me, ready to bury the hatchet, or at least place it on the ground for now.

"It was okay. I liked the girl who was showing us around."

"She was cool?"

"She had pink hair."

"Fair enough. Did you ask any questions?"

Emily shook her head. "No, Alice asked about sororities, and Will asked about balancing a job and college, and someone asked about engineering."

"Did it feel like somewhere you might want to be?"

She was irritated. "Mom, I have no idea. I spent all of an hour on campus. How am I supposed to know anything about it? If I dated someone for an hour and then said we were moving in together for the next four years, you'd have me committed."

She's not wrong, of course, but I said, "Look, I only want you to make a good impression," then wondered why on earth I'd said that. I hoped she'd roll on by, but of course not.

"On the pink-haired girl? Mother, she didn't even know our names, she's not paying any attention." She looked at me angrily. "Or do you mean on the other parents? That's who you really care about, right? Making sure I look good so the other parents won't think you did a bad job." Her tone was disgusted, but at least she lowered her voice. I glanced around the table and saw an echo of our conversation happening all over, parents and kids talking quietly in pairs, the kids looking irritated and hungry, the parents looking hopeful or frustrated, presumably depending on how long they'd been talking. I suddenly put my hand on Emily's and smiled.

"I'm sorry, baby, you're totally right. I'm being pushy, I'm sorry."

She was surprised but pulled her hand away and opened the menu. The college process makes you think in terms of points or scores, as if everything they do in eleventh grade is subject to ranking. Please, god, let that not be true, because unless they're looking for champion sulkers with a minor in toneless insolence, Emily isn't going very far.

And then I felt guilty about thinking that and hid behind my menu, too.

EMILY

Mom was being pushy again, so I told her I liked the girl who was showing us around, even though she was actually kind of a bitch, and kept saying, "Well . . . IF you get in," which wasn't exactly encouraging. Now we were waiting to order lunch. I might have been dying of hunger, btw, just saying. Presumably if I died right here and now, Mom would prop me up and carry me around on the tour like nothing was wrong. God forbid we stand out in any way.

I wish Mom would realize there's nothing I'd like more than to walk onto a college campus and feel immediately at home. That would be awesome, because right now all I know is I don't know. I don't even know what I like anymore. I used to like drawing and horses and taking things apart. I used to like reading books about wizards and witches and talking animals. All that really stuck from that time were horses and drawing, although I do still have my Pokémon card collection. It's going to be worth money someday.

I know Mom wants me to be happy, and if I knew what happy looked like, I'd be glad to help her. The happiest I've ever been was hanging out with my grandmother at the country place, the smell of her cigarette smoke sticking to my clothes along with those fuzzy little cannonball weed things that get everywhere. We built forts and dug holes. There was a stream we could dam up, or redirect, and we'd get covered in mud and sit there and smoke—her, not me. I'd eat candy. Her pockets were always mysteriously full of candy, although I never saw her eat any. She taught me how to unclog a toilet and use power tools. We never talked about anything except the job we had in front of us, and it was fantastic.

But lately everything feels like it doesn't fit right, and I don't honestly know if the misfit is everything else, or me. And seriously, if I didn't get food soon, I was going to expire.

JESSICA

I kept smiling behind the menu and counted slowly. I've read that there are over two thousand accredited universities in the US. Surely to goodness one of them will appeal to Emily? Then we can start actually trying to get in, which these days is part political campaign, part *American Ninja Warrior* competition. I swear to you my parents didn't do any of this. My dad managed to convey the importance of working hard in school using a subtle blend of emotional blackmail (*I'm paying for the best high school in New York, don't make me regret it*) and fear (*if you don't work hard now you won't get into a good college and you won't get a good job and you won't meet a nice man and you'll end your life filled with regret and fast food*). It was incredibly effective.

He was right, of course. I went to a very good high school, filled with the daughters of professionals both male and female, and a lot was expected. Having run straight As the entire time, I met with the school counselor once. She asked me what I wanted to do. I laughed and said, *Not disappoint my parents*, which she didn't think was funny, so I coughed and said, *Become a lawyer.* She said, *Columbia will take you. Your grades are very strong and their law school is first-rate.* I said, *Fair enough*, and I swear to you that was it. I think I applied to four other colleges, but Columbia let me in, so I couldn't even tell you what they were. Bear in mind I was not only running As but also trying to make the Olympics, and there are whole swaths of eleventh and twelfth grade I literally don't remember because I wasn't getting enough sleep for my brain to function properly. And where was my mom in all this? She was busy with her own projects and only ever said, *Choose work that makes you happy while you're doing it, because you'll be doing it a lot*, which might be the best life advice ever.

When Emily started eleventh grade, the school sent out an email letting us all know that college was now a thing we needed to think about. This was funny, of course, because we'd all been thinking about it, on and off, since the moment the obstetrician cut the cord. I'd dutifully attended every informational session, read everything they told us to read, and tried not to get infected with the panic that was palpable every time a dozen mothers got together—which of us was going to be triumphant in the grocery store, loudly and clearly announcing all the Ivies her daughter was admitted to? Which of us would be pretending not to care at carpool when the news wasn't good, or wasn't *as good* as everyone else's? Conversations at Whole Foods were about schools and majors and empty nests, but the subtext was how well you managed your children and how secure their trajectory would be now. As if the future is ever secure for anyone. As if anything your own parents did mattered now, thirty years on.

I'd started this process a year or so ago, convinced I was going to be calm and Zen and 100 percent real about it all, emphasizing the wide variety of colleges and encouraging Emily to follow her heart. But honestly, right now I'd be satisfied if she expressed any interest in the college process at all. When I give her my opinion she just shrugs. She's certainly not scared of disappointing me, that's for sure. I couldn't tell you if that means I'm a worse parent than my dad, or better.

Then my phone rang and I had to step outside to take a work call and ended up on the phone for forty minutes while everyone else ate. I should have fully, openly quit for real, then maybe I'd get ten minutes of peace to completely freak out. As it was, I had to fit panic attacks in around everything else, which wasn't the best way of doing it.

6

EMILY

I swear to god I'll be graduating college and Mom will be on a call. I watched her nervously through the window at first, but it was clearly the office; she looked base-level stressed and didn't throw any accusing glances my way. She'd missed pretty much everything I did in elementary school because of work, and although I totally support her, girl power and all that, it's irritating. She complains about her work all the time, too, so I can't help noticing I'm coming second to something she doesn't even like. She came back into the restaurant when we were all done, and it was just as well I'd saved half my sandwich for her. Sometimes she forgets to eat, she's so busy saving the world with the power of the law, or whatever it is she's doing when she's walking back and forth talking on the phone. When she took the sandwich I noticed she'd started picking at the skin on her fingers again, a nervous habit I thought she'd gotten over. Adults are so messed up.

After lunch we all took the Metro to Foggy Bottom to visit George Washington University. For some reason my mother finds the name Foggy Bottom hilarious, and I had to use my Bitchy Voice to get her to stop making stupid jokes. She's such a child.

This time the kid showing us around was nicer, and for a moment I tried to imagine myself playing Frisbee under the cherry blossoms. It didn't work, and suddenly Alice appeared, like a lion creeping up on a limping antelope or whatever.

"This is boring," she said. "Are you even interested in GWU?"

I shrugged. "I don't know. I don't even know if college is what I want to do."

Alice was surprised. "Why not? It's four years where your parents pay for you to sleep in and party. Who wouldn't want to do that?"

I looked at her and raised my eyebrows. "Well, I think the schools actually want you to work as well, Alice."

Her expression changed. "Oh . . . don't you have good grades? I hear community college is a good alternative." She tried on a tone of supportive enthusiasm, which suited her about as well as a party hat suits a rhinoceros.

Nice try, but I shook my head. "My grades are fine. I don't like school."

"No one likes school, Emily." Alice checked her phone absently. It was almost like blinking. "Besides, my mom says college is way more fun."

"I thought she didn't go to college."

"She didn't, but I've never dated a movie star and I still know it would be fun."

I decided not to waste any more mental energy on Alice's Guide to College. She's an idiot.

Alice asked, "Where did your mom sneak off to earlier? Secret boyfriend?"

I gazed at her. "Yeah, she got a match on Tinder."

Alice giggled. "Can you imagine?"

I shook my head. "No. She had a work call."

"Oh," said Alice, losing interest.

The guy leading the tour had stopped to point out the engineering building, and we all concertina'd together again. Engineering buildings all look the same, what's up with that?

Alice yawned hugely and stared around. She lowered her voice. "Did you hear about Becca and Lucy and that other girl? They got suspended."

"No," I lie, "what for?"

Alice shrugged. "Who cares? Bad grades, probably, they're all dumb as bricks." She looks over the group of kids. "I think I'm going to try and hook up with the blue-collar guy."

I frowned. "Will? How do you know he's blue collar?"

"You knew who I meant, didn't you? He needs to work through college, doesn't he? His parents may not have even graduated high school for all we know. I've never slept with someone in a different social class, it might be fun." She fake shivered. "A little rough around the edges, if you know what I mean."

I shook my head. "You're an asshole, Alice."

Alice grinned and nodded. "I know, I'm a terrible person." Will happened to turn around at that moment and caught us both looking at him. He raised his eyebrows at us and then, when Alice smiled flirtatiously, smiled back. Then Alice did that stupid thing where she looks at the ground and bites her lip, which I guess she thinks is totally hot, so she missed the moment when Will looked at me and briefly rolled his eyes. I laughed but managed to turn it into a cough.

Alice said, "Do you want to bet I can bag him before the end of the week?"

I said, "How on earth, your mom is here, his dad is here, it's not like we're going to get a lot of free time."

Alice snorted. "Are you joking? Did you actually read the itinerary?"

"Uh, no. I leave all that stuff to my mom." This was a fairly embarrassing admission, and Alice pounced on it.

"How grown up of you," she said sarcastically. "There are several periods where we can all hang out, only the kids. Side trips, visits to the mall, whatever. It's totally doable."

"Well, I'm not betting on it. I don't care what you do."

Alice said, "Really? I saw you looking at him, too. Maybe we should both try and see who wins."

I felt myself blushing but said no pretty firmly. "He's a person, Alice, not a prize. Did you miss all those lectures about consent?"

Alice snorted. "Oh please. You're saying guys hate being offered sex with no strings attached?"

"You'd sleep with him to win a bet?"

"No, I'd sleep with him because this trip is a total bore and I need something to occupy my time. I don't even know why I'm here. I'm going to USC. My dad went there, he's on the board, and the admissions director has been to our house and has a boner for my mother. I'm so good."

I stared at her, wondering how we'd ever been friends.

Then Alice said, "I bet you think me and my whole family are hideous, horrible people, but the thing is, Emily, everyone would do whatever they could to get ahead. I'm just being honest about it." She shrugged. "If you don't think your mom would blow the dean of Harvard to get you in, you're an idiot."

I wondered if Alice was right. Was everyone else playing the system every way they could? They seemed so nice. Will and another kid were standing nearby, laughing at something on their phones—were they hacking into the school's mainframe to boost their chances? Were they blackmailing the admissions person? They suddenly both laughed and it seemed unlikely. I'm not naive: The process is a crapshoot; I know that. Colleges get millions of applications from kids with 4.0 GPAs and up every year, and I've watched enough college acceptance videos online to know that getting in is as much luck as anything else. We all put a lot of faith in the shibboleths of academic success (not sleeping through Comparative Religion, either; check that vocabulary); we're like compulsive gamblers who wear their lucky shirt or who only place bets on even days, or brides who wear something blue. We get this grade. Take that AP class. All so our raised hand stands out and we'll be the one pulled from the ocean. Suddenly I'm completely exhausted and turn up my palms at Alice.

"I don't think your whole family is hideous, your little sister is really quite sweet."

Alice laughed. She never takes offense; it's another aspect of her character I envy. Maybe she's a sociopath who has no human feelings whatsoever, or maybe she's so incredibly self-confident that other people's opinions simply roll off her beautiful plumage.

"Do you know why you and I never became real friends, Emily?" she asked, leaning close enough for me to see the sheen of highlighter on her cheekbones, the dab of lighter shadow at the inner corner of her eye.

I shrugged. The group had moved off again, and in a moment I was going to walk ahead and lose Alice. "I don't vape? I don't know the lyrics to rap songs? I get blackheads and dandruff like every other normal teenager?"

"Well, yes, all of those, but the biggest problem is you have no sense of humor. You take yourself so seriously." Alice giggled. "Who the hell cares about penmanship anymore?"

I was annoyed. "I have a sense of humor, I can be fun."

"Oh yeah? Prove it."

Just then the tour finished, and I saw the parents group standing across the street. My mother smiled at me, as she always does when she first sees me. *There she is*, my heart sang, *there's my mother*. Don't tell her but seeing her makes me feel safe.

I turned to Alice. "You know why you and I never became real friends, Alice?"

Alice shrugged. "I'm too pretty?"

"No, it's because I do take myself seriously. You think you're here to party, and I know I'm here for something more interesting. If you want to call that having no sense of humor, then fair enough, I'm cool with it." I pivoted to walk away. "Good luck with your project, Alice. Have fun."

I nearly banged into Will, who, it turned out, had left the other kid behind and was apparently about to speak to me. He had his phone in his hand—either the cat video was so good he had to share, or he was offering to let me in on the hacking.

I muttered an apology, praying he hadn't heard Alice talking about him, and pushed by to make my escape. Always so smooth, Emily.

JESSICA

So, while Emily was pretending all is normal, clearly something had happened across the street. I could tell from the way she paused to let a driver by, waving her hand impatiently, that she was upset.

"How was the tour?" I said, wanting to hear her speak a bit before deciding if I needed to dig deeper.

"It was good," said Emily. "I liked it better than Georgetown. The lecture halls were very pretty. The dorms were nice. I like the school colors."

Huh, that was a lot of detail. I examined her covertly. "What's wrong?"

"Nothing," replied Emily. "I'm tired."

"Alright," I said, knowing that wasn't true. Or maybe it was true, because teenagers are permanently exhausted, but it wasn't the whole story. I looked across the street and saw the rest of the kids approaching, so I turned and nudged her.

"Let's go get coffee or something. We don't have to stay with the group all the time."

One of the selling points of E3 is that they take care of everything on the tour; you just have to pay a ridiculous sum of money. They offer dozens of different tours, some regional like ours, some hop-scotching the country to cover a particular major (best colleges for engineering, etc.). Once you've picked a tour and handed over your credit card, they do the rest, booking all the tickets, arranging and paying for meals (except where noted and excluded—always read the small print), hotels, transportation, and such. For those of us with no time to ponder the variables, it seemed like a worthwhile exchange. All we had to do was show up and check "college tour" off our list. But it wasn't like touring North Korea; you could always leave the group, as long as you made it back in time for the bus.

I walked alongside my daughter, noting the pace of her steps, the set of her shoulders. As a little girl Emily had been shy and reserved, a little bit clingy and interested in staying close. She was the kid sitting on the side twenty minutes after everyone else was in the pool. When I'd expressed concern to her preschool teacher, the teacher laughed and told me to be glad she wasn't first in the water.

"She's not scared, she's watching. She's evaluating. When all her friends are doing drugs, she'll be the one who calls the ambulance, don't worry." As Emily wasn't quite four at the time, the thought of her actually being able to use a phone was as surprising a concept as her doing drugs, but I'd clung to this advice tightly, especially during middle school.

I missed her being little. Little-kid problems are so much more easily solved than teenage problems. I'm fully aware I'm not the first parent to notice this. I was working full-time, but in the evenings and weekends I had string cheese and cookies, cartoons and hugs, kisses and stuffed toys. I took Emily to baby gym and then toddler gym and then kinder gym on Saturday mornings; later I drove her to dance lessons and piano lessons. I felt competent and quietly proud that I managed to stay patient most of the time.

I'll be honest, though, there were days in the office, or in the courtroom, where I forgot I even had a child. Not all day, just periodically. I loved my work. I loved solving problems that were complicated and thorny, that no one else had yet solved. And working hard also meant I was building a wall of protection for us, Emily and me, and if it meant I had less time for Emily, then it was the small price we had to pay until the wall was high enough. Once she was in school and we had Anna, I could convince myself she was fine. But bit by tiny bit the wall I was building ended up between us.

In the last several years any feeling of competence I ever had has completely eroded. I wake up most days unsure of myself, stressed about work and anxious about Emily. She needs help more than ever before but refuses it with every ounce of the self-assurance I'd foolishly encouraged her to develop. I spent over a decade acquiring advanced Emily-decoding skills, like one of those profilers they bring in on TV cop shows, able to look at a crime scene and tell you where the criminal grew up and whether or not he wears hats. But one day, somewhere around Emily's thirteenth birthday, I'd woken up in enemy territory, having apparently parachuted in overnight, and none of those skills were any use at all.

"Did Alice say something to you?" I asked carefully. Not looking at her, like approaching a skittish horse.

"No," said Emily. "You know, we barely know each other anymore."

"You used to be friends."

Emily shrugged. "Back in ninth grade, for about ten minutes. I don't think you remember how time behaves in high school, Mom. Something can happen one week and be totally forgotten by the following one. Every six-hour school day has about fourteen hours in it." She was still looking ahead, walking quickly to put distance between herself and Alice. "It's a miracle of physics."

I nodded, though I wasn't sure I completely knew what she meant. My own life seems to be getting faster every week. However, I do remember my mother grounding me at fourteen, for something predictable like throwing an illicit party, and how the sentence of a month seemed impossibly long. I remember thinking no one at school would recognize me when I got out; they'd stand in the hallways and mutter to each other, *Who's the girl with the unbrushed hair and overgrown fingernails? She looks a little bit like Jessica . . . but didn't Jessica move away or something?* My mother had relented after two weeks, doubtless worn down by the endless whining and stomping about. As every parent of a teenager knows, grounding is a double-edged sword.

"Are you hungry?" I asked Emily.

"No," my daughter replied firmly. I wasn't fooled for a second. Emily is never hungry . . . until her blood sugar suddenly drops through the floor and she turns into a total monster.

"Well, I am," I lied. "Let's stop here." We'd reached a reasonable-looking café, and I turned in without waiting for an answer.

The waitress turned out to be the pink-haired girl who'd shown the kids around Georgetown that morning, but she didn't recognize Emily. She'd probably already had a busy day, what with showing a bunch of idiots around school and then rushing here for her afternoon shift. I'd waited tables in school; it was actually far more instructive for becoming an adult than anything I'd studied at Columbia.

"What can I get you ladies? Start with a drink?" The waitress was shooting for perky but falling slightly short. I felt sorry for her.

"I'll have coffee and a pastry," I said. "What do you recommend?"

The waitress looked at me and probably wanted to suggest cutting back on the baked goods, but instead said, "People love the donuts. They're baked."

"Okay," I said, "I'll take one of those."

"Me, too," said Emily.

"I thought you said you weren't hungry?" I asked innocently. Why do I do that? Why must I always comment? I knew she was hungry, I'd maneuvered her into eating, why couldn't I leave it at that? No, I have to make a point.

"I changed my mind." Emily smiled up at the waitress. "I'll have an iced coffee, too, please." She didn't seem annoyed by my comment, but she dropped her smile once the waitress glanced away. Honestly, I feel like a spy in my own life sometimes, trying to figure out what's going on using tiny clues, body language, menu choices.

The waitress nodded, looking towards the door as the rest of the tour group came in. Damn, now Emily wasn't going to tell me anything. Well, at least I got her to eat something. Despite my close call with ruining the moment, I took a second to fist-bump myself for my masterful ninja parenting. In some ways Emily reminds me of bosses I'd had when I was younger, the kind of out-of-date leaders who needed to think an idea was theirs before they could accept it. I'd quickly learned to propose something after lunch when they were at their most genial, to act mildly confused when I made a mistake and hope their avuncular bullshit sexism would kick in. Emily is like that; her interest in something wanes in exact proportion to the interest I express in it. It's probably a law of nature. Someone should fund a study.

"Do you mind if we join you?"

We looked up to see Will, the boy from the tour, with his father. He was the one who'd spoken.

"Not at all," I said, doing that thing where you shift your chair a little bit, indicating your willingness to make room.

Will smiled at Emily and she smiled back, and I could see she thought he was cute. It was the same smile as the one she wears when she shows me an outfit she already knows looks awesome. I love that smile. That smile gives me hope she knows how wonderful she is, rather than doubting herself. But it comes and goes.

The boy sat next to her, and I realized he was a full head and shoulders taller than she was. I wondered anew at the enormousness of teenage boys. They go home the summer after sixth or seventh grade and come back in the fall seventeen feet taller. Having never had a son, I usually imagined that the kid's poor mom comes in one morning, drops her tray (she's carrying one in this imaginary scene; go with it, okay?), and screams to discover her son is barely fitting in his bed. She flies to get a crowbar to help him get up, then rushes to Target to buy everything three sizes bigger. It's probably not that sudden, but it seems that way to me.

The boy's father smiled at Emily. "So, you're Emily, right?"

"That's right," Emily said.

"And you're Jessica," the man said to me, proving that he may not have gone to college but he certainly outstripped me in the name-recall contest. "I'm Chris, and this is Will."

I smiled at him and said, "I remember from this morning."

There could have been an awkward silence at this point, but as both Chris and I could see the kids liked each other, we bounced the conversation along like a doubles beach volleyball team headed for the regionals.

"What are you thinking of studying at school, Emily?" Chris asked, his clear green eyes regarding my daughter steadily.

Emily blushed slightly. "I'm not sure, maybe engineering?"

"Oh," said Chris brightly. "You like building things?"

Emily said, "Well . . ."

I jumped in, again unable to help myself. "She always did, you should have seen the Lego cities she built. She likes fixing things, she was the classic take-it-apart-to-see-how-it-works kind of kid. Engineering would suit her down to the ground." I suddenly realized I'd interrupted Emily, and turned apologetically. "Not that you need to decide right now, of course." Emily was still smiling, but her eyes warned me that I'd come dangerously close to embarrassing her. I subsided.

Chris looked at his son. "Will was like that, too, but now he wants to study computer science."

Will grinned at Emily. "I hear the internet is going to catch on."

"You think?" She smiled back.

Suddenly Chris said, "You know what, you two should move to another table, otherwise it's going to get overcrowded once the food arrives."

"That's an excellent idea," I said, "and then we can show each other pictures of you two when you were small, which would be painfully embarrassing for you if you had to sit through it."

"Definitely not into that," said Will, looking at Emily. "I had a haircut in fourth grade that would be social suicide if anyone saw it."

Emily nodded. "I dressed like Dora the Explorer for three months straight in second grade, and she has pictures."

Will grinned. "They don't realize the power they have."

"Yes, we do," said his dad. "Go sit somewhere else so us adults can actually have a conversation."

EMILY

Well, that wasn't awkward at all.

First my mom dragged me into this stupid café, although I was a bit hungry, and then Hot Boy and his dad showed up. And now I was sitting with him all alone and I had zero to talk about. What if he heard what Alice was saying about him? What if he asked me about it and I had to stab myself with a fork in order to cause a diversion?

The waitress showed up with my donut.

"You changed tables," she said accusingly.

"Sorry about that," I said.

"Will you be wanting a separate check?"

Oh, great, more awkward. "Yeah," said Will calmly, "we'll take separate checks, and can I get a coffee please?"

The waitress eyed him dubiously, but he smiled at her and she softened. He has a freaking dimple on one side of his face that I could honestly use for storage. It is so cute I can't even.

The donut was huge, so I cut it into pieces, nudging the plate towards Will. He took a piece and said, "Do you really want to study engineering?"

I shrugged. "I don't know." I chewed a segment of donut and swallowed. "You know, there's a reason why donuts are usually fried and heavily sugared. My eyes were so happy to see a donut, but my mouth is now sorely disappointed."

Will grinned at me—score—and nodded over to where our parents were sitting. "That's funny," he said. I turned and saw that they, too, had cut their donut into pieces and were sharing it. "I guess you and your mom are pretty alike."

I shook my head. "Not really. Maybe we both have small appetites."

"Or maybe you're both nice and like to share?"

"Maybe. She's nicer than I am."

"Probably. Moms usually are, right?"

I made a face. "Do you read the news? Watch movies? Moms can be evil incarnate."

Will laughed. "You have sugar on the side of your mouth."

I licked it, but he smiled and said, "The other side," so I licked that, too, and he nodded. "You got it." He handed me a napkin. "My mom left when I was little, so I guess I should have a lower opinion of mothers, but I don't. My dad's fine, but he works all the time, so he can be pretty cranky. He also has this weird obsession with chores. What about yours?"

"Same."

"Chores?"

"Not so much chores, but same working. She's a lawyer and she works all the time. We have dinner together maybe twice a week."

"And your dad?"

"I don't know him very well. They weren't even together when she found out she was pregnant. He lives in London now, he sends me Paddington Bear stuff every so often." I smiled. "I think he thinks I'm still ten, but it's reasonable seeing as he hasn't actually seen me in years." I looked at him. "Are you an only child?"

"No, there are four of us, but my older sister left home already." He said it casually. "My grandma lives with us, so she's watching my brothers while we're here. My dad's spending half his time on the phone, yelling at employees."

"What does he do?"

"He's a contractor." He took another bite of donut. "What about you? Why are you on the tour if you don't want to go to college?"

"What makes you think I don't want to go to college?"

He waited. "Am I wrong?"

"Everyone goes to college."

"Not everyone."

"Well, everyone I know does."

"And you have to do the same as everyone else?"

I shook my head and didn't say anything. I suddenly can't decide if I like this boy or not. He's cute, but he asks a lot of questions I don't have answers to. I looked over at my mom, but for once she wasn't watching me like a hawk. I dug a dollar out of my pocket and started folding it into a butterfly for the waitress.

"That's cool," Will said. "Where did you learn that?"

"My grandma taught me. She taught herself origami after she quit smoking to give her something to do with her hands."

"My dad used to smoke. He quit, too."

"Does he do origami?"

"No, he cracks his knuckles."

We both shuddered. I finished the butterfly and spread out its wings, balancing it on a sugar packet.

"Wait," said Will. He took the sugar packet, tore the corner, tipped out a little sugar, and replaced the butterfly so it appeared to be eating the sugar.

"Funny," I said.

"Amazing what a little scenery will do, am I right?"

He smiled at me and I felt a bit like a butterfly myself, not to be all gushy about it.

JESSICA

It turned out Chris and I got along very well, which was a pleasant surprise. In general he was a pleasant surprise, because it also turned out he was the most no-bullshit person I had met in a while.

"You're much nicer than I thought you would be," he said, for example.

I laughed. "Uh . . . thanks?"

Chris chewed a piece of donut and nodded. "You look like one of the moms at school, friendly but judgy at the same time. Do you know?"

I wasn't sure I did know but nodded. "I look judgy? That's not good." I wanted another donut. Why am I always so hungry? I looked around for the waitress.

He shrugged. "*Judgy*'s too strong a word. I take it back."

I asked, "Are the moms at your school not nice?"

"Oh, no, they're nice. But for some reason the fact that I'm a contractor and not, you know, a fancy doctor or lawyer messes with them. They assume we don't have money, and although they're all good liberals and want to treat all people with equal dignity, they also don't want to be insensitive and invite Will to play polo and discover he doesn't have his own pony, you know?"

I laughed. "It sounds to me like you're the one doing the judging. How many families in Los Angeles play polo?"

He grinned. "You're right, I'm being unfair. A little bit. But, here's a good example of what I mean: Back in ninth grade, when we started there, one of the moms in Will's class offered me a bag of hand-me-down clothes, right?"

"Sure, that's not unusual at all. I have a friend whose daughter is two years older than Emily and she passes stuff down all the time. The kid has excellent taste. Em loves it."

"Yeah, but this kid was no bigger or older than Will, these were extra clothes they didn't need. And when I said no thanks, which I did because he has plenty of clothes, she looked embarrassed and I realized she thought I was being proud and that she might have offended me." He caught the waitress's eye and signaled for another coffee and two more donuts. I could definitely like this guy.

I shrugged. "So? Did you clear it up?"

Chris stared at the table. "No, actually. I guess word got around that the guy with the dusty boots is sensitive, so nobody ever offered me anything again." He made a face. "Will isn't bothered by any of this, none of the kids seem to give a crap about parents anyway. I ask Will what his friends' parents do and he looks at me like I'm nuts. Why would they talk about old people, when they have themselves to talk about?"

I grinned at him. "This is why children are our future."

He grinned back. "We should teach them well and let them lead the way?"

"Yeah, if we don't mind following someone who's looking at their phone all the time. Was Will always into computers?" I asked.

"Yeah, if by computers you mean video games and *Minecraft*," Chris replied. "It's not like he's been building microprocessors in the garage, he likes computers the way other kids like sports." He sighed. "I think he wants to do computer science because it's a good career, not because he's deeply passionate about the future of programming."

"And you didn't go to college?"

"No, I was sick of school. I wanted to get on with my life, you know?"

The coffee and donuts arrived, and I took a bite while I thought back to that time.

I said, "I never considered not going, it was what everyone did. My sister was already at school, it seemed like fun."

Chris looked at me. "And was it?"

"Sure. I made good friends, we're seeing a few of them on this trip." I shrugged. "And I had archery, which I was really into. It was fun. I hope Emily has as much fun as I did . . . They take things so seriously these days. And the debt is nuts."

Chris nodded. "Yeah, I never had any debt. I worked in my family business for a few years, then started my own."

"As a contractor?"

"Yeah. My parents focused on houses, I do larger buildings and stores, but it's the same work." He shrugged. "I like it. It pays well, and because my mother-in-law helps with the kids, I can afford better schools. I couldn't do it without her." He laughed. "And compared to all those fancy doctors and lawyers, I think I have less stress. What do you do?"

I said seriously, "I'm a fancy, overstressed lawyer."

Chris made a face. "Whoops."

I laughed. "It's fine, I love it. I started out wanting to defend the defenseless, right, like you do when you're twenty, but then I got pregnant with Emily and had to switch to plan B, which was go into corporate law and make a load of money so I could afford to be a single parent." I noticed Chris hadn't asked me about Emily's dad, unlike everyone else. "Work kind of expanded to fill all my available time, though, so I'm not sure I'm doing all that well on the parenting front."

I looked over at the kids. They were laughing at something on Emily's phone and seemed fine. I turned back to find Chris looking at me.

"I'm sure you're a good mom," he said. "We all worry."

I shrugged. "I'm lucky, I have a great nanny who takes amazing care of Emily while I'm stuck at work, but now I worry that I missed all of it."

"Well, I have a mother-in-law and feel the same way."

I hesitated, because I wanted to ask where his wife was, but it's a minefield. He took pity on me.

"My wife left us when the kids were younger. She'd been leaving slowly for a couple of years and her mom had been there a lot, so I'm not entirely sure the kids were as traumatized by it as I was. Her mom took it worst." He paused and looked over at Will. "He's always had his head on straight, but my older daughter is a disaster already and she's only twenty." Another bite of donut, another sip of coffee. "But I guess like mother like daughter."

I ignored his comment about his wife because, you know, hos before bros, and said, "Emily's a pretty good kid, probably because of the nanny."

"What's her name?"

"The nanny? Anna."

"Well, Anna might take care of the day-to-day but you still laid the groundwork, right?"

"Yeah, I guess. And Emily's not super challenging, she does her work, she goes out with her friends, she comes home when she says she will." I smiled wryly. "Or she's got a really good cover and she's actually running a drug-smuggling ring."

Chris said, "You never want to give up on a kid. But my daughter's making it hard not to, and it puts more pressure on the others, too." He looked at Will again. "He seems fine, but I thought she was, too. Right up until she wasn't."

7

JESSICA

Emily and I decided to go to the optional Ford's Theatre tour, which turned out to be the least disappointing tourist experience either of us ever had. If you haven't gone, you definitely should. The guide was amazing, the story—bearing in mind we all know how it ends—was tense and dramatic, and the gift shop was outstanding. I love a good museum gift shop; it makes it possible to both spend money and feel erudite. Sure, some people would argue that museums are for education and inspiration, not the purchasing of assassination-themed merchandise. But they would be wrong.

Back at the hotel, Emily threw herself down on the bed and sighed. She'd bought a T-shirt that read "That is SO four score and seven years ago," and we'd had fun together, without even a hint of teenage angst or perimenopausal agita. But now I felt the air change a little and got ready to be patient.

She pulled her backpack over and got out a little model kit my dad had sent her. These were little sheets of metal with shapes punched into them, for making buildings, cars, bugs, all kinds of things. I've got about three dozen of them scattered around the house, and let me tell you, stepping on a three-inch model of the Brandenburg Gate at 2:00 a.m. in bare feet is no joke. Thank god it wasn't the Chrysler Building, or I'd still be limping.

Then, without looking up, Emily said, "I like the city a lot, but neither of those colleges really appealed to me. Not that I could even get into them."

I walked across the room and turned on the bedside light, getting a short static shock. Why does that happen so much? I shook my hand and waited a moment before saying, "Well, honey, I'm sure you'll get in somewhere, and you can't have a career these days without a college degree."

"Not necessarily." She'd dug out the little pliers she carries everywhere and was working on the model.

"Well, yes. All I want is for you to keep your options open."

Emily was silent. We'd had this conversation a dozen times lately. As usual, I could feel Emily wanting to say something, but not. I glanced at my watch. Was there time for a quick power nap before dinner? I realized Emily was looking at me from under her lashes.

"What is it?" I said, sitting down on the edge of the bed.

"Nothing," said Emily. "I'm getting kind of burned-out at school. I'm not really the academic type." She was focusing on her pliers again, having drawn me back in.

"I know," I said, trying to be supportive. "You've always been

94

more hands on, you like to do things." I gestured at the model, but she didn't see me.

Emily suddenly frowned at me. "You know, it's really annoying when you tell me what I'm like. I know who I am, I don't need you to narrate my internal experience."

I took a breath. Then: "Sweetheart, I'm sorry. I didn't mean it like that. Just that you've always liked building things, exploring outside, that kind of thing."

"I know, Mother, I was there, remember? I'm actually living my life, I don't need an explanatory voice-over to understand it."

Another breath. She's not *being* a problem, she's *having* a problem, I reminded myself. "Are you hungry, honey?"

Emily sat up. "No! I'm not hungry, Mom, sometimes I can get irritated on my own, without low blood sugar, lack of sleep, or too much screen time. Sometimes there isn't a reason, alright? I understand what I'm feeling, no explanation needed. I can manage myself, I don't need handling like a four-year-old."

I bit my tongue to stop myself from pointing out that this was clearly untrue, based on current evidence. I decided strategic retreat was probably called for, so I got up to take a shower.

"Where are you going?" asked Emily.

"Uh, to take a shower?"

"You're mad at me."

"I'm not mad at you. I wanted to take a shower and you didn't want me to 'handle you,' so I thought it was alright if I left the room."

Emily glared at me. "You're being sarcastic."

I felt a familiar wave of exhausted sadness wash over me. It's so hard to know which Emily is going to show up for any given conversation. She's capable of so much happiness and calm, and then in an instant she gets enraged by anything and everything I say. Conversations would veer off the rails like cartoon chase sequences, regardless of how slowly I took the curves. However, Emily is right about one thing. I do tend to look for explanations that feel more comfortable than the obvious one: My kid is an asshole.

"I'm sorry, Mom." Emily had her hands over her face as she lay on the bed. "I'm sorry." Her voice cracked, and I'll admit it, I rolled my eyes. It's not that I don't have enormous sympathy for the hormonal and emotional roller coaster that is sixteen; it's that the whiplash is killing me. I went over and sat next to Emily on the bed again.

"Baby, it's okay," I said softly, stroking her hair. "I know it's hard to be your age."

"How do you know? It's completely different than it was when you were sixteen." She pulled away her hands and her face was angry again. "I mean, physically it's the same, but it's a completely different world. You didn't even have computers."

This was, of course, untrue, but I doubted this was the time to split hairs. You cannot win this argument, I reminded myself, because she is irrational and actually couldn't be less interested in what your teenage experience was like any more than I had been interested in my mother's. Her brain is awash in chemicals and her prefrontal cortex is as smooth as a hazelnut, and she's looking for someone to blame for how she feels and you're sitting right there.

Emily was still going, her voice thick with tears. "You could make mistakes at school and it didn't ruin your entire life. You could get into college with like a 2.4 GPA and do fine. You could get drunk and stupid and it wouldn't show up online the next day and follow you everywhere you went your whole entire life." Her hands were back over her face, and now she rolled over and started sobbing into the coverlet.

Oh, for crying out loud. "I know, honey, I'm so sorry." I rubbed Emily's back and thought longingly of the shower. I'd been so close . . .

EMILY

I got a great T-shirt and the theater tour was really good; I loved it. I posted pictures and we got back to the hotel in plenty of time to chill out. I was planning on having a shower, but Mom decided to push me about college and got all upset about it. She doesn't understand that things are so different now, there's so much pressure to be perfect all the time, perfect at school, perfect online, plus a little bit different, to make yourself stand out. A learning disability is good, or maybe freckles all over your face, or a little bit plump but sexily body positive . . . you know, something that says you're not basic. While still meeting the basic criteria, obviously, and not messing up in some catastrophic way.

I stood in the shower and tried to clear my thoughts. I'll admit I'd gotten a little bit bent out of shape when my mom was interrogating me, and I didn't want to look puffy at dinner. I was still freaked out about the girls in my Statistics class, but even before that, I felt anxious all the time. Maybe I have a disorder; maybe a specialist can write me a note getting me out of life for a few years, so I can recuperate.

The shower helped, though, and maybe dinner would be fun. I hoped Mom wouldn't bug me again.

JESSICA

In the end there wasn't time for both of us to take a shower, so Emily took one and came out totally recovered and in a good mood. And me? Well, still feeling grimy from all the walking we'd done, I had to content myself with fresh deodorant and brushing my teeth. At least I'd been able to vent to Frances while Emily was in the shower.

I texted, "Emily has lost her mind."

Frances replied, "How can you tell?"

"She says she hates me, then she says she's sorry and cries, then she hates me again."

"Sounds normal to me. Two minutes ago Sasha asked me if she could Postmates a Venti iced chai from Starbucks, and when I said it was less than ten minutes away on foot, told me I didn't care about her future."

I smiled. "The connection being . . . ?"

"That she was doing Vitally Important Studying and the half hour she would lose by fetching her own drink—and please note, we have chai in the fridge—could mean the difference between getting into college and going on the pole."

"Totally reasonable."

"Right. The fact that your child even occasionally apologizes to you is amazing. Quit your bitching."

The dinner that night was at El Presidente, and dancing had been threatened. El Presidente was clearly a DC institution, with adobe walls painted pink and the scent of forty thousand tortillas hanging in the air. My tummy rumbled, but thankfully, chips and salsa came immediately once we sat down. The E3 group had a long table to ourselves, and Cassidy had arranged the seating in order to separate parents and children, "the better to get to know each other." As the parents at least had our kids in common, we did fine, but god knows what the teenagers were going to talk about, especially once Cassidy insisted they put away their phones.

"Oh my god," said one parent, in an undertone. "They're going to have to actually speak to each other."

"I think my kid's forgotten how," said another. "He texts me from the room next door to ask me something. On the one hand it's ridiculous, and on the other hand it's so much better than shouting back and forth."

Chris nodded, and said, "Sometimes I think it's easier for Will to text 'I love you' than it would be to say it to my face."

I thought about the texts Emily and I sent each other. Even if we'd bickered all evening, we would declare a truce over text. I would sit in my bed and she would sit in hers, at the other end of the hall, and we would send each other funny pictures, say sweet things, discuss plans . . . It was lower stress, being able to talk without having to deal with body language, having time to think about how you wanted to say things. People lament the amount of time teenagers spend online, but there's a lot to be said for old-fashioned, written communication.

After ordering, the parents' end of the table began engaging in gentle but insistent competition over social status, as expressed through the medium of children. Of course, Dani was leading the charge, which started out disguised as general conversation.

"So, where is everyone at school?" She might as well have said, *So, let's rank each other by socioeconomic status and potential social power, shall we?* but listing schools was much quicker and equally effective. Once you've entered a city's educational system, it doesn't take long to work out the pecking order. I imagine going to jail is a similar process. A week or two of getting the shit beaten out of you followed by a rapid self-placement in whatever subgroup offers the most protection.

Dani smiled. "Jessica and I are both parents at Westminster, but I don't think anyone else is, right?" Westminster is the best all-girls school in Los Angeles, and one of the best in the country. It is cripplingly expensive, very hard to get into, and fiercely competitive once you had dragged your poor child over the barbed wire to get in. Don't get me wrong, there are great kids there, some of the brightest and best of the city, but there are also enormously entitled, wealthy kids who make life difficult for the nice ones. But if you have a very intelligent kid, or one with medium intelligence but lofty ambitions, Westminster is a good choice.

Dani scanned the table. "Phillip-Daniels?" She was going down the standard list; PD was the best co-ed school in Los Angeles, extremely academic and competitive. Four other parents raised their hands.

"Northridge? Plummer? St. Jude's? Hedgewood? Camberly?" She was only naming private schools, a safe assumption based on the expense of the tour, but I thought she was revealing more about herself than she probably wanted to. The rest of the table slowly segregated themselves, with only Chris unaccounted for. Dani turned to him. "And you're in public school?" Ouch.

Chris smiled at her. "No, we're at Clarence Darrow." Clarence Darrow was a small private school for academically gifted children, set midway between Los Angeles and Pasadena.

Dani paused. "Really?"

Chris laughed. "That's hard to believe?"

"No . . . I'm just surprised. Darrow is very . . ." Dani trailed off, apparently experiencing a moment of self-awareness that took her by surprise. Maybe she realized she sounded like a snob and a total bitch, but for whatever reason, she closed her mouth, confused. I tried not to enjoy her discomfort, because that would make me a bad person.

Chris had clearly had conversations like this before. "Expensive? Exclusive? Yes, it's both of those things, but Will is very smart and apparently the principal at his elementary school, which was public, knew the principal at Darrow and reached out. They have an incredible program and Will really likes it."

Before things got out of hand, Cassidy intervened. "So, did everyone enjoy the colleges today?"

"Yes," said one of the parents, "I thought Georgetown was charming."

"I preferred George Washington," said another parent, "particularly the dorms, which I thought were very nice."

"Oh yes," said Cassidy, congratulating herself on regaining control of the group. "Are most of you assuming your children will live on campus for the first year or so?"

The conversation bubbled on, and I saw Chris taking a deep breath to calm himself. He looked over at me, and I smiled, trying to convey supportive non-judgyness. The whole stupid conversation reminded me of elementary school, where I'd had a totally miserable time and always felt like a big fat loser. I was born with a club foot; it's pretty common, especially if your mother smokes like a fiend while she's pregnant (not that my club foot stopped her; my sister had beautiful feet, she said, and she'd smoked during that pregnancy, too, ipso facto, not her fault), and although they'd fixed it, I still had trouble running or playing sports very well. It wasn't even PE that bothered me, it was recess, when everyone was friendly enough but had me mind the jackets while they all ran around playing whatever ball-based fad was sweeping the playgrounds of the East Coast that month. I'd sit there, surrounded by foothills of coats, reading and trying not to listen to everyone else having fun. Eventually my dad took me to archery class because it was something I could do as well as anyone else, and it clicked for me. But I've never forgotten third grade.

It's entirely possible that somewhere there is a group of people in their forties who can drink a lot of wine, then do tequila shots, then dance like Beyoncé, but we were not those people. The teenagers of the E3 tour group sat at their end of the table in frozen horror as several of the parents, egged on by Dani, who actually could dance annoyingly well and therefore never missed an opportunity to do so, took to the dance floor. There was a live band that was playing a medley of pop classics flavored with a Cuban beat, and until you've seen a middle-aged woman get down to a reinterpretation of "Independent Women" on trombone and cowbells, you haven't lived. I imagine several of the teens will never be able to hear the song again without experiencing PTSD flashbacks.

Eventually, inevitably, one of the parents fell, and Cassidy declared our evening over. We walked back to the hotel, which was only a few blocks, and most of us were pretty sober by the time we reached our rooms. I'm not going to say all, but most.

"Did you have a nice time?" I asked Emily as she climbed on the bed fully dressed and settled down for some serious phone time. She pushed her shoes off her feet without untying them, which explained why she needed new ones so often. I decided to chalk up her inability to undo laces to parental failure, and let it go. I was too tired to nag.

"Yes," replied Emily, already flipping through her feed or watching porn or whatever it was she was doing. It suddenly reminded me of those kids at school who would curve their arms around their work if they thought you could see it; all this looking at screens no one else could see was as defensive and slightly aggressive. *Don't look at what I'm looking at; it's not for you.* No sooner had I had this thought than Emily turned her screen around to face me and grinned.

"Oh my god, check this out." It was a baby animal of some kind— I couldn't really tell from the bathroom door—maybe a bear? It had its head stuck in a bucket and people were trying to help it. Eventually it popped off and the baby—it *was* a bear—rolled over backwards several times before loping off into the woods.

"So cute," said Emily, turning the phone back.

I gazed at her for a moment, watching her mouth curve up into a smile at whatever she was looking at, and felt that certainty of love that lives in your bones, an awareness you would give your life for someone and not regret it for a second. I remember reading to her at night, her little body settled in my lap, the smell of her hair and her tiny fingers wrapped around my thumb. Back then I was the one introducing her to everything, the one gatekeeping her experience of the world. Now I'm no longer necessary, my daughter doesn't want a mediator and, in fact, was sharing new information about the world with me. Without Emily I'd never have known baby bears could get their heads stuck in buckets, although I probably could have surmised it.

Suddenly, just as I was feeling pretty sorry for myself, Emily looked up at me. "Did you have a good time, Mom? At dinner?"

I was surprised. "It was fine."

Emily frowned. "Only fine? What did you guys talk about?"

"You guys, of course. What else is there to talk about?" I turned away and went into the bathroom to brush my teeth. "The part where that other mom did the robot was pretty funny, largely because I thought you kids were going to die of embarrassment."

I started getting ready for bed, wondering if Emily was even listening.

EMILY

I couldn't hear Mom's voice any longer; she was running water in the bathroom. I have no idea what she really thinks anymore. She used to be so easy to get along with, all my friends loved her, she was generally agreed to be the cool mom, the one who made cookies on the weekend and didn't care if you cursed. She was tired a lot, and worked all the time, but when she wasn't working, she would take me to museums and buy me toys and we'd go to Disney or the beach . . . but in the last few years, she's changed. She's not anxious, exactly, just more . . . pinched. I wish there was a way to pause your life so you could stay in the good bits. Nine had been perfect. I could have stayed nine forever.

I had a load of good photos from tonight, including some potentially viral gold. I managed to capture the moment when that kid's mother moonwalked herself right off her own feet, and I was far enough away that you can't tell who she actually is. No need to ruin someone's life because his mom can't look where she's dancing.

My mom came out of the bathroom, dressed in one of her many comfy nighties, smelling of face cream and a hint of toothpaste. This is how she would smell at night when she read to me; I remember it so well. Her lap was the comfiest place in the world, not that I could fit in it anymore, plus that would be weird. When she heads out to work in the morning, she smells of perfume and makeup, moving fast and taking her coffee to go. But at night she smells of roses and mint and seems to have all the time in the world for me. For a moment I got the crazy idea to ask her to read to me and opened my mouth to ask.

The phone rang. She looked at the screen, and answered. "Hey, Valentina, what's up?"

I watched her for a moment. When she's working her face changes. She gets focused, interested. Whenever she looks at me she looks tired, resigned. I guess I'm less fascinating. Perhaps I should sue someone or attempt a complicated corporate arbitrage of some sort.

Well, don't respond at all, she said to Valentina, who's this woman at her office I've never met, but who seems to be Mom's work daughter. It doesn't matter if we're in the middle of something, if Valentina calls, Mom gives her her full attention. I'm not jealous; whatever gave you that idea? Mom was still talking on the phone: *Wait him out, let him come to you. Be busy whenever he tries to reach you, tell your assistant to intercept your calls and tell him you're unavailable.*

Eventually, Mom got off the phone, then tapped at the screen for a moment.

"Why is your school calling me?" she asked. "I've missed three calls today."

I froze.

"Wait," she said, "I know. It's fund-raising time again. They want a check, and because I'm on a college tour, I am raw and fearful and open to persuasion." She grinned at me. "They are professional sharks, your school, I have to hand it to them. Your tuition is bigger than the library budget of some small towns, but they're never too shy to ask for more."

I shrugged. "I guess."

She turned back to her screen. "I'll email them that I'm away, which they should already know, for crying out loud, and deal with it when I get back."

"What's up with Valentina?" I asked. I don't even know why I asked; I don't really care.

Mom looked surprised. "Valentina? She's up for partner at work, and I'm trying to help her get there, that's all."

"That's very supportive of you."

Mom looked quizzically at me. "It's my job. She's my mentee, I take care of her."

"You're her boss?"

"Not exactly, it's different than that. I look out for her. I anticipate problems, I give her guidance, I lobby for her with senior people at work." She frowns at me. "Like Angela was for me, remember?"

"Angela?"

"Angela was my mentor when I was younger." She looks hazy for a moment. "I guess it was when you were very small."

Why do I feel so annoyed about this? "So, Valentina is like your kid."

Mom shook her head. "No, she's another adult who's professionally more junior than me."

"But you make time for her. You listen to her. You answer her calls and emails. You think about her future." Suddenly I was angry. "You treat her more like a daughter than you treat me."

Mom waited a second, then clearly decided to take the bait. "That's not true. She listens to me more than you do."

"Because she's paid to."

"Or because she knows I know what I'm talking about and appreciates my advice."

"She doesn't know you as well." Wow, that was a little harsh, Emily. I suddenly felt too tired to have this fight. I wish I knew why I lost my temper like this. I understand I'm a hormonal mess, that my brain is bathed in a soup of conflict, but it would be nice to be able to rise above it. "Never mind," I said, shooting for conciliatory and ending up with huffy. "I'm going to watch a show and go to sleep."

I put my earbuds in and pretended to be super focused on the screen. Luckily I don't think Mom could see it from where she was, because she might have wondered why I was watching *Monster Truck Rally* with such commitment.

JESSICA

I had no idea what had just happened, but it seemed to be over. Why Emily was so interested in monster trucks was beyond me, though. I'm too tired and old for this. I decided to go to sleep.

Tuesday

Washington, DC, Baltimore, and Philadelphia

8:00 a.m.: Theme breakfast: Dreams!

10:00 a.m.: American University

Drive 1 hour and 4 minutes on the E3 College Coach—
*packed lunch included! (Please advise us of dietary restrictions,
allergies, etc. E3 is a nut-free company!)*

2:00 p.m.: Johns Hopkins University

Drive 1 hour and 43 minutes to Philadelphia on the
E3 College Coach—*snack included!*

5:00 p.m.: Check into hotel in Philadelphia

6:00 p.m.: Optional group visit to the Philadelphia Museum of
Art, and a chance to run up the Rocky Steps and take photos!
(Tag us and win a tote!) Note: The museum itself will be closed.

7:30 p.m.: Dinner at the hotel

Overnight in Philadelphia

8

JESSICA

The next morning E3 was hosting breakfast in the same small conference room as the day before, and according to the itinerary, there was a theme.

"A theme?" asked Emily, pulling on her socks. They might have been my socks; she was a little furtive about it.

"Yes." I nodded. "Dreams."

"Dreams is the theme?"

"Yes." Not sure why she's struggling with this, but I woke up ever so slightly hungover and she needs to stop asking questions. I felt as if a pillowcase had been filled with dirty socks and tied around my head, and if I didn't get a cup of tea soon I was going to cry.

Emily reached under the bed for her sneaker and started untying it. Slowly. "Huh. I dread to think what teenage boys dream about. It could get pretty steamy in there."

I frowned, wishing she would hurry up. "I don't think they literally mean dreams. I think they mean it in the aspirational sense."

"Okay." Both shoes on now, Emily stood. "Shall we make stuff up? I could say I dream of being a jet pilot or a firefighter."

"You could."

"Or a mountaineer or fashion model."

"Sure."

She looked at me as I held the hotel room door open for her. "Are you feeling alright? You seem a little cranky."

"I'm not cranky."

"Maybe you're hungry?"

I checked that the door was closed all the way. "I'm not hungry."

"Sure, Mom. Whatever you say."

Oh my god, I was turning into my daughter.

Instead of pastries there were bagels, and the chairs were different, arranged around small tables. People grabbed their breakfast and drifted to chairs, looking slightly nervous. Several of us looked a little worse for wear, which made me feel better, and the mom who'd fallen on the dance floor didn't show up at all. Her son was there, still slightly red from the embarrassment of the night before, and I felt bad for him. If teenagers were anything like they used to be, it was going to take a while to live that down. Especially now, because it was permanently recorded and instantly shared, making a brief moment of shame something you had to live down over and over again. He'd probably said as much to his mother through the bathroom door as she'd thrown up, and I couldn't decide whom to feel more sympathy for.

EMILY

I saw the kid whose mom fell on the dance floor last night and decided to delete the clip I had. He looked like crap, even though no one blamed him for his mom's deeply embarrassing behavior. You can't blame kids for their parents, any more than you can blame parents for their kids, though they all seem to feel responsible for everything we do. We do have autonomy, you know.

Will and Alice were chatting next to the coffee machine. They were probably discussing the variety of pods available, but I wasn't convinced Alice needed to touch Will quite so frequently in order to choose between French roast and hot chocolate. I couldn't decide whether to go over there or not, and then I reminded myself that I was allowed to get coffee, too, for crying out loud. I was losing my mind. I needed to text the group chat and get talked off the ledge.

JESSICA

With shaking hands, I looked at the itinerary—Emily said she'd get me tea, but she was talking to the other kids and I AM DYING HERE—and prayed I wouldn't throw up on the bus. If I'm driving I'm fine, but several family vacations with my parents were paused for me to throw up on the side of the road, much to Emily's horror. I made a mental note to get Dramamine. And Advil. And possibly a hip flask.

"Emily?" I tried to keep my voice reasonable, but from the way she jumped I guess I sounded more desperate than I felt. Actually, I was pretty desperate. She came over with the tea, which was delightfully strong and sweet, but then she went right back to the other kids. I sipped my tea and ruminated on getting old.

I've become painfully aware of my age lately. I'm not springing back the way I once did, and if I've been sitting for a while, I make sad noises when I stand and start walking. People I grew up with are starting to die of cancer; the children of celebrities I'd loved in my teens are becoming famous. Is this what aging is? A gradual loss of the faces you remembered, and as gradual a replacement of those faces with ones whose names you can't be bothered to discover.

Just as I was sinking into a genuine decline, Cassidy blew into the room, moving with determination, verve, and the accompanying scent of coconut shampoo.

"Good morning, people!" Cassidy was clearly a morning person. "Quick housekeeping: Any minibar or video purchases you made are your responsibility, so be sure to settle up with the hotel before we all check out. I see all the bills, and I don't want to chase you for a packet of M&M's." She grinned mischievously, but none of us wanted to see Cassidy's dark side. I wondered if any of the parents had bought embarrassing movies they suddenly realized Cassidy would know about, or decimated the minibar because they thought it would be their secret. *Huh*, Cassidy would say to herself, *Mrs. BlahBlah and her son Barry BlahBlah bought* Air Bud, Air Bud: Golden Receiver, *AND* Air Bud: World Pup *while completely emptying the minibar. Yet they seemed so normal.*

Cassidy had moved on, even if I couldn't. "We'll be leaving to visit American University at nine, the tour starts at ten, so please gather in the lobby. If you're not there on time, we will leave without you, so consider yourself warned." She looked as if she hoped her smile conveyed the friendliness of the warning, but the glint in her eye made it very clear to everyone that getting left behind was not an option. "After American we'll be getting on the E3 bus and driving an hour or so to Johns Hopkins. The tour there finishes with a question-and-answer session with current students, so please bring at least one question each. Last year nobody wanted to know anything, and it was pretty embarrassing. Then we will be boarding the bus again to drive to Philadelphia, where we will check into the hotel."

I was exhausted simply hearing about the day to come and tottered over to the bagel selection in the hopes that a sudden spike in blood sugar would propel me through the darkness.

Cassidy beamed around. "In order to foster closer friendships, breakfasts from now on are going to be in small groups. I'm going to switch the seating around every morning so we get to meet as many of our fellow parents and kids as possible during the week. Won't that be fun?"

A short but heavy silence, interrupted by a mother who'd clearly not been listening, and who suddenly said, loudly, "Fantastic." Then she clapped a few times before sinking back into silence. Her child got to his feet and left the room and, for all we know, the country. That's not true. He just wanted to.

Then Cassidy read off the morning's happy little groupings, and Emily and I were with a boy and his mother I hadn't spoken to yet. The boy was fairly nondescript, apart from his T-shirt, which featured the table of elements. His mother was slender and small, with pale golden hair curving under her chin. She looked like a fourteen-year-old pretending to be a librarian, but she probably wasn't.

"And to break the ice, I'm going to pose a question for discussion: What are your dreams for college?" Cassidy beamed around. "Take it away."

EMILY

Mom and I ended up sitting with Casper and his mom, who honestly didn't look old enough to be on a college tour for herself, let alone her son.

"I'm Jessica," said my mom, reaching across the table. "And this is Emily."

Casper's mom nodded. "You failed to qualify for the Olympics and she folds origami." She smiled at us. "My name is Jennifer, and this is Casper."

"We met last night," mumbled Casper. "Well, Emily and I did."

"At dinner," I added, in case they thought we'd had a secret assignation by the ice machine.

"That's nice," said Casper's mom.

"And so, Casper, what are your dreams for college?" Mom sounded chirpy, but I could tell she wasn't quite sure how to handle being reminded of competitive failure this early in the morning.

"To graduate with honors, to get an exciting job, and live a life of exploration and discovery," replied Casper. He turned to me. "What about you?"

I shrugged. "No clue."

He raised his eyebrows. "No clue?"

"Nope. No idea what subject, what college, what time frame, what anything."

He didn't look critical. Just puzzled. "Huh."

There was a pause. My mom tried again, turning to Jennifer. "So, do you feel ready for the whole college application process?"

Jennifer nodded. "Yes, it's all taken care of. We create a schedule for the children several months in advance, so I know we'll have time for everything. We put it in a Gantt chart, of course."

"What's that?" I asked. Might as well keep the ignoramus theme going.

Casper was surprised. "Oh, you'd know one if you saw one. It's a chart project managers use to organize work and time, represented visually. It allows you to see how one job leads into another, and therefore, how one thing is dependent on another."

"Really?" said Mom politely. "That sounds helpful." She added another spoonful of sugar to her tea, which was unusual, seeing as she'd drunk half of it already.

"It is," said Jennifer enthusiastically. "We use it all the time, for all of us. We plug in the kids' schedules, my husband's work schedule, mine, everything. Then we can see how it's all going to come together and we don't need to worry about any of it." She smiled serenely at my mom, and I suddenly wondered if she was stoned. "It's very efficient."

I looked at Casper. "And you use it, too?"

He nodded.

"Yeah, it's good. It has my school schedule, right, and it estimates homework times, keeps track of due dates, etc. I input everything throughout the day, and the system automatically updates."

My mom took a really long drink of her tea. "And you created this?"

Casper muttered, "Mom works at Caltech." He smiled at me and mouthed, *Super nerd.*

I laughed but shut it off when Mom shot me a look.

"Yes," Jennifer said, nodding. "When Casper was a toddler my husband and I read an article in *Scientific American* about children not having sufficient downtime for their intellectual growth." Her eyes widened. "So we wrote a program and have been refining it ever since." She nodded. "Having a second child really helped, obviously."

My mom nodded back. "Because you get more relaxed about everything?"

Jennifer frowned. "No . . . because you get a whole new data set."

"Right," said Mom, "that's what I meant."

"The chart even has blocks of time set aside for doing nothing, for playing Magic: The Gathering, for practicing the piano . . . everything." Casper grinned. "Sometimes I think it's developed a mind of its own. I noticed it started scheduling 'room cleaning.'"

His mom laughed. "And made everything else a dependency!"

They cracked up. Nerds.

"Wow," I said. "Do you ever do anything unscheduled?"

"Sure," said Casper, "there are blocks of free time at regular intervals."

I narrowed my eyes at him. "You schedule unscheduled time?"

Casper and his mom both nodded. I didn't dare look at my mom, but luckily she's tough.

"That sounds fantastic," she said. "Do you know what you want to study in school, Casper?"

"I want to be a geologist," he replied earnestly. "My grandmother gave me some iron pyrite when I was, like, three or four, and it was like a lightbulb went off over my head. Since then it's always been my dream." He smiled around. "I'm the president of the Minerals and Gems Club at school."

I gazed at him, not quite sure what to do with that information. I couldn't tell if I was amazed at how truly nerdy he was, or jealous that he'd achieved such power and influence in his school's semiprecious and igneous subculture.

He added, "And I'm the president of the California Young Geologists Association. We meet twice a year to compare samples."

I said nothing because, frankly, what can be said to that?

I was jealous, though, because I really, really wish I had half his certainty. When the college counselor at school asks me what I'm interested in studying, I go completely blank. I'd love to tell her the truth—I'm interested in studying how to get out of school, but I doubt she has a leaflet or podcast recommendation for that. I mean, I know what I'm supposed to do, we all do: I'm supposed to finish high school and go to college. In college I'm supposed to make several romantic errors and have one meaningful relationship and maybe question my orientation.

Then, having amassed the appropriate mix of rueful/hilarious memories and life experience, I'm supposed to take a job in a field related to my degree, struggle for a few years to perfect my adulting skills, then launch a real career (this can be related to my degree or an interesting change of direction, either is acceptable), get married, have kids, grow old, and push my kids through the whole cycle all over again. This is how capitalism perpetuates itself; I learned it on Khan Academy.

JESSICA

I need more caffeine. Those people are insane.

9

JESSICA

We arrived at American University. I'd tell you all about it, but honestly, you can google it. It's a university. It's pretty. I had a headache.

Ignoring Cassidy's warning, Dani shamelessly flirted with the admissions director, who appeared to be doing his best to get away. She literally had her hand on his arm, and the poor sap was leaning back at an angle of at least forty-five degrees. I looked up their admissions numbers on my phone (yes, I have an app). They got about twenty thousand applicants last year—did Dani really think she could flirt her way into memorability against that kind of overwhelming competition? The poor man looked dazed; Dani's charm is of the high-wattage-bulb variety. I've seen it take down fathers, grandfathers, and teenage boys indiscriminately.

I'm very aware that there are parents who have files on the admissions teams at particular colleges, who work their LinkedIn networks and alumni connections in order to gain any small purchase on the solid wall of incorruptible entry. I can't play that game. I'm not good at it; I'm more likely to mess it up than help. What if you paid for a library and your kid still didn't get in? Not to mention the horror of cheating the system and getting caught: *Sorry, honey, I didn't think you could make it on your own, so I bribed someone and now I'm going to jail. I'll probably get released in time for your wedding.* As if the relationship between mothers and teenagers wasn't hard enough. I text Frances, hoping she's awake.

"Dani Ackerman is trying to sleep with the admissions director. Do you think I should throw my hat in the ring, too? Do you think it would help?"

There was a pause. "Not sure it would help or hurt."

"Ouch."

"No offense. But if Dani is flirting outrageously, which is the only way she does it, then a more subtle approach might be more effective. Cheese of the month club, maybe?"

I grinned and wished Frances had come on the trip; it would have been so much better. My phone rang. Emily looked at me and arched her eyebrow. It's an unfortunate side effect of busting her hump for being on the phone all the time that every time I'm on my phone she takes the opportunity to bust mine.

"Really?" she said softly. "You left the ringer on?"

I narrowed my eyes at her and stood up to take the call outside. I could see it was the office.

"Hi," I said, walking over to a bench and sitting. Work calls are rarely short.

"Good morning, Jessica," said a familiar voice. John thinks his Southern charm makes up for a lot. He's wrong.

"Good morning, John," I said. "How can I help you?" I crossed my legs and started bouncing the top one. Cardio for the day.

"Well, Jessica, you can actually help me quite a bit, because Arthur Ostergren is getting rather difficult, and you're around the corner."

"I quit, remember? Ostergren was Jackson's client. It's international shipping and maritime law. I don't know anything about it. Can't someone else deal with it?"

"No," said John. "And he is your client, because you're a partner in the firm and all the firm's clients are your clients. You quit, but you said you wouldn't make it official until you got back." He paused. "I scheduled a board call to discuss it, by the way. I'll do what I can for Valentina."

"And Janet."

He sighed. "And Janet."

I frowned. "Ostergren is in Baltimore."

"Correct."

"I'm in Washington, DC."

"Again, nothing gets past you. Baltimore is less than fifty miles away. Eloise is sending a car now. You'll be at their offices before lunch."

I checked my watch. Damn it, he was right.

"But, John, I'm in the middle of something of my own here."

"I'm sorry, Jessica, but with great power comes great responsibility." This was a favorite joke of his, usually cracked when he was getting you to do something he didn't want to do himself. "Call me in ten minutes and I'll bring you up to speed. I'm giving you back to Eloise now. Give her your location and she'll sort it all out." He went away, presumably to go back behind his curtain and work the controls of that giant floating green head.

Eloise, his assistant, politely gathered information from me, and told me a car would be there in fifteen minutes. No one gets angry at Eloise, but she clearly got that I was annoyed, because she apologized for the last-minute notice.

"No problem, Eloise," I said, "but I need to rejoin the group."

She assured me it was all in hand, as she had a copy of the tour itinerary (which I hadn't given her, so that was weird, but Eloise knows everything), and I went back into the lecture room to tell Emily. She was going to be thrilled.

"What about dinner with Grandpa?" She was whispering, but still managed to sound annoyed. "And what about drinks with your friend? I can hardly have drinks with a total stranger without you."

"I'll be back in time, I promise."

"You always do this."

I opened my mouth to say (a) what is *this*, and (b) how is it possible I *always* do it, but then I remembered the futility of arguing with her when she's pissed. I grabbed my bag and went in to kiss her. She ducked away. I love it when she does that; you can see everyone wondering if they should call Child Protective Services.

My phone buzzed. The car was outside. It would have been funny if it weren't also so deeply, deeply irritating.

"See you later," I said.

"Whatever," said Emily, not even looking at me.

I sat in the car as it moved across campus, and watched the students walking to class, filled with their own thoughts, their plans for the day, the week, their entire future. They knew so little and hoped so much. From the other side of youth things seem far grayer, the ups and downs of life softened into the folds of a quilt rather than the mountains and valleys they appear to be when you're twenty. That's the thing with data; if you pull any graph out far enough, the peaks and troughs flatten out. Live long enough and life averages out.

The phone rang. It was John. "Jessica, are you listening? Ostergren is peevish about his representation. I need you to go over there and smooth his feathers."

"Jackson's been gone for months. Ostergren's feathers should be totally glassy."

"Well, they're not. It's not a big enough account for me to fly someone out, but you're right there. You're good at placating clients, it's those Mom skills."

I rolled my eyes. This kind of drive-by, benevolent sexism is completely invisible to those who use it, and women are as guilty of it as men. If you're a mom, it's assumed you have people skills others, non-moms, don't have. If you're a man with children, no one makes the same assumption. I remember when I was made partner, one of the older women cornered me in the office.

"In my day," she'd said to me, "you had either a career or children, never both. I had to make the choice." She'd regarded me coldly, her St. John business suit as much a uniform as camouflage and khakis. "I had two abortions in the eighties and still didn't make partner until I was fifty."

"Uh . . . I'm sorry?" I had said, my coffee growing cold in my hand.

"I don't regret it," she replied, "but if I think you're slacking at work, you can rest assured I'll come down on you like a ton of bricks. I voted against you for partner, you know, and I'll vote against you for a board seat when that rolls along." She pointed her finger at me. "What if you're needed in court and your child is dying? You'll pick the child, we'll lose the case." She shrugged. "And the kid will probably still die."

"Um . . ." I'd said, not sure what I was supposed to say to that. She went completely gaga a year or so later and had to be gently but firmly removed from the board. But she wasn't alone: It was made clear, in dozens of subtle ways, that I was theirs first, my daughter's second.

I realized John was waiting for me to speak. I said, "You promise you'll talk to the board and make them change their position?"

"Yes."

I sighed. "Okay, send me any background I need."

"Eloise is taking care of it. Call me after the meeting."

He hung up and moments later a file buzzed into my in-box. I pulled it up and started reading, trying not to think about Emily.

EMILY

Unbe-fricking-lievable. My mother has left the building. She vanished to do some stupid work thing, leaving me to deal with two colleges, a bus ride, and a hotel check-in. Thank god Cassidy was there. Her eyes glittered when I pulled her aside to tell her what had happened, and I could tell she's into a suddenly missing parent. She has prepared for this; it's the tiny emergency she goes over in the middle of the night. She patted me on the arm as we toured American, and told me not to worry. I hadn't been worrying, but as she hadn't told me not to seethe, I kept seething.

The mood definitely picked up when we saw the E3 College Coach. With one fluid motion we all pulled out our phones and started snapping. It's a regular coach-type bus, right, quite a nice one, like a rock band on tour or something, but someone had the brilliant idea of painting it like a school bus. At first glance it worked—we were all like, *Huh, an oversized school bus*—but then it suddenly dawned on us that the proportions were all wrong. Will said it was like an episode of *The Magic School Bus*. It's a school bus . . . and yet also a blue whale. He's funny.

Inside it was pretty cool, actually. I spent a year on the soccer team at school—don't ask, it was hideous—so I'm an expert on school buses. This was nothing like. The seats were comfortable and actually had seat belts, and there was a bathroom and a shower, although why on earth we'd need a shower is beyond me. I saw Alice eyeing it thoughtfully; maybe she's hoping to join the bus equivalent of the mile-high club. What would that be? The twenty-feet-off-the-ground club? Less impressive.

"Don't forget to tag us when you post," called Cassidy. As if realizing it was unlikely any of us would be giving her free publicity and admitting we were on a college tour, she then gathered us at the back for a group shot and tagged it herself. The parents have all been posting up a storm, of course. At one point the previous day we'd all compared embarrassing *"Can you believe s/he's looking at colleges?/ tearful emoji"* posts, to which all their friends added shocked faces and commented on the passage of time, yawn. Some of them went for the comparison post (*Here's a picture of little Wanda in her Dorothy costume at four, here she is at sixteen; Oh my god I feel so old because this rite of passage is about me, not the one actually passaging*), while others went for the sarcastic shot of their kid on their phone with a caption about looking forward to the future. They love to criticize us for being on our phones, despite the fact that their generation created the phones, marketed the phones, and are profiting from the phones. They're drug pushers making fun of the junkies, which, if you think about it, is lame AF. Besides, any day now those same junkies are taking over the street corner, so they should try being nice. I'm not actually sure what I mean by that; don't judge. And why do they all have phone cases that open like little books and make it difficult to take photos in the first place? They created the monster and don't even know how to use it properly.

Anyway, after the posed shot, we all ended up sitting in the back of the bus together, which was good, because the enthusiastic parental questioning after each university is exhausting all of us. Will sat next to me but spent the whole trip talking to Casper, so that was confusing. I would have joined in but they were talking about *Zelda*, about which I know nothing. I know I'm supposed to be into video games, but I'm not. Only *Minecraft*, which I still enjoy from time to time, no shame. The kids kept giving me dollar bills to fold. It was fun. Even Alice gave me one, although of course she gave me a twenty. I folded her a pig, which may be the smallest act of rebellion ever recorded.

JESSICA

I'd never been to Baltimore before; it turns out it's really pretty. Ostergren's offices were near the harbor, and his windows were filled with the masts of yachts and flags. It resembled a highly festive forest. He was less festive.

"I don't like it, Ms. Burnstein, I don't like it at all." He was one of those old men who thinks he's still good looking; he wore a handsome tie and matching pocket square, and his shoes were handmade and polished by someone whose only job it was to polish his shoes. "I realize I am only a relatively small account for your firm, but when Mr. Jackson left the firm—after apparently wasting my fees on drugs and loose women—no one really stepped up to fill his spot. I have only associates on my account." He shot his cuffs, presumably so I could see his fancy cuff links. "If the acquisition I'm planning goes ahead, our annual revenues will more than double."

I smiled at him and felt relieved I had worn appropriately professional clothing to the tour that morning. I'd debated jeans, then decided I lacked the confidence to be casual, if you know what I mean, and had stuck with slacks and cashmere. I was even wearing pearls; thank god for fashion insecurity.

"Firstly, let me reassure you that Mr. Jackson didn't spend any of your money, only his own. There was certainly bad behavior on his part, but no hint of financial impropriety."

"Humph," said Ostergren.

"Secondly, the lawyers on your account are highly capable, and all accounts have access to a partner whenever it's called for." I leaned forward. "Having said that, have you come across a lawyer called Valentina Guerrera?"

He nodded. "I think she was on a call once, advising about a specific tax issue."

I nodded back at him (mirroring body language, very important).

"Valentina is about to be made a partner and is extremely capable. Brilliant, in fact. You should request her. I happen to know she'd love to run an account as interesting as yours."

"Really?"

"Yes. The intricacies of international shipping are like catnip to her."

"Really?"

"Yes, only the other day she was talking about the Abandoned Shipwreck Act of 1987 with a great deal of enthusiasm."

He frowned and for a moment I panicked. I'd literally googled "important maritime laws" in the elevator, and that was the only one I could remember.

He relaxed. "It is incredibly fascinating."

Oh, thank goodness.

"Guerrera, you said?"

I nodded. "You'll love her."

"And she's a partner?"

"About to be. You should definitely call John today."

Once I was in the car on the way to Philadelphia, I called John and prepared to press my advantage. I'd learned early on in my career that the simplest way to succeed at work was to talk like a man, which means removing all warmth, doubt, and softness from every sentence. Try it; it's surprisingly difficult.

"Hi, I calmed Ostergren down, but he insists on Valentina being put on his account. He wants a partner."

John's frown could be heard in his voice. "Valentina isn't a partner."

"Well, I told him she was going to be. Now he wants her." I looked out the window at the world sliding by. "You told me to smooth his feathers, John, so I smoothed them."

"And made things hard for me at the same time."

I smiled. "Hiding in every problem is an opportunity, remember?"

"Really? Who told you that?"

"You did, John. Goodbye."

I hung up and immediately called Valentina. "Hey there, what do you know about international shipping?"

"Not all that much."

"Well, you might want to brush up." I told her about Ostergren. "Any word from John on the partner thing?"

"Nothing." She sounded uncharacteristically uneven. "It's unofficially going around that Will Maier and Jeff Mako are getting it." She added, "They totally deserve it."

"Yes, they do. So do you, Valentina."

"Maybe it's not my year."

"It is. Don't get ready to fail."

"I can wait."

"Yes, but don't."

There was a silence long enough to tell me she was thinking about saying something. "Spit it out."

"Someone said they aren't making any women partners this year because of Jerkwad."

Jerkwad, obviously, was what we all called Jackson the ex-partner and total douchebag who'd been fired.

Now I hesitated. "Why would that make sense?" Not an answer, but hopefully she wouldn't notice.

"I don't know. I never even worked for him."

"Listen, Val. Hold fast. Don't let any of this get in your head. Tell me about your caseload." As she started telling me about her work, I heard her voice settle. I see this in myself; work is not always my happy place, but it is my confident place. I know what I'm doing with law, it behaves in predictable ways, it takes its time. It gives me a feeling of competence and mastery I don't get anywhere else.

I let Valentina talk out her work all the way to Philadelphia. As we approached the hotel, I told her we had to break it off.

"Thanks, Jess," she said, clearly feeling much better. "I'm going home." She laughed. "It's strange not having you here. Usually when it's time to go I can still find you in your office."

"Well," I said wryly, "not sure that's very admirable."

"I am," she said. "I do admire it. You're a great mentor, Jess. Thanks."

The car pulled up in front of the hotel. "You're welcome, Val. Gotta go face Emily now."

"I'm sure she admires you, too."

I laughed. "Current evidence suggests not, but never mind. I'll call you tomorrow." She hung up, and I gave myself thirty seconds to feel good about myself. My colleagues let me help them, and it's such a good feeling. When Emily was little she needed my assistance constantly, asking me to do up a shoe, to make her a sandwich, to show her how to work this small machine or that one, and when she stopped wanting my help it was like missing a step in the dark. I still reach for the jar she can't open, the object that's too high on a shelf, the thorny problem my weathered hands can untangle. But where she used to smile and run off, happy with the open jar, the tied shoe, the sandwich, now she turns angry eyes on me and tells me sharply she can do it herself: *God, Mom, just stop, will you?*

I walked into the hotel, feeling my confidence rubbing off on the carpet with every step. Every day the culture shock of leaving the office omnipotent and walking into my house incompetent threatens to overwhelm me. I had hoped this trip would even things up a bit, but so far it's a bit of a bust.

10

JESSICA

When I walked into our room I found Emily already dressed and ready to go out.

"How was your work thing?" she asked. "Did you save the whatever?"

Her voice was a hair trigger, impossible to judge. I tried smiling. "I did. I saved the whatever and then on the way back I fixed the thingy and talked to Valentina about the whatyoucallit."

She'd started off smiling back at me, but it was clearly a mistake to mention Valentina. "Valentina gets a lot of your time," she said, turning away.

"Not really," I said, taking off my shoes and sitting on the bed. "What time are we meeting your grandfather?"

"Eight," she said, "but we have drinks with your friend first, remember?"

Damn, I had totally forgotten. I was exhausted and would happily have canceled the drinks part at least, but for some reason she was all gung ho. The whole hanging-out-with-my-friends thing was Emily's idea; she'd suggested it when we were originally planning the trip.

"Hey, don't you still have college friends on the East Coast?"

I'd stared at her across the dinner table and frowned. "Uh, yes, I think so. Not sure . . ."

"That's great, let's go see them."

I was surprised. Say what you like about Emily, she's not particularly nosy about my life. I could be explaining my latest case to her, hoping she might like to understand what I do all day, but then I realize she's basically listening for her name, like Alexa, and ignoring everything else.

"Really?" I said. "We'll be seeing Amanda and Robert in New York."

"I know, but I think it would be fun to meet more people who knew you when you were in college."

I'd duly wandered onto my Facebook page to see who was still around. Not as many as you'd think. Several of us had stayed in New York after graduation, including me, but after two-plus decades, most of us had abandoned the city for more affordable digs. I reached out to David Millar, who was in Philadelphia; Helen Gonzalez, another friend, was teaching at Vassar, for crying out loud; and of course my best friend, Amanda. I'd stayed in touch with her anyway; that one was a no-brainer. She'd married another college friend, actually, which was efficient and helpful of her. She and Robert were still in Manhattan, having had the good luck to buy a brownstone before the market went bananas. For once the stars had aligned and all of them had been excited to get together.

Now we were going to have drinks with David Millar before having dinner with my dad, which had seemed possible when I set it up, but now seemed like an exhausting overreach. But I could tell Emily was still vexed with me about disappearing that morning, so I took a very deep breath and pulled it together. Maybe it's not lifting a car off a small, bloodied child, but it felt pretty heroic to me.

While I got dressed I asked Emily about the tours I'd missed, the rest of the American University tour and Johns Hopkins. She seemed more enthusiastic about the bus trip in between, to be honest.

EMILY

Mom thinks more about Valentina than she does about me. Maybe she prefers her because she's essentially a mini her, whereas I am a failure. She asked me about the tours, of course. I told her the truth: I liked Johns Hopkins a lot, but then I checked the admissions requirements and there's no way. Never mind. I liked Philadelphia in general; it's a city I could totally see myself living in one day. Not that I can really imagine living anywhere except where I live and maybe some TV town like Stars Hollow. Then I told her about the bus, and it's possible I seemed more into the bus than anything else on the trip so far. Sorry not sorry.

Mom was trying really hard to keep it light, especially as she was attempting to do a cat-eye eyeliner for the first time in several years, but eventually she couldn't hold it in.

She blurted out, "Do you have any sense of what you might study, yet?"

I shook my head.

"Lots of places don't make you pick a major, right?"

I nodded.

"So you could choose a college and then take a gap year, and not pick a major until the end of the first year, so that would give you actually three more years before you need to decide what you want to study. You could even take a year off after high school and go live in London." She paused. "Or somewhere else, doesn't have to be London. Who knows what you'll want by that point?"

Probably just to shoot myself, but I didn't say that. "Mom, I don't want to put off my future, I want to start living it. I'm not sure what to study yet."

This shut her up, as I knew it would. She's trying hard to be cool, my mom, but I could see the warring impulses on her face. It is a face I've been studying closely for sixteen years, after all. On the one hand she's worried I'll end up living in the garage because I can't support myself, and on the other she doesn't want to be the kind of mom who pushes her kids too hard and drives them away. Remind me not to have kids; it's hell on your figure and gives you heartburn.

Eventually her good angel won. "Fair enough, baby. You'll let me know when you work out what you want." She went back to trying for that perfect cat eye.

I wanted to say, *Mom, you'll be the second person to know, after me.* But I'm not sure she isn't tired of hearing it.

JESSICA

I managed to get dressed for dinner without grilling Emily more than once, which I think is a bit of a triumph. Of course, I had a headache, which weakened me. And I'm nervous about seeing David Millar this evening, because he was the first guy I dated in college, and Emily doesn't know that.

David and I met literally on the first day of school. He sat next to me in a lecture, and by the end of it I was more aware of him than I'd ever been of any man in my life before. Not that I'd known many men, to be fair, I was all of nineteen and I'd only lost my virginity the previous year, but still. There was something about him that appealed to me on a cellular level, and by the end of the first week we were having the kind of sex I'd only seen in movies. He blew my tiny little mind, and I blew his tiny little mind, which is even hotter, as you know. We spent so much time in bed we both got a C in that class, and it was totally worth it.

But anyway, it's not like I can lean over and say to Emily, *Hey, the guy we're seeing later is a sexual god, would you like to hear some of his moves? Would you like to hear about all the places we had sex? Would you like to hear about how hot sex can be between two nineteen-year-olds who are insane with lust and in peak physical condition?* She'd probably take a crowbar to the hotel window and throw herself out.

EMILY

It turned out that old friend of Mom's was actually good looking, in an older-teacher-the-moms-flirt-with kind of way. We have a biology teacher like that; it's hilarious. They think we don't notice, but please . . . biology isn't that funny.

Mom also thinks I didn't notice she put makeup on and got dressed more carefully than usual. I didn't say anything, just loaned her my mascara, and then some makeup wipes when she got it all over her eyelids. Honestly.

She asked me how she looked and I told her the truth: good. My mom is still pretty slim, and she has great arms. Well, whaddya know, she'd packed a sleeveless top I'd never seen before, and she put on slightly nicer-than-normal dark jeans, and even boots. She's always bugging me to take up archery, which is where she got the arms, and maybe I should.

Anyway, we went down to the hotel bar, and when the guy waved across at us, I was pretty impressed.

"Wow, he's kind of cute for an old guy," I said.

"Oh please," replied my mom. "He's not old. He's my age."

"You said it, not me," I said, but then we were at the table so I stuck out my hand and introduced myself.

The guy grinned and said it was nice to meet me, but then he came around the table and gave my mom a full up-and-down look and pulled her into a hug. And I'm not talking the kind of hug adults usually give each other, but the kind of hug I don't think he would have given her if she'd been married.

And that's when I realized they used to date, and that, even worse, this asshole still fancied my mom.

JESSICA

Uh, so David Millar is still really hot, which caused a minor problem in my body for a moment, but my brain was able to get it together. I simply wasn't prepared for him to look so attractive. Mind you, if I were being honest, I would point out that I had dressed as nicely as I could under the circumstances—the circumstances being two decades having passed since the last time he saw me naked—and that it was shamefully satisfying to see his eyes widen when he saw me. I'm so shallow.

All this went over Emily's head, thankfully, and she was being charming and chatty, which is my favorite kind of Emily. I don't want to be the kind of person who beams proudly at the achievements of their kids, as if the parent had more than a passing influence, but it is very nice when your kid is being the polite version of herself in public. Again, so shallow.

I did that thing where you gaze around for the waiter to buy yourself time, while Emily and David got to know each other a bit.

"So," asked David, "you're touring colleges?" I glanced at his hands where they lay on the table, and tried to cool down. Since when did my libido get so independent?

"Yes," said Emily, "we're going up the East Coast looking at eleven different schools, it's a bit nuts."

"Sounds fun." His hands were still gorgeous, still strong, still . . . wait, no ring.

"Kind of."

"Only kind of?" He had definitely been married. No question.

Emily shrugged. "Well, it's kind of speed dating, for a start, it's not like you really get any more than a first impression. And I'm not really sure what I want to study."

"You'll find something," I said, unable to stop myself from chiming in. "College is fun, isn't it, David?" I had been so certain he was married; if he was single, that was a whole other problem. Married, it was a problem of *damn it, you're still hot and there's nothing I can do about it, oh well*. Unmarried, it was a different thing. Not that he had shown any interest in me.

He smiled at me. "Sure, if you meet a supersexy girl on the first day of class."

Scratch that. Definitely interested. I looked at Emily. "He's joking. It's good whoever you meet. You meet lots of people, not all of them are sexy. Some are, some aren't. But they're all interesting, and you meet lots of them." That didn't come out right.

Emily raised her eyebrows very slightly. "So, you meet people at college, that's what you're saying?"

"Yes."

"Good to know," she said, clearly deciding I was losing my mind. "I'll make a note."

The waiter came over to take drink orders.

"I'll get another scotch," said David, which was when I noticed he was finishing up a pretty substantial drink. I ordered a glass of wine and a Sprite for Emily, and hoped he wasn't too drunk. He'd always enjoyed a drink.

"So," said Emily, "what was my mom like in college?"

"Oh god," I said, "can we not do this?" Please don't mention . . . oh, so many things.

David smiled at me. "She was not what she appeared to be."

Emily said, "How do you mean?"

"Just that. She seemed one way, she turned out to be another. She was very self-assured, very disinterested, very cool. She was unexpected and delightful."

Emily's eyes widened. "Oh my god, you two dated." She raised her eyebrows at me. "You did, didn't you?"

David frowned. "She didn't tell you?"

I blushed. "I didn't think she'd be interested." I glanced at Emily, willing her to drop it. "It's not a big deal."

"It was a big deal to me," said David. "She was one of the most beautiful women I ever took to bed." He looked at me. "She still is."

Oh my god. Suddenly the attraction I felt for him began to fade. It was fun when it was hypothetical, or even simply one sided, but now I frowned. "David, Emily doesn't want to hear about this."

"Wait, maybe I do," said Emily, although her face was difficult to read.

David looked at me for a moment, then said, "So, Emily, do you want to be a lawyer like your mom?"

"Absolutely not," my daughter replied firmly. "She works too much. And I've heard her on the phone, it sounds stressful." She took a sip of her Sprite. "Are you a lawyer, too?"

"I was," he replied. He'd been a very successful lawyer; I'd read about it in the alumni newsletter. It hadn't mentioned the divorce, or the continued incredible hotness. Alumni newsletters aren't really exhaustive, to be fair.

"You quit?" I asked.

He nodded. "After my divorce I kind of stepped back a bit, do you know what I mean?"

I didn't, yet, but said, "Sure," to be supportive.

"I realized I'd been busting my hump for twenty years to get somewhere I no longer wanted to go." His eyes were serious, and I wanted to nod thoughtfully but kept remembering things we'd done in bed. I reached for my wine.

Emily spoke. "Where did you want to go?"

He shrugged. "I wasn't sure. So I quit the job and spent a year in the Peace Corps."

"You are joking," I said, stunned. This guy had been good in bed, sure, but he had also been insanely good at law, graduating at the top of the class despite that early C, clerking for a top-tier federal circuit judge, golden ticket all the way.

David laughed. "Nope, not joking. It was great, you should try it. It really cleared my head."

I shook my head. "Not until she's safely through college," I said. "Then I can cut loose."

Emily frowned at me. "You could do it now. I wouldn't care."

I laughed. "You would when you couldn't afford college." Let's pretend I didn't just put that at risk.

She started to say something else, but David spoke again. "Emily, you should consider traveling before college, if you can. It's very . . . clarifying."

"I'd love that," she said, "but I don't even know where I would go. What do you do now, then, if you're not a lawyer?"

"I run a nonprofit. We connect really great lawyers with people in trouble. The clients get the best lawyers in the city, and the lawyers get to feel less guilty about their success." He laughed. "It's really fun to see a Harvard Law School graduate walking into court for a battered wife who's trying to protect her kids." He shrugged. "As I'm sure your mom has told you, the law was written by and designed for the benefit of rich white men. I'm trying to balance it up."

"She never talks about her work," said Emily.

I gazed at her. "I talk about it all the time."

"You do?" She shrugged. "I guess I'm not listening."

There was an awkward pause, and David changed the subject. "Did you know Amanda and Robert got married?"

I nodded. This was conversation I could handle. "Yeah, we're seeing them in New York. We stayed in touch."

"Really in touch, or Facebook in touch?"

"Really. Amanda is Emily's godmother, actually."

The waiter brought David's drink, and he took a healthy swig of scotch. I sipped my wine and checked my watch. Half an hour until we could politely escape.

"So," said Emily, putting her elbows on the table. "Do you have kids? What did they think about you disappearing for a year?"

David matched her posture and smiled. "Yes, and I'm not sure they even noticed. My kids are slightly younger than you, but not much. Thirteen and eleven." More scotch. "I don't have to think about college yet, thank goodness. The older one wants to be a professional video game player, which is apparently a thing now, and the younger one wants to be a vet, like most young kids at some point."

"I never wanted to be a vet," replied Emily. "We had a dog when I was little, but I never really got the animal bug."

"Really?" David looked surprised and turned to me. "I thought you were such a dog lover? Remember Peanut?"

"Who's Peanut?" asked Emily.

"A dog your mom had in college. She found him behind the lab building, eating trash, and adopted him." He paused. "The dog was eating trash, not your mom."

Emily turned to me. "You like dogs?"

I nodded. "I love them. I didn't have Peanut for very long, though. He went to stay with your grandparents because you weren't allowed dogs in the dorms, and by the time I was off campus, your grandma refused to give him back."

"Why didn't I know that?"

I shrugged. "You're allergic to animal dander, remember?"

"Bummer," said David. "And you never married?" He looked pointedly at me. "How is that possible? A gorgeous woman like you shouldn't be single." He narrowed his eyes in what he clearly thought was a sexy manner. "Maybe you like a lot of variety in the bedroom. You were always pretty . . . open minded."

I couldn't look at Emily, and simply smiled at the table, trying to pretend he hadn't said that. Hello, idiot, my teenage daughter is *right there*. "I'm too busy. Too busy having a small child, then too busy working. I've dated from time to time, but nothing serious." I wasn't even going to go near the bedroom comment; I was going to pretend it was never said at all.

Emily said, "She dated some real losers."

"Thanks, Em."

"Tell me about them," said David, reaching for his glass.

"No, don't," I said, meaning it.

Miraculously, she dropped it and pushed her chair back. "I'm going to run to the ladies' room."

EMILY

I was so steamed right then. I called Ruby from the bathroom.

"Hey, bitch," she said. "What's up?"

"Hey," I said, half whispering. "I'm stuck in a bar with a friend of my mom's and he's totally trying to get into her pants."

"Ew, that's gross," she said. "Like, how?"

"Telling her she's hot and staring at her, it's repulsive."

"Is she into it?" She laughed. "Maybe you're cockblocking her and should leave them to it."

"No," I said, "that is not happening."

"I'm sure your mom can handle herself. Isn't she, like, fifty?"

"She's forty-five."

"Same difference. Besides, Jessica Burnstein is a bad MF, right? My dad said she's a ballbuster."

"Ew, also gross. But true story."

I hung up and peed, and washed my hands, because I've been properly raised. Then I took a deep breath and headed back to the table.

As I got closer, I saw the guy was holding Mom's hands, but then she pulled them away. He reached out for them again, and that time he didn't let go, and that, I'm afraid to say, is when things got a bit awkward.

JESSICA

After Emily left the table, I leaned across and frowned at David.

"Hey, what's the big deal? Stop talking about me like that. How would you like it if I told your kids how good you were in bed? You'd be pissed, right?"

David looked for the waiter again. "We were both good in bed. I miss you, that was the best sex I ever had."

"You're drunk. We were nineteen years old, of course it was good. What's wrong with you?"

"Nothing," he said. "I got divorced, I got lonely, and then you emailed me and I can't stop thinking about you." He gazed at me and, for a second, just for a second, I met his eyes and remembered how they clouded when he was deep inside me. He took my hands and ran his finger across my palm. "I'll get a room at the hotel, and when she's asleep you can come find me. Just one night, Jess, I promise it'll be worth it." He kissed my wrist.

Oh, for crying out loud. I pulled my hands away. "David, this is all very flattering, and even tempting because, sure, great sex is a fantastic thing, but on the other hand, are you out of your freaking mind? I'm with my daughter, and there is no sex on earth worth doing the walk of shame in front of a sixteen-year-old. I barely hold her respect as it is."

"You're forgetting how good it was between us." He reached out and caught my hands again. "We spent days in bed, finding out new ways to make each . . ."

"Let go of her hands, asshole, before I call security."

Emily was back.

David let go. "It's fine, we were only catching up."

She frowned at him. "She pulled her hands away and you grabbed them again. Consent isn't an ephemeral concept, you know?"

I looked at my daughter and tried not to get distracted by her excellent vocabulary. "Em, chill out. Everything's cool."

She sat but glowered at David across the table. In an ideal world, or even in the world most of us live in, we would have simmered down and struggled through the remaining ten minutes or so until we left. Maybe David and I would have attempted to make conversation about something neutral, like old friends we'd lost touch with, or things to do in Philadelphia. We would pretend she hadn't called him an asshole, or implied he was a sexual predator. But this wasn't that world. To be fair, it wasn't Emily's fault; it was David's.

"Emily." His voice was firm but sugarcoated, not that it made any difference. "Your mother is her own person, you know. I expect you feel the world revolves around you, but it really doesn't. When you get older, you'll understand."

There was a brief pause. In the back of my head I imagined the sound of a bowstring being stretched and braced myself.

Then Emily said, "When I get older?"

David nodded. "Yes. In many ways you're still a child. Maybe it's time you grew up a little bit." He paused. "Maybe if you spent less time on your cell phone and did something useful instead . . ."

I reached up my hand and waved furiously at the waiter.

"In fact," said David, reaching across the table. "Why don't you give me your phone now and I'll put it away?"

I stood up and yelled across the bar. "Check, please!"

EMILY

In the cab on the way to the restaurant, I suddenly had a terrible thought. What if my mom *had* wanted to sleep with that guy? What if Ruby was right and I had cockblocked her? I mean, he was a total idiot, but he was good looking, and adults can be so superficial. She'd seemed as keen to leave as I was, but maybe she was trying to avoid a scene. She hates a public spectacle.

I decided to ask her. I took a deep breath.

"I suddenly realized I might have messed up your plans. I'm sorry." I felt bad, and hungry, and a little bit tearful, but I was holding it together. "You're my mother, not the other way around."

Mom frowned at me. "I'm not sure what you mean . . ."

"Well, maybe you wanted to sleep with that guy. You know, he was good looking for an old guy and, you know, helping the poor and everything. I don't know anything about your . . . romantic life."

Mom burst out laughing. "Emily, I had no intention of sleeping with him, and I appreciate that you defended me, despite the fact that we can never go back to that hotel bar again. For future reference, I can take care of myself, I'm a fully grown woman, but that doesn't mean a little support isn't appreciated." She checked her watch. "Besides, what a dick."

I still felt upset. "I'm sorry. I never really think about you . . . like that. Maybe you have a very active . . . life. Maybe after I go to sleep at night you're on Tinder, swiping away and creeping out for secret hookups."

Mom snorted. "Oh yeah, that's me. When you come in to kiss me good night and I'm already in bed with the lights out, you think maybe I'm fully dressed under the covers, waiting to spring out and climb down the ivy outside my bedroom window?"

"There's no ivy outside your bedroom window."

"I was speaking metaphorically. Do you think maybe it's a pillow under the cover, and I'm out at a sex club?"

"Not really. And, ew."

"You've seen me go on dates." Mom was smiling at me. "You helped me fill out my online dating profile."

I grinned at her. "Yeah, but, you know, it wasn't super successful. You insisted on putting in that part about only being available between 7:00 and 8:30 p.m. every other Wednesday."

"Well, I didn't want to leap into anything. I really am very busy at work, Emily, and what free time I have I want to spend with you." She shrugged. "Look, that sucked, but now we're meeting Grandpa, so let's pretend it never happened. You didn't do anything wrong, we're good, okay?"

I nodded, not completely convinced. But then we pulled up outside the restaurant, and I saw Grandpa, and things started to feel better.

11

JESSICA

I'll be honest, it was good to see Dad. He's old, he's ornery, he refuses to quit smoking his hideous pipe or move closer to my sister and me, but he still feels like a safe place when I hug him. I wonder how I feel to him.

After Mom died I assumed Dad would simply fade away, because she was always such a driving force. But after wandering aimlessly around their big DC apartment for a couple of months, he pulled himself together. He moved to a smaller place in Philadelphia, worked a bit for old colleagues and clients, played bridge competitively, and still drove the ridiculous sports car he bought himself for his sixtieth birthday. He cooked for himself, or he went out. He got bored eating alone, so he dated, largely because there were more single women his age than single men. But he told me once that he still loved my mother and would never marry anyone else. And now, nine years after her death, it seems he spoke the truth.

Emily clambered out of the Lyft and ran to him, hugging him

much the same way she'd hugged Anna, back at home. It's weird, watching your kids having relationships with other people, especially people who loom large in your own life. For the first few years after Emily was born we'd lived in DC, close to my parents. I dropped off the baby at their house almost every day and went to my job. If it weren't for them, I would never have been able to continue working, and even though I don't think single motherhood was a dream they had for me, they made it possible because it was something I wanted. I'd appreciated it at the time, but not as much as I did now. Back then I appreciated the help with Emily, I really did. Now I realize my baby was very much their secondary concern; their own baby was the one they were caring for.

I watched Dad now, talking to my sixteen-year-old about the little metal model kit he'd given her. (Sidenote: On the one hand I love the fact that this is a bonding thing between them, and I appreciate how good she is at making shiny little aircraft or tiny wooden buildings or whatever, but it's my house that's filling up with all these pointy little objects. How many of you—be honest—have stood with a black plastic trash bag in one hand and a child-made creation of question-able value and struggled with throwing it away? Right, all of us.)

Maybe I was jealous. I don't remember him talking to me very much at all when I was sixteen, except to ask about school. My sister Lizzy was the sociable one, and he always seemed to have time for her. Mind you, she's easy to hang out with; it's not her fault. I wanted to debate Big Questions with him, like the LA riots and police bru-tality, whereas she wanted to show him her Breyer horses. I know which one I'd pick at the end of a long day arguing in court. Now that I had a teen of my own, I realized how reasonable my parents had been, twenty years too late. This is why grandparents look so happy all the time: They know they've made their point.

Dad had chosen Harrisons, one of those classic chain steak restaurants that haven't changed in fifty years. This one, in Philadelphia, was pretty indistinguishable from the one in Washington, which we'd visited maybe once a month throughout my childhood. It was my mom's favorite, even after they banned smoking at the tables. She'd always had filet steak, rare, creamed spinach, french fries with gravy, and a slice of cherry cheesecake. Emily had always loved it, too, and as we'd gone to DC several times a year throughout her childhood, going to this place was a highlight. We'd come less since my mom died because at first my dad couldn't face anything that reminded him of her. But eventually it morphed into Emily's favorite restaurant and shook off its sadness.

EMILY

My grandfather is pretty cool. He was standing outside the restaurant, hands behind his back, rocking back and forth on the balls of his feet, looking exactly the same as he always has. Maybe once you get really old you stop aging, if you know what I mean.

Grandpa and I have an excellent relationship, despite his bizarre attachment to Facebook. I think he's stoked to have mastered social media, and I don't have the heart to tell him Facebook is for old people. Plus, he is an old people, so, you know . . .

I ran over and gave him a hug. He smelled of pipe tobacco, probably on account of the pipe he smokes, and even though I've told him a million times about mouth cancer (I even sent photos), I kind of like the smell. No one else I know smells like that. Probably because they're all dead.

"You're still smoking?" I asked accusingly.

"Sweet Emily," he replied, "I am seventy-nine years old. I smoke a pipe once a day, and don't inhale. The tobacco scares away the germs. I'm fit as a flea."

"You saw the pictures! Your teeth will fall out!"

Grandpa leaned closer. "Sweetheart, I take my teeth out every night, they're almost certainly cleaner than yours."

Then he straightened up as my mom came over, and beamed at her. Mom claims Grandpa likes Aunt Lizzy better than her, but it's not true. Aunt Lizzy is a lot sweeter than Mom, possibly because she's not as smart (sorry, truth) and she's very easy to like. Mom takes more work.

"Dad," she said, and hugged him. I'm surprised, but she holds it a little longer than usual. Maybe the scene in the bar upset her more than she let on. Adults are such an enigma.

I spent a fat three minutes outside Harrisons, taking pictures, because that place is a half-timber Disney dream of Olde England. They even have a red mailbox, which England doesn't even have anymore! We used to spend a month every summer with my grandparents; they had a house in Lost River, in the Shenandoah Valley, with acres of woods and grass and streams and actual deer and things like that. But we'd fly in and out of DC, so we started and ended the trip at Harrisons.

Not this one, the one in DC, obviously. When I was a kid, I thought it was genuinely magical, and even now I'm stoked, no lie. Mom likes it, too, even though she totally misses the point of a steakhouse and gets the pork chop. She says she never makes them herself, which I get, but still. It's got steak *in the name.*

It was only after we sat down and ordered—I always get the same thing, steak, rare, creamed spinach, french fries—that I realized Grandpa was about to make a speech. Shoot me now. No, really, take me outside, blindfold me, let me say something memorable, then shoot me.

Grandpa was a lawyer, like my mom, but I think he spent more time in court or something, because he loves to give a speech, and it's impossible to interrupt him. I guess years of rolling right on over the objections of opposing counsel (not sleeping through *Law & Order*, that show is a classic) gave him plenty of practice.

"So, Emily," he began, and I knew right away I might as well rest my elbows on the table and get comfortable. "You're here to look at colleges, correct?"

"Correct," I replied, and glanced over at Mom. She was looking at Grandpa with one of those little lines between her eyebrows. She was wondering where he was going. She's always slightly on edge around Grandpa, I've noticed, even though he's completely harmless.

Right then he had his serious voice on. "I want to give you some advice."

As this was not a shocking development, I nodded.

"College is a wonderful opportunity," he said. "A time to really dig deeply into a subject that interests you, and hopefully discover the calling in your work we all really need. For me, and for your mother, it was the law. I have long suspected that law isn't something that interests you, am I right?"

I squirmed a bit. How to tell the truth without being savage?

"Not really, Grandpa. I don't think I'm smart enough, for one thing. I'm a pretty solid B student." Apart from those Cs, of course, but we don't need to get into specifics.

"But you can get your undergraduate degree in anything. You could study art history or something pointless like that."

I frowned at him, ignoring the diss to, you know, the entire creative output of humankind. "Well, not really. Most lawyers study political science or criminal justice or psychology as undergrads."

He frowned back, then asked my mom, "Is that true?"

She nodded and shifted in her chair. "It's not like it used to be. It's not even like it was for me. These days getting into college and law school is like a blood sport. It's insane."

She sounded tired and irritated, and gazed around as if hoping the bill would miraculously appear before the actual meal.

He nodded thoughtfully. "Well, I know the deans at several excellent schools. I'm sure I could put in a good word."

I had to cut this off. "But, Grandpa, I don't want to be a lawyer. It's not my jam, all that studying and memorizing."

"What, then?" The waiter came and refilled Grandpa's wineglass. Grandpa raised it at me. "Where are you going to triumph?"

Crap. How about nowhere?

"Uh, I'm not sure, Grandpa. I really don't like school very much, not sure four more years of it is . . ."

"College is nothing like high school. You'll love college."

The food arrived, thank god. Grandpa always chills out after he eats and has some wine. He also has a strict rule never to discuss serious matters while eating, so we talked about baseball, which I happen to enjoy talking about more than most girls I know—not a sexist comment, just an observation. I wish I could talk about baseball for a living, but I can't imagine that working out for me. When I went to the bathroom I googled it. As I suspected, I'd still need a bachelor's degree in journalism or something.

Everyone tells you middle school is fun, and then you get there and it sucks. Then high school is going to be fun, but you get there and it both sucks and is really hard. Now, apparently, college is going to be fun, but it really seems like one more hurdle standing between me and actual happiness. Whatever that is.

JESSICA

So, Dad started grilling Emily about college, which is not the best way to get anything out of her. But I couldn't exactly interrupt his flow to say, *Dad, wait, you're going about this all wrong. She won't tell you anything if you come at her head-on; you have to approach her obliquely, sneak attack.* Besides, she never tells me anything anyway, so my way isn't exactly coming up trumps.

I remember the conversation my dad and I had about my decision to become a lawyer, like him. It went like this:

    Me: I've decided to become a lawyer.

    Him: Are your grades strong enough?

Me: Yes.

Him: Good choice.

That's it. That was the whole thing. I finished my degree, I got into Columbia Law, which was a lot easier back then, especially for Columbia graduates, and was about to start my first job when I got pregnant with Emily. I remember that conversation, too:

Me: I'm pregnant.

Him: You're about to start work.

Me: Yeah, I know.

Him: Are you going to have an abortion?

Me: No. I don't think so.

Him: You'll ruin your career.

Me: No, I won't. I have it all figured out. I'll work part-time. When she's older I'll work full-time. It's fine.

Him: Good luck.

And again, that was it, the whole thing. The conversation with my mother was slightly different:

Me: I'm pregnant.

Her: Are you keeping it?

Me: I think so.

Her: Do you know who the father is?

Me: Of course, but he's not interested. If I keep it, I'm doing it alone.

Her: Aren't you worried you'll end up a lonely single mother
who no man will ever want?
(Pause)
Me: Well . . . I wasn't.

And that was it, her version of the conversation. It wasn't that they didn't have any faith in me, it was that I was twenty-eight. I was an adult. I was expected to know my own mind, and I did.

EMILY

Dessert might even be my favorite thing about Harrisons. You can have Spotted Dick, lol, which is actually a super-yummy spongy cake thing with raisins, or cheesecake, or chocolate cake, or that thing where they cook the top with a tiny blowtorch right at the table. You'd think the sprinklers would go off, and I kind of always hope they will. I had cheesecake. Cherries are my go-to berry. Are they a berry? (Googles under table.) Go-to drupe, new word of the day.

Grandpa took a forkful of chocolate cake and said, "But really, Emily, what's your plan for the next few years?"

I swallowed my cheesecake and shook my head. "I'm not sure, Grandpa. Go to college, I guess."

Mom jumped in. "She doesn't have to decide until the fall, Dad. Part of the point of this trip is for her to look around and see which colleges appeal to her." The irony of the Great Questioner defending me from interrogation is not lost on me.

Grandpa pointed his fork at my face, which was rude. "If you're not sure what to do, pick a major you can live with and go to the best school you can. The people you meet are far more important than what you study. You'll make the connections that matter."

I wanted to talk about how elitist that is, and how it perpetuates inequality (two semesters of sociology elective) but decided to nod thoughtfully and eat my cheesecake. Did I mention it had cherries?

After dessert I escaped to the bathroom again and ended up FaceTiming with Sienna for about ten minutes. She was over the Becca thing because something more serious has happened: She got a B on her test and thinks her life is over. She was literally in tears. She's dramatic at the best of times, but now she really gave it her all.

"Cornell's out of the question now," she sobbed. "They haven't taken anyone with less than a 4.2 in over twenty years. I might as well take Northwestern off the table, too, and UPenn isn't happening." She's a madwoman, of course; one B isn't going to make any difference in an otherwise perfect record. Sienna kept going but I kind of drifted off. Everyone wants to get into a "name" school, one that when you tell people you got in, they make that face, the face that says, *You won the game, you're set for life.* Of course, only very few get in, which makes those schools even more special. They're like the girl who turns everyone down, so everyone wants to date her and no one ever discovers she's completely boring.

"Did Mrs. Bandin call anyone else in?" I asked suddenly.

"No," said Sienna, "are you even listening to me?"

"Yeah," I said, "what about your safety schools?"

After another few minutes I suddenly remembered where I was

and shot back out to the restaurant, surprised Mom hadn't come looking for me.

But they were talking and hadn't even noticed my long absence.

JESSICA

Emily went off to the bathroom, and my father cleared his throat. "Is Emily a good student?"

I looked at my dad and wondered about his definition of good. "She maintains a steady B. She tries hard, she does her work. I don't think she's a rocket scientist. She's still better and happier drawing and making stuff than she is at schoolwork. Always has been."

His eyebrows drew together the way they did at least once in every conversation we'd ever had.

"Sure, but now she's a young woman, not a child. Time to put aside childish things, correct?"

I tried to channel my mother's neutral tone. She frequently disagreed with my father, but never made him frown the way I did. "News flash, Dad, adults draw and make things, too."

"Maybe she could be an architect?"

I sighed to cover my irritation. "Dad, she's sixteen, she doesn't know yet. She's struggling right now, you need to leave her alone."

"We left you alone and look what happened."

I frowned at him, my eyebrows a perfect echo of his, not that I could see it. "What happened? I got my degree, finished law school, moved to LA, succeeded despite being a single parent, and now I'm a partner and making a frankly ridiculous salary. Isn't that what you wanted?"

He was silent for a moment. "It's what I wanted for you. Your mother thought you would have been happier staying in school."

I laughed. "What, forever?"

He shrugged. "She thought you were too deep a thinker for the law, not pragmatic enough for the constant compromise."

I was surprised. "This is news to me. She never told me that." My mother had talked to me constantly, her voice the birdsong of my childhood. I wish I could remember more of what she actually said. Listening might have helped.

He shrugged again and moved the knife on his plate. "You never asked her opinion. You went off to college and we rarely saw you, then you were at law school and we saw you maybe twice a year, and then you were pregnant." He drank his wine, unable to sit still for a moment. "At least then she felt needed. Helping you with the baby made her very happy, although it was bittersweet."

I refilled my glass, largely to give myself a moment to think. My mom had only rarely given me her opinion, whereas my dad had an opinion about everything. He and I argued all the time about this and that, starting when I was around nine and really settling in once I was a teenager. My mom used to roll her eyes when we started and go outside to smoke (later on I'd banned her from smoking in her own home when I was there with Emily, something I feel a little guilty about now). I regret not going and sitting with her outside every time she left the room; I wish I'd spent more time asking about her rather than telling her about me. We'd spent time every summer with my parents at their country house in West Virginia, but I'd seen it as a chance to rest while she played with Emily and watched her build her forts or make dams in the stream. She and Emily were so happy together, I felt fine leaving them alone. Now I wish I'd joined in more.

Dad was still talking. "She always felt she'd given up a lot once she had you two, and she wanted you both to have as much freedom from responsibility as possible." He cleared his throat. "Not that she regretted having you two, she loved being a mom. But when Emily came along, she was sad, not because she didn't love children, but because she loved you. She wanted you to have more time to yourself. More space."

I wasn't sure how to process that, so I said, "Did she miss working?" My mom had been a graphic designer, working in an advertising agency in New York when she met my dad. He was already in DC; they'd met at a wedding. For a year or two they'd dated on and off, then she'd moved to an agency in DC and they got married. I realized I'd never heard her talk much about her career. Maybe I wasn't listening, the same way Emily wasn't listening to me.

Dad nodded. "Sometimes, although she never really loved her work. She was much happier puttering around the house, putting up shelves, or whatever it was she did in that workshop she had. Besides, this was the seventies, remember? Everyone thinks it was a time of social revolution, but after taking a few years off when you two were small, it was really hard for her to find another job she actually wanted." He caught the waiter's eye and signaled for the check. "Employers knew women would put their children first, and felt comfortable not hiring them because of it." He looked at me. "These days I would probably get fired for saying that, despite the fact that it's true."

"Not all women, Dad."

He shrugged. "Your mom used to say she'd made a trade, and

sometimes it felt worth it and other times"—he made a face—"like when you stayed out all night in tenth grade and she nearly called the police, it didn't."

I smiled. "Emily certainly wouldn't get away with that. I track her every movement on her phone."

He made a noise under his breath. "Well," he said, pulling out his wallet to pay the bill. "I can't imagine that's very much fun for either of you."

12

JESSICA

When we got back to the hotel, I felt like I'd spent the previous four hours pushing a rock uphill or attending an endless PTA meeting. I was wiped. I checked my watch. Wow. Nine o'clock.

As soon as we got to the room, Emily threw herself on the bed and opened her computer. God forbid ten minutes should pass without connecting to the internet. I went to the bathroom and texted Frances.

"You there?"

I waited a moment, and then, thankfully, she appeared. "'Sup, dog?"

"OMG you are not going to believe the evening I just had."

"Spill the tea."

"David turned out to be super hot, super drunk, and super into sleeping with me. It was extremely awkward." I start removing my mascara, taking half my lashes with it. I don't remember that happening when I was younger. Do eyelashes grow back?

A pause, then: "No way. That's awesome. How often does DHG stay D and H?!"

Let me back up a bit. I had told Frances about David ages before, of course. About how we'd had this supersexy relationship, how we had slept together on and off throughout college, even for a few years after. Frances had christened him Dangerous Hot Guy.

"We all have one," she'd said. "A guy who blows our buttons off in bed but who is in no way suitable for an actual long-term relationship."

Now she was delighted. "I was expecting him to be twenty pounds heavier, married, with three kids and erectile dysfunction."

I texted, "Well, he looks much the same, is divorced, left a highly lucrative job in government law to help the dispossessed, and at least to hear him tell it, has zero dysfunction."

"So . . . ?"

"So nothing. Emily saw him holding my hand and went totally ballistic. It was beyond embarrassing, and then he patronizingly suggested she spend less time on her cell phone."

Frances said, "Wow, I bet she loved that."

"Yup, we left the hotel bar, then she and I had a follow-up question-and-answer session about the state of my sex life that I could definitely have lived without." My fingers couldn't tap fast enough; I kept having to go back and fix autocorrections. "And then, to cap this challenge of fire, we had dinner with my dad. I spent the whole time deflecting the kind of questioning I'm usually on the other side of."

There was a pause while she presumably digested that. Then: "And now?"

"Now I'm hiding in the bathroom texting you!"

My phone buzzed with another text. "OMG David texted me, hang on."

"Hurry!"

I swiped over. "My offer still stands, Jess. I'm in the lobby."

I swiped back. "He's in the lobby!"

"No! Stalker!"

"Yes!" I suddenly felt panicky and slightly nauseated. "I'm freaking out."

"Don't freak out. Just tell him you're not interested." A pause. "You're not interested, right?"

I swiped back. "David, go home. This isn't going to happen."

I swiped back to Frances. "No, it's not going to happen. I don't want it to happen."

"To be fair, you were complaining only last week about your lack of sex!"

"Yes, but in the context of discussing vibrators, not hooking up with stalker ex-boyfriends!"

"Good point. Go watch TV with Emily and lock your door."

"It's a hotel, it's already locked."

"Another good point. Text me tomorrow."

Another text came in from David, but I blocked him and shut off my phone. I could feel an intense desire for my own bed, my own house, my own safe space. So I crawled into bed next to Emily, and together we watched TV and I felt better.

EMILY

I ate so much at Harrisons I kind of thought I'd crash out once we got to the hotel. But when I checked my phone in the car, I had dozens of texts from both Becca and Sienna, which, you know, ruined my potential food coma. After pondering it for a while, I decided to take the decisive step of ignoring them both; I'll deal when I get home. Meanwhile, life online has continued, with Ruby trying to cheer Sienna up by posting a funny picture of her, which, it turned out, Sienna hated because it looks like she has no butt at all. We all swiftly posted pictures that were more butt flattering, and slowly the drama simmered down. Sometimes social media feels like a runaway train, or an out-of-control team of horses in a western movie. Other times it's so boring I could quit it forever, once I've made sure there's no more good stuff over here on this feed . . .

I sent a picture of my room, so they're all jealous, which they wouldn't be if they could see how tiny it really was. But I stood on the desk and put a good filter on, and by the time I was done it was amazing. Not that anyone cares anyway, though I did get over a hundred likes. Pretty standard.

Thank goodness for *Friends*; it's my favorite show. It's open on my laptop all the time, nestled in the background. It's like one of those apps that make ocean noises or whatever. Chandler Bing is my ocean noise.

I could hear my mom's phone pinging away in the bathroom while she was in there, and wondered if she was talking to that guy. But when she came out she was in her flannel nightie and had taken off her makeup and was my regular mom again. Phew. I even put away my phone, and I'm not ashamed to say we snuggled and watched *The Land Before Time*, which is not in any way historically accurate. I also finished the metal model Grandpa gave me. It's a dragon. My mom has kept all the models I've made over the years and I really hope she doesn't expect me to take them to college. If it were up to me I'd chuck the lot, but you know how sentimental parents are.

After the movie was over and the lights were out, another thought occurred to me.

"Mom?"

"Mmm?" Her voice was sleepy.

"What exactly is the Peace Corps?"

She turned over in bed, tugging the quilt tighter. "I'm too tired to explain it in detail, but basically it's this thing where people, usually young people, sign up to spend a year or more in a country where they're needed, to do whatever work is asked of them, in order to help local people."

"Wow, that's a pretty detailed explanation, for a tired person."

Her voice was sleepy. "I'm a highly trained professional."

"Would you ever do it?"

She paused. "Not now. Maybe when I was young. But it's kind of a luxury, to be able to spend a year not working on your actual life. People do it, of course. People take their kids and stuff, even."

"He did it."

"Sure, very noble, but all I could think about was that he'd wandered off for a year to find himself, leaving his ex-wife alone with two young kids who've just gone through a divorce. Kind of a dick move, right?"

"I hadn't thought of it like that."

She mumbled something. She was drifting off.

"What kind of things do they do?"

"Not sure . . . build schools, dig wells, that kind of thing." She half snored and caught herself. "Google it." Then she fell asleep completely.

······················▶

Wednesday

Pennsylvania

8:00 a.m.: Theme breakfast: Fears!

9:00 a.m.: Check out of the hotel

10:00 a.m.: University of Pennsylvania

12:00 p.m.: Lunch at the Philadelphia Museum of Art—
café meal included! Note: The museum is open this time! Art it up!

2:00 p.m.: Drive 25 minutes on the E3 College Coach

3:00 p.m.: Swarthmore College

Drive 1 hour and 4 minutes to New Jersey on the
E3 College Coach

6:00 p.m.: Check into hotel in Princeton

7:00 p.m.: Dinner at Einsteins—a math-themed diner!
(Two courses included.)

◀·······················

13

EMILY

This morning the breakfast was back to pastries, and after a bit of a scuffle over the limited number of cinnamon rolls, people stood about uncertainly, waiting to be told where to sit. I was too slow for a cinnamon roll, but I did snag a chocolate croissant, the silver medal of pastries. I got a cup of tea, too, because I had what Mom calls an emotional hangover from the previous evening. I'm sure you've had one: Everything is a little bit loud, you seem to have lost a few layers of skin, and tears are a distinct possibility. I think Mom has one, too; she and I have barely spoken, but not in an unfriendly way. Just in a not-speaking way that could go either way any second. Mom taught me that emotional hangovers need four things to dissipate: caffeine, sugar, space, and time. Sometimes she's very wise; don't tell her I told you so.

I walked over to Will. He'd snagged a cinnamon roll, of course, but he tore off a piece and offered it to me. I waved the croissant at him.

"How was the Rocky thing?"

"The steps? Surprisingly fun." He lowered his voice. "It was a classic example of the gap between perception and reality."

"How so?"

He grinned and leaned in a little closer. I could smell the hotel soap on him, as if he'd been in the shower with me not thirty minutes earlier.

"Well, in the movie, he runs up the whole flight of stairs, right, which is not what happened last night. People stationed someone at the top, sprinted up the last few, and then raised their arms for the picture." He took a bite of cinnamon roll. "Although Sam and Casper decided to actually run the whole thing and Sam had to stop halfway to pull out his inhaler. Casper made it to the top in record time, then revealed the other school office he holds is secretary of the cross-country club."

"Sam is . . . ?"

Will narrowed his eyes at me. "Sam is Falling Mother. Casper you already know." He chewed. "We're all actual people, you know. It's not only you and Alice on the tour."

I was surprised, and started to ask him what he meant, but Cassidy launched into her speech.

"Good morning, tourists!" (She'd probably come up with that in the shower and was clearly pleased with it.) "Here are today's seating groups."

Oh, fantastic.

JESSICA

Looking across the table at Alice, I realized a lack of eye contact was a constant for teenagers. It's not that they won't look at you, it's that they have many other things to look at and, to be honest, they've seen you before.

When Cassidy put us together, there was a highly awkward exchange where we all pointed out we knew each other and therefore the avowed intent—getting to know new people—wasn't going to work.

"But I pulled names at random," said Cassidy.

"Right," said Emily, "but we all know each other already. Can't you pick again?"

Cassidy wasn't having it. "But you're friends."

Infinitesimal pause while we all internally debated refining her definition, then realized we should have been rushing to confirm it.

"Of course," I said, smiling at Dani.

"Good friends," she replied.

"Well then," said Cassidy, turning to deal with a nut allergy at table four.

"So, Alice," I said, "are you enjoying the trip?"

She shrugged and flicked a glance up at me. "Sure. It's better than school."

I looked at Dani, and for the first time ever our eyes met in perfect mutual comprehension.

We both tried to engage the kids in conversation, but they weren't having it, and as soon as possible they bounced away to talk to other kids, leaving Dani and me alone.

"More coffee?" she asked as she got up to refill her own cup.

"Thanks." I watched her walk away, realizing I'd never seen her in sneakers before. She was still very tall, but somehow more human without the towering stilettos.

She sat back down. "My feet are killing me," she said. "All that walking."

I nodded, taking the coffee from her and smiling. "LA really makes you soft."

"Who walks?" She laughed ruefully, "Turns out I'm only in shape from the ankles up. My feet are a mess."

We sipped in silence.

Dani sighed. "Do you think your daughter likes you?"

I was surprised by the vulnerability implied by the question. "I'm not sure, I'll be honest. Some days she's lovely. Other days she treats me with utter disdain."

Dani pursed her lips. "Yup. Me, too. If I'm giving her what she wants, Alice is totally lovely. But if I thwart her plans in any way—which is not hard to do these days—she's so amazingly mean."

I looked at her lovely face sympathetically. "Emily has thrown some truly amazing insults my way, I promise you. It was maybe even slightly worse a couple of years ago. Twelve to fourteen was pretty hideous."

"At least you get to go to work." Dani was gazing glumly into her coffee cup. "I could have kept modeling, but I wanted to give my girls the best start possible." She flicked a glance at me, and tried to backtrack half a step. "Not that working full-time is a bad idea, of course."

"Well," I replied drily, "it's a better idea than starving to death."

She laughed uncertainly. "Mind you, I keep myself busy. I'm on three different committees at school, as you know, and I do a lot of philanthropy, of course."

"Of course," I replied, trying to remain neutral. In the past, Dani—and other moms like her, moms I thought of as professional mothers, who tackled parenting like a full-time career—had made me feel guilty for going to work. When emails went out calling for library volunteers, or chaperones for field trips, the same subset of parents would leap forward. *Of course*, they would say. *I'm available. Happy to!* Those of us who worked outside the house would be bummed out, briefly, but—and I'm being honest here—accompanying twenty-two fifth graders to the Natural History Museum isn't my idea of a good time.

Now Dani looked at me. "You know, I thought I was doing the right thing, staying home with Alice and her sister. I thought it would be fun, and it was fun, for ages. When they're little, when they're cute and let you dress them up. But now it's just a pain in the ass. Despite everything I do for them, they treat me like a combination chauffeur/ATM/punching bag, and it's getting on my nerves."

"Why did you come on this trip?"

Dani shrugged. "It seemed like a good idea at the time. I thought maybe Alice and I would hang out, like we used to." She laughed at herself. "I thought maybe if she was away from her friends, she'd have to talk to me." She examined her acrylic nails, checking for chips. There weren't any.

I nodded. "Same here. But it isn't working out quite how I wanted it to. Not yet, anyway."

Dani leaned across the table. "I've spent the last sixteen years doing everything for her, and she treats me like crap." She eyed me. "Maybe if I'd been less available, she'd treat me with more respect."

I shrugged. "I wonder if I'd been around more, Emily would be nicer to me."

"Maybe if I'd been more disciplined," said Dani.

"Maybe if I'd been less disciplined," I replied.

Emily appeared suddenly at my elbow.

"I'm going up to pack up and get ready," she said. "Are you coming?"

I nodded, but she turned and walked out without me. Dani and I watched her go, and then I turned to her and grinned.

"See? Pure charm."

Dani laughed.

14

EMILY

We were on the bus to UPenn. My mom was on her phone, as usual, probably texting Valentina something important. After breakfast we'd gone up to the room and had the following stellar conversation:

Mom said, "I never thought I'd say this, but Dani isn't as bad as I thought."

"Really?" I replied.

She nodded.

"Well," I said, "Alice is still a total bitch."

But now, on the bus, Mom was ignoring me again. I thought about David Millar, the night before. Normally, and I don't mean to sound weird, most people I meet with my mom are more interested in me. They're being polite, usually, but they ask about school, or these days about college, or about social media or whatever. The guy last night looked right through me and was only interested in my mom. I looked at her now, staring at her phone, and tried to imagine what she was like in college. Apparently she was sexy and unpredictable, two words I would never have applied to her.

"Mom," I said.

"Yes?" She turned away from her phone and smiled at me.

"Do you miss being . . . single?"

She frowned. "I am single . . ."

"I meant, without a kid."

She shrugged. "No. I love being a mom, even if you don't like having a mom."

I turned back to the window. "I like having a mom. What kind of thing to say is that? I love you."

"I know. I love you, too." She paused. "Are you still thinking about last night?"

I nodded but didn't say anything. My throat had gone tight again, for no good reason I could see.

She put her hand on my leg and squeezed. "Don't worry about it. I promise not to desert you and run off to the Peace Corps."

I felt the tension ease a bit. "Are you sure? You're not secretly harboring a desire to build latrines in the developing world?"

"Well, obviously that would be fun, but no, I'm quite happy with things as they are."

I nodded. "Me, too."

We rode the rest of the way to UPenn in silence. But it was nice.

There is no way I'm ever getting into Penn, not even sure why they include Ivies on the tour; it's depressing. However, we went to the Philadelphia Museum of Art for lunch, and it might be my new favorite place. There was half an hour before lunch, so I wandered off to look at this one thing I'd seen on the website. They have an entire room from a nineteenth-century town house, and I wanted to see it. The room was beautifully furnished and ornate, filled with vases and sculptures, richly colored furniture and rugs. I read the card on the wall: Apparently the room had belonged to a woman who survived the sinking of the *Titanic*. She'd probably been full of beans, but her drawing room was kind of cold.

"The tapestry at the back tells the story of Cupid and Psyche, you know."

I turned and there was Will, standing behind me with his arms folded. He continued, "The way I heard it, Venus was jealous of Psyche's good looks so she sent her son, Cupid, the god of love, to make her fall in love with the biggest loser he could find. However, Cupid fell for her himself, hid her away so he could seduce her, and eventually, after much drama, was able to make her immortal and date her, you know, on the regular."

I laughed. "That's how you heard it?"

He nodded. "That's the story."

"I thought Cupid was a fat little cherub with an arrow."

"Yeah, but before he was that, he was a totally fit guy who hooked up with Psyche."

"Huh."

We were silent for a moment, then Will said, "Is this what your bedroom's like at home?"

I turned and grinned at him, nodding. "Yeah, exactly."

"Mine, too, except mine's more red and gold, you know."

"More regal?"

"That's what the decorator was going for."

We turned and started walking slowly along the galleries. "Are you enjoying the trip?" I asked, suddenly aware of his arm swinging next to mine. He was deeply cute, and we did seem to keep ending up talking all the time. I guess Alice's plan wasn't working out the way she'd hoped. Sorry . . . not sorry.

"Yeah, it's interesting." Will smiled at me. "It's like visiting a series of really big high schools, where the kids are taller and the subjects are harder."

I laughed. "I really hope college is more different than that. My mom always makes it sound like an incredible adventure of new people and casual sex."

Will looked puzzled. "She's excited for you to have casual sex?"

"Well, not explicitly. But she says things like *college is a great time to get to know lots and lots of different people*, and then she'll look at me meaningfully, which is, like, the most embarrassing thing ever."

"Wow, that's super awkward."

"Yup. She means well, I guess . . ."

"My dad gave me a giant box of condoms and said, 'Pants off, jacket on, end of story.'"

I raised my eyebrows. "Wow, also awkward."

"Very."

"At least it was a big box. Awkward, but optimistic."

Will smiled at me, my god the dimple. "He bought them at Costco, he lives for bulk savings."

"Interesting. My mother is more of the 'get a good one that will last a long time' shopper." I made a face. "Not really applicable to condoms."

We'd reached a gallery where many Mary Cassatt paintings were hanging, and paused before a sketch of a mother and child.

"It's hard to imagine my mother being young like that," I said, nodding my head at the picture. "I mean, I can only remember because I see the photos, right?" I wondered whether to tell him about my mom's ex-boyfriend the night before, but decided it was too weird. But looking at the picture, I realized the guy still saw my mom like that—not a drawing, obviously, but a young woman. He couldn't see her any other way, any more than I could see her as anything other than my mom.

My phone buzzed. "Speak of the devil, my mom's bugging me to come eat."

"Gotta eat. It's not like you've got a lot of reserve, you're like a bird."

I narrowed my eyes at him. "Are you making an uninvited comment on my physical appearance?"

Will shrugged, unconcerned. "Yeah, if comparing you to a hollow-boned but beautiful creature is unwelcome."

I stuffed my phone back in my pocket. "I'll have to think about it."

He grinned and looped his arm through mine. "Well, let's eat while you think."

JESSICA

Emily disappeared off into the museum, muttering about something she wanted to see, and I trailed to the Museum Café with the other parents. Valentina had needed help while I was on the bus, but there were no more texts from her. It was time to check email again.

I scrolled past the usual school communications, invitations to donate to worthy causes, and reminders of meetings I'm not physically available to attend, and came to rest on one from Arthur Ostergren. Jesus, I'm not even on his account. I just happened to be handy.

"Dear Ms. Burnstein," it read, which was a reasonable start. "Please contact me privately at your earliest convenience."

I sighed. He's not an idiot; he must understand that asking for privacy over corporate email is dumb. I started to write back, then looked at the time and decided to call. Hopefully he'd be at lunch; then I could leave a message and ignore his call back, and we could go back and forth like that until I returned to Los Angeles and could actually focus on work. Look at me, devious corporate superstar.

He picked up immediately. Damn him.

"Ah, Ms. Burnstein, how good of you to call."

I realized it's not so much Bond villain as it is Mr. Burns from *The Simpsons*.

"No problem, Mr. Ostergren. How can I help you?"

Around me the other parents and kids were getting lunch, and now I was hungry. There were a few mothers with young kids, too, and I found myself watching them enviously. The days when a trip to a museum would fill the space before a nap or dinner, when simply being in such a big place would keep Emily amused for ages, those days were dreamy and, now, long gone.

Mr. Ostergren cleared his throat. "Well, it's rather a delicate matter."

Oh crap, he was being sued for sexual harassment.

"Well, perhaps one of your own lawyers would be . . ."

He interrupted me. "No, that's the point. I wanted to ask if you would be at all interested in leaving Lexington to take a position as our corporate counsel."

I watched a toddler throwing a tantrum on the other side of the café. His mother was simply sitting there, watching him sympathetically, giving him space. I would have traded places with her in a heartbeat.

"Uh, well, that's a surprising question, Mr. Ostergren. You know very little about me." I thought of something else. "Are you unhappy with our services? I'm sure John would be happy to . . ."

"No, I'm not unhappy, per se, but I'm trying to acquire a competitor, and for the amount I pay in fees, I could have someone in house." He huffed. "It turns out the competitor has an in-house counsel, and she's been making my life pretty difficult during the acquisition process."

"Well, if you make the acquisition, presumably she'll become your in-house counsel. Problem solved."

He said firmly, "No, I want one of my own."

I'm sure he didn't realize how childish he sounded. I chewed my lip. This was a problem. I didn't want to offend him and potentially lose a client, but of course I might be leaving the firm, in which case I could use the job, but then on the third hand, stealing a client isn't a good way to start a new firm, although on the fourth hand, if I were just his in-house counsel then it was less . . . I stopped thinking; it was all a bit too much.

He had continued. "After we met, I googled you. You have a very impressive résumé."

"I do?"

"Yes. Graduated near the top of your class at Columbia Law, a year or two in Washington as an associate at a very good firm, then out to Los Angeles, youngest partner at Lexington, several landmark cases and state precedents. For a single woman, it's all very impressive."

I took a breath. Why was there always that qualification? What if every time I commented on a man's success I said, *for someone whose genitalia is dangerously housed outside of their bodies, it's a reasonable effort.* I chose to deflect.

"It probably would have been harder if I'd had someone else's career to consider."

"Possibly."

"I do have a child, Mr. Ostergren. Leaving Los Angeles isn't possible for me right now, I'm sorry."

There was a pause while he considered this. The toddler on the other side of the café had calmed down and was happily playing with a plastic dinosaur, and for a moment I met the eyes of the other mother. I smiled at her, and she smiled back. *Congratulations*, my expression said, and, *Thanks*, said hers. Complete conversation, three seconds.

"Well, that's acceptable. You don't have to move to Baltimore right away. You could work remotely, there's not really any need to relocate." He had clearly realized he would save on relocation costs and was warming to this idea.

"Uh, I don't know, Mr. Ostergren. Your firm specializes in international shipping, it's not an area of law I'm very familiar with."

"You'll learn." He paused. "I'm a good judge of people, Ms. Burnstein. I know you can do it. I assure you the salary would be attractive, the benefits comprehensive." Then he mentioned a sum of money far in excess of what I was currently making, which, I won't deny, changed the tenor of the conversation somewhat.

"Mr. Ostergren, I'm very flattered you even thought to ask me. I need to think about it for a while. I'll get back to you next week, once I'm in LA again. Will that work?"

"Certainly, Ms. Burnstein."

I hung up, then texted Emily that she needed to come eat something.

Good lord.

15

EMILY

After lunch it was back on the bus. Swarthmore was pretty, but I probably shouldn't pick a college based on looks; it would confirm my mom's worst suspicions about the Instagram generation. Right now I can't imagine wanting to spend another minute in a classroom, given the choice. When I graduate high school I will have been in school for thirteen solid years, not even counting preschool. I'd get a shorter sentence for armed robbery.

The admissions lady was nice, though, and she was wearing, like, platform saddle shoes with bright green laces. I was obsessed.

JESSICA

Emily seemed very interested during the Swarthmore admissions talk and told me she thought it was a really pretty campus. I'd wandered onto Columbia's campus and felt immediately at home. Was it too much to hope Emily would have a similar experience some-where?

It was a bit rushed at Swarthmore, unfortunately, and then we piled into the E3 bus to head to New Jersey. I guess they wanted to try to miss the traffic, but that was a pretty epic fail and we spent three hours on the bus instead of the hour or so the itinerary said. Not that it mattered.

Emily sat next to me on the bus, although I'd noticed she and Will had had their heads together all through lunch. I decided to try to sidle up to the topic.

"So, you and Will seem to be getting on. Is he nice?" Not a subtle sidle, to be fair, but it worked.

"Sure," Emily said. "He's very nice. He knows a lot about art and history."

"Really? Then why isn't he studying that at college, rather than computers?"

She shrugged. "No clue. Ask him."

"No, you can ask him."

She frowned at me. "You know, it's weird what you think I talk about with my friends. We never ask each other what our parents do for work, although you always ask me. We don't talk about college, either, unless we're forced to, like by Cassidy at breakfast. We talk about ourselves, about what we like, movies, books, the usual conver-sational stuff. It's not a constant interview, which is what seems to happen when two adults get together. *What do you do for a living? Where did you go to school? What does your wife do?*" She looked out the window. "You guys are weird, you don't know how to communi-cate, you're too busy stratifying."

I looked at her. "Nice word."

"Thanks," she said, not turning around. "I learned it from Casper."

"Who's Casper?"

"Geology Boy." She frowned at me. "We had breakfast with him yesterday, remember?"

"Oh yeah, sorry."

She turned back again. "See? You don't even know their names."

I fought back gently. "It's not like they've been coming up to me all the time, introducing themselves and curiously asking me my opinion and thoughts on everything."

"Alice talks to you."

I shook my head. "No, Alice hasn't actually spoken to me directly. She doesn't like me, because she can tell I don't like her." I lowered my voice, suddenly worried Dani could hear me. She was at least eight rows ahead, but the last thing I wanted was for her to know the truth. Truth is a deadly foe when you're trying to get along with hundreds of other parents for a dozen years.

Emily's mouth twitched. "How can she tell that?"

I narrowed my eyes at her. "Because she possesses the native cunning and sense of self-preservation all mammals do. She can smell my disapproval."

"Like a horse?"

"I think that's fear. I don't think horses care if you approve of them or not."

"Why don't you like her?"

I made a face. "Because she's not a nice person, she's mean to you, she's a narcissist and a power-mad queen bee." I paused. "Apart from that I'm sure she has many sterling qualities."

"Not really."

"Well, there you go." I watched the Pennsylvania countryside sliding by. We passed a classic red barn, a man walking a cow back into it on a rope, presumably leading his best farming life. He was unaware of our passing, and for all I knew he was filled with concern about his own kid's entrance into college, but it seemed more likely he was thinking about his cow. Not getting her into college but getting her into the barn. Often when I'm driving around, I look at other people and wonder about their lives, about how we all go about our day with our minds swirling with hopes and plans for disaster, unaware of everyone else's concerns. It made me feel better, knowing I was one of many, because most of the time I feel very much on my own.

I'd made that choice, of course. When I'd found out I was pregnant, which was a surprise, I'd immediately known I wanted to keep the child. The guy in question was not a candidate for marriage, and although we'd been dating for a few months, it was simply a mildly pleasant liaison. We liked the same movies, enjoyed chatting about inconsequential things, amused each other in bed, but . . . nothing beyond that. He wasn't quite as smart as me, I wasn't quite as good looking as him, and neither of us had a desperate urge to couple up at all costs.

When I told him the news, he was completely on board with my keeping the baby as long as I didn't expect him to do anything about it. He didn't want kids, didn't want to share custody, didn't want to babysit, didn't want any of it. That was fine with me. I was nearly twenty-nine, didn't see any opportunity for marriage in my future but had always wanted to have kids—or kid, at least—and didn't want to wait any longer. I hadn't been tapping my foot, impatient to get pregnant, but once it happened I felt completely confident I could handle the baby.

And I was mostly right, because although babies are a lot harder than they look on TV, they are still only babies. I gazed lovingly at my daughter's jawline, so much firmer than it had been at six months, but still adorable. She turned, caught me looking, and raised a single eyebrow before rolling her eyes. It's just as well parents get a decade of cute and cuddly children before they turn into teenagers, otherwise humans would have died out long ago.

Then we hit traffic, and Emily got hungry, and the packet of gum I had in my bag was apparently the wrong kind of gum, and suddenly I wished I were anywhere but on this bus. I'd even have traded places with the cow on a rope.

EMILY

You'd think the tour people would provide a snack; it's kind of bullshit. My mom usually has nuts or something, but she had nothing but crappy gum. I knew I was hungry and it was making me bitchy, but knowing it is useless. My mom telling me I have low blood sugar doesn't raise my blood sugar, and if she told me one more time to chew some gum, I was going to get off the bus, possibly without even asking the driver to slow down. I gazed out the window: Maybe one of those four thousand cars standing between me and food had a sandwich in it.

Honestly, Mom drives me up the wall sometimes. If I complain I'm hungry, she points out other kids are starving, as if the fact that they're hungrier than me means I'm not hungry at all. That's not how it works! If she came in and told me to clean my room, and instead I told her about hundreds of other rooms that were far messier than mine, I can assure you she wouldn't say, *Wow, you're right, I should be grateful for what I have.*

Then Will appeared, smiled at me, said hello to my mom, and asked me if I'd like to share a Twix. We're getting married next week.

JESSICA

Oh my god, The Boy showed up and offered my furious daughter some chocolate. There goes her virginity.

Then she and Will went off to sit with the other kids, and I leaned my head gratefully against the window and tried to work out what I'm feeling. I've gotten used to describing my state as "tired" and letting it go at that, but lately I've noticed other adjectives have been pushing forward. Sad. Frustrated. Confused.

Dani suddenly plopped into the seat next to me. "Can I join you?"

Seeing as she was already sitting, I didn't think I could say no, but at least I could rely on her dominating whatever conversation she had in mind. The worried Dani of breakfast seemed to be gone; this was the usual Dani, casually expensive clothes, layered necklaces, contoured bone structure. That Dani.

She leaned forward and lowered her voice. "So, I've been meaning to ask . . . do you have a plan for college?"

I frowned. "How do you mean? Do you mean like a savings plan? Like a 529?"

Dani flicked a glance over her shoulder and lowered her voice further. "No, I meant an actual plan of attack. For getting in where you want. You know the school always plays it straight, but there are ways to make it easier."

"Make what easier?" I was clearly missing something.

She looked at me with raised eyebrows, clearly resetting her assessment of my intelligence. "Getting into college, Jessica. It's not an even playing field, you know that."

"I guess. I haven't thought about it that much." This was a lie, of course, but I wasn't going to give her the satisfaction of knowing how freaked out I was.

"Liar," she said, which was irritating. "Well, I have a friend who can be very helpful."

"Like a college adviser person?"

She nodded. "Yes. He can make calls, pull strings, that kind of thing."

I wondered why she was telling me. "Emily doesn't even know where she wants to go to college." And, I thought to myself, *I don't think you like me any more than I like you.* Or was she so starved for friends that one bonding conversation over breakfast was enough to bring me into her secret inner circle? I was definitely overthinking this, as usual.

Dani snorted. "None of them know anything, they're idiots. Alice is going to USC, we've already laid a lot of groundwork, but it wasn't like we gave her much choice."

I was surprised. "Alice strikes me as the kind of kid who doesn't like to be told what to do."

Dani shook her head. "She doesn't like it, but in this case our interests aligned. Lots of influencers go to USC, apparently." She smiled at me. "But anyway, if you need help, let me know. I'd be happy to introduce you to my friend. He knows everybody. There are back doors everywhere, and all you need is the right key."

"Are you talking about cheating?"

She looked horrified and amused at the same time. "Jessica, wash out your mouth. Of course not!" She lowered her voice again. "I'm talking about taking advantage of the existing holes in the system. It's not illegal to know people, right?"

I shook my head.

"And some kids need more help than others." She suddenly sucked in her breath. "Oh my god, I completely forgot, did you hear about what happened at school?"

"No." I remembered those emails from the head of eleventh grade and felt mildly guilty.

"They suspended several juniors for cheating. Or rather, planning to cheat. On their APs."

"Really? Is that even possible?"

She laughed. "Of course, anything's possible. Not sure what their plan was, exactly, but their parents weren't involved, so I doubt it was that good." She looked at me. "How are Emily's grades?"

I frowned at her. "Emily's grades are fine, she'll be able to get into college."

"A good college?"

Man, she was pushy. "Well, probably not an Ivy, but a good school."

She shrugged. "Well, things have changed since your time. My husband's personal assistant has a degree from Yale, and she's fetching coffee for a living. He told me over a third of their interns this year are Ivy League graduates, and one of them has a master's in chemical engineering."

I frowned at her. "And now she's an intern at a movie studio?"

Dani got to her feet. "I guess chemical engineering wasn't as glamorous as she thought it would be." She stepped into the aisle of the bus and looked down at me. "So nice to talk, Jessica."

I smiled and lied. "Yes, lovely."

"Let me know if you want to meet my friend." She paused. "I think you're so brave, letting the future take care of itself." She smiled at me. "I think it's my job to take care of my daughter."

I said nothing, letting that piece of bullshit settle in my heart and watching her sway to the front of the bus. I guess she forgot she showed me her soft insides that morning. Then I closed my eyes and leaned my head against the window, suddenly exhausted.

We finally arrived in Princeton, and Cassidy apologized for the traffic and told us we had fifteen minutes to change for dinner if we wanted to.

"Are jeans okay?" asked Chris.

Cassidy nodded her head. "Of course, it's a math-themed restaurant. I simply thought some of you might need to freshen up after the journey."

"I brought a special T-shirt," I heard Geology Boy say to Emily. "With three thousand digits of pi on it."

"Awesome," replied my daughter, with apparent sincerity. "I wish I'd thought of that."

"Oh," said the boy, "I have one with Einstein, Alan Turing, Ada

Lovelace, and Grace Hopper crossing Abbey Road, you know, like on the Beatles album cover. You can borrow it, if you like."

There was a pause, and then Will, who was standing next to her, said, "Wait, can I borrow it? It'll be too big for her, but I could totally rock it."

The boy—his name is Casper, I remembered, brain like a steel trap—looked thrilled to share with Will, who was definitely cooler than he was, in the way teenagers view these things. But Emily frowned up at Will and shook her head.

"No, he offered it to me first."

Casper got excited. "It's okay, I have another one, too. I have one with a really nice unit circle on it, you can borrow that, if you like."

Emily asked, "What's a unit circle?"

And, I kid you not, Casper appeared surprised she didn't know and said, "It's the circle of radius one centered at the origin in the Cartesian coordinate system in the euclidean plane." (In the interest of honesty, I had to go look it up on Wikipedia to make sure I got it right.)

Emily said, "I thought you said you brought a special shirt, like, a single shirt. Are all your shirts math related? I thought you liked geology?"

Casper looked confused. "Yeah, I have those, too." He unbuttoned his flannel shirt to reveal a T-shirt that read "Geologists know their schist."

At that point I turned and went into the hotel. Emily could handle this one on her own.

I checked in and went to the room and then called my sister. She'd texted me earlier that she had news, and I wanted to hear both it and her voice. Our outsides might be very different, but our insides are as thick as thieves.

Lizzy sounded happy to hear my voice. "How's it going? Is Emily being nice?"

"Well, she's ignoring me."

"Sort of the same thing."

"Is it?" I stretched my neck and wondered if it was too late for a cup of coffee. Probably; the last thing I need is another night lying in bed rehearsing conversations I'll never actually have. "We saw Dad last night. You'll be impressed to hear I didn't argue with him about anything."

She laughed. "Was he weakened by illness? How was the old fart?"

I grinned. "Fine. The same. Did you realize Mom missed her career? I had no idea."

"I wouldn't say she missed it. Who said that? Dad?"

"Yeah."

"She didn't miss advertising. She joked about wanting to be a plumber, remember? It wasn't a thing women did, back then, not that they do it much now. She loved fixing things, she loved doing it herself. She missed her workshop in the country, she talked about it a lot when she was sick."

This was a thing between us, a thing we didn't talk about because there was nothing to say. When Mom was dying, my sister went back to DC to take care of her. I came as often as I could, but Lizzy stayed. My dad was working, and someone needed to be with Mom. They'd discontinued treatment, and Mom was on a lot of pain medication, and the two of them sat together in the dining room that had become a hospital room, and talked. At the time I'd had a kid in school and was working seventy hours a week; I couldn't have been there. But I regretted it more and more. Regret is one of those emotions that outpunches reality: Even if you 100 percent could not have done things differently, it still pops up and takes a jab.

"She always did love fixing a toilet," I said, smiling. Then I changed the subject because this one hurt. "How was your day?" I imagined my sister sitting at her kitchen table, piles of homework being held down by one of her family's two elderly, constantly sleeping cats. She had long, dark hair, and sometimes when she was working it would drape across a sleeping cat and you couldn't tell where it ended and the cat began. I'd asked her once if she dyed her hair to match the cat, and she'd simply said she would no more dye her hair than she would dye the cat, and laughed at what a daft question it had been. Lizzy isn't like me; she doesn't care about getting older.

"It was okay. Teddy has strep, Paul had a callback, the other two did nothing shocking or remarkable, so, you know, a win."

"And what did you do?"

"Changed all the bedsheets."

"You know how to party."

"You're not wrong."

"What's the callback?"

"Ad for beer."

"National?"

"Yeah."

"Fingers crossed."

Emily walked in and threw her bag on the floor. "Who are you talking to?"

"Aunt Lizzy. Do you want to talk to her?"

Emily sat on the edge of the bed and reached for the TV remote. "No, say hi and tell her I love her."

"Your niece says hi and that she loves you."

"Of course she does. I'm adorable."

"Nicer than me, for sure."

"Shit, hang on a minute." The phone clattered, and there was a long gap where Lizzy went AWOL, so I put the phone on speaker and laid it on the bedside table.

Emily was flicking around the unfamiliar menu with ease and found a marathon of *Friends*. I think it might be a law that at least one channel needs to be playing *Friends* at all times. I'm showing my age; thanks to the internet, I guess everything is playing everywhere all the time. If I were the editor of *TV Guide*, I'd be reading up on how buggy whip manufacturers retrained for the future. I watched the show lazily and wondered how it was still funny, twenty years after I first watched it, mildly stoned and sitting on my tiny apartment sofa in New York. I'd been the same age as the characters, and in some ways it felt like an alternative version of my own life, with better lighting and wardrobe.

I watched Jennifer Aniston and tried to decide if I'd been able to warn her about the future—*Hey, good news, you're going to marry Brad Pitt, but then it's all going to fall apart, and the world will spend the next twenty years obsessing over whether or not you're going to have a baby and end up collectively feeling sorry for you*—would it have changed anything? Does knowing something in advance make it more or less likely to happen?

I often find myself musing on useless things like that, because I can't help thinking how weird life looks in reverse. When I was Emily's age, I thought I was going to become a world-class athlete and a Supreme Court justice, but neither of those things panned out. A relatively happy, professionally successful single mother of an unfriendly only child . . . the seventeen-year-old me would not have been impressed. She had much higher hopes for herself. I looked over at Emily and wondered what hopes that sixteen-year-old had for herself. I hope hers work out better than mine.

My sister reappeared. "Sorry, Teddy threw up."

"From strep?"

"Yeah . . . I guess I overdid it on the consolation ice cream."

I smiled at the phone, like my daughter did. "You lead a very exciting life." I was getting tired and wondered if I could persuade Emily to go for room service instead of going out.

"True story."

"Didn't you have news? You texted me."

"I did?" She paused. "Nope, I have no idea what it was."

"Probably not that you're pregnant then, you'd remember that."

She laughed. "I hope so. Oh, wait, I remember. I spoke to the other Jessica, not the Harvard Dropout Jessica, but the other one, Moldy Nose Ring Jessica . . ."

"I know which Jessica you mean . . ." (Jessica was a very popular name when I was in school. I was Pushy Jessica; let's not dwell on it.)

"And she said Tim Martinez was getting divorced."

"And this is news because . . ."

"Because you guys dated in high school."

I frowned. "And so . . . what? I'm supposed to move back home and marry my high school boyfriend?" All I remembered about Tim Martinez was that his was the first erect penis I'd ever seen. The rest of him was far less memorable, which didn't bode well for a reunion tour.

"No, silly. He's in Los Angeles."

I sighed. "I don't have time to date, you know this."

"Your vagina is going to close up."

"It's not, because that's not how biology works, and also I didn't say I didn't have time for sex. I have sex."

"With whom?"

"None of your business."

I suddenly realized Emily was looking at me and frowning. I shook my head at her. "I don't really have sex. I'm lying to your auntie so she'll stop bugging me to date someone."

"You don't have time to date," said Emily, returning to her screen.

"I told her that."

"You don't have time for anything," she added, swiping upwards like someone flicking dust.

"I've got to go, Liz," I said. "Was there anything else?"

My sister sighed. "No. Call me tomorrow."

"I will, let me know about the audition." A national ad campaign was a lot of money; it would make a real difference in their year.

"Okay."

We hung up and I tried to decide whether to ask Emily what she meant by saying I never had time for anything, and then decided against it. If I took the bait every time she dangled a potential argument in front of me, I'd have been hooked and landed years ago. We can always argue later, and probably will.

EMILY

So I borrowed a math shirt from Casper, and Einsteins turned out to be really fun. Who knew? I mean, math is okay, I don't hate it, but you know. We ordered Fermat's Prime Burgers, Fibonacci Fries, and Infinite Shakes, which came with endless refills. This last part prompted a totally ridiculous argument between Casper and Sam (falling mother kid; he and Casper are at the same school) about whether or not milkshakes could be truly infinite, because that would also mean infinite cows, infinite vanilla plantations, and infinite refrigeration, and Will and I sat there and did our best to not get a headache. I realized I wasn't mad about any of this; maybe college wouldn't be so bad. Assuming it's mostly hanging out with smart people and eating themed food. There's probably more to it than that.

JESSICA

Emily seemed to be having a good time with the other kids, and I'm not exactly miserable myself, hanging out with several of the parents and eating Cartesian Chili and Newton's Apple Pie. I was a little bit worried the servers were going to deliver the pie by dropping it on our heads, but they handed it over in the usual way.

I mentioned my concern to Jennifer, Casper's mother, and she looked at me quite seriously. Mind you, she looks serious most of the time; it might be a job requirement if you teach at Caltech.

"I'm not sure that story isn't apocryphal, anyway." She reached for her phone, presumably to look it up.

"Well, it doesn't really matter if it's true or not, does it?" I asked. "It only matters if they need a reason to drop food on customers' heads."

She regarded me curiously. "Why would they do that?" I suddenly realized she had no sense of humor at all, and probably regarded me as a subject for study.

I began to regret opening the topic. "Uh, because customers can be really annoying? Didn't you ever work as a waitress?"

She shook her head, and a little flare of doubt appeared in her eyes. This was a challenging conversation for her, apparently. The flowchart hadn't prepared her for this one.

I wrinkled my eyebrows. "What did you do in the summers and through college? I did waitressing, some of my friends worked in hotels . . . you know?"

"I interned at NASA."

"Oh."

"And then after high school I worked on my dissertation whenever I could, of course."

"Of course."

She tried. "In the last summer of college I worked at Disneyland."

"Dressed up as a character?"

She shook her head again. "No, rewriting their security system."

There was a pause. Then I said, "Does Casper have any brothers and sisters?"

"Yes, a younger sister. Wendy."

"And is she into geology, too?"

"No, not at all. She's more normal." She paused. "She's into Latin."

I studied the other woman carefully; was she actually joking now? "Isn't Casper normal?"

Her face was still completely devoid of expression. "Well, he's obsessively into geology, math, fractals, and cross-country running. There aren't any other kids like him at school, so I've always assumed he wasn't normal." She paused. "In the nonjudgmental sense of the term. Not usual. Uncommon."

I nodded. "Fair enough. Maybe he should go to Clarence Darrow, like Will. There are probably lots of kids like him there."

"Yes, almost certainly, but then Wendy would be at a different school, and the disadvantages of two different commutes would outweigh the benefits of going to Darrow." She smiled, finally. "We ran the numbers."

There wasn't a great deal I could say to that, so I turned to Lisa, who was the mother who'd danced overenthusiastically on the first night. She'd been quiet throughout this exchange, focusing on her pie and coffee. "And your son? He's at school with Casper, right?"

"Yeah, they're friends. They're co-presidents of the Fibonacci Society."

"Is that the math club?" I won't lie, I was super proud of myself for correctly remembering who Fibonacci was. I could just as easily have asked if it was an Italian cooking club.

Lisa nodded.

"And they need to share the presidency?" I was really struggling. Did Emily's school even have a math club? I resolved to ask later. "There's that much to do?"

Lisa nodded. "Oh yeah. Math Olympiad is a real thing." She lowered her voice. "Last year the team from Westminster tried to mess with our team by slipping them a printout of pi to three hundred digits with two transpositions." She was clearly scandalized. "They couldn't put it down until they found them."

Jennifer nodded. "Who could?" And then she asked me, "And what's Emily into?"

I hunted for the waitress, needing more pie. "Her phone. Her friends. Netflix."

They were fascinated. "Oh . . . she's normal."

I nodded. "I'm afraid so."

"Lucky."

I thought about their brilliant children with their assured futures and tried not to be envious. "I guess so."

16

EMILY

Back at the hotel, Mom was all bent out of shape.

"Emily," she said from the bathroom. "Does your school have a math club?"

"Yeah," I replied. "We came in third in the Math Olympiad last year." I snorted. "Darrow won, naturally."

"Do you know any of the girls on the team?"

"No, they're seniors. There's one junior on the team, I think. Not sure."

I checked my phone. I'd posted pics from the dinner, and all my friends had commented. I liked all their comments, added responses, and opened the group chat. The general consensus was Will was cute and I should go for it. There was also a subthread about whether Casper was cute, in that supernerd, suddenly-cute-best-friend way you see in movies. We know a lot of boys, despite the all-girls school vibe, because we went to regular elementary and stayed friends with those boys. Sienna and Francesca both have serious boyfriends—well, as serious as you get at sixteen, which isn't as serious as adults think, although yes, hooking up—and Ruby dates whoever she wants to. I'm not all that interested . . . At least I wasn't. Will really is cute, and anyone who pulls out a Twix at the right moment deserves consideration.

Mom appeared from the bathroom, still dressed. "Do you belong to any clubs?" She's stuck on the club thing, god only knows why.

"No, Mom. You know that."

"Is there an engineering club? You could start one."

I rolled my eyes at her, clichés be damned. "Mom, and commit social suicide? Are you out of your mind? Why don't I start an Asperger's Virgins Club?"

"Asperger's isn't funny, Emily."

"Yes, Mom, in the context of a club, it's funny."

"Well, I think you should engage with school a bit more."

She has got to be kidding. I gazed at her, exasperated. "What are you talking about? I'm taking three AP classes and the rest are honors. I've got SATs in three months and haven't gone out during the week this entire year. I couldn't be more engaged in school, and I couldn't be more freaking miserable about it." I flapped my hands at her and noticed a broken nail. I was falling apart.

She wasn't hearing me. "Some of these kids have all these extracurricular activities, you don't do any of that stuff. How's that going to look on your college applications?"

I started to feel a bit attacked. "Mom, this is my life, remember? I have two evenings a week when I'm allowed to go out, and one full day to have fun. I have homework every evening and Sunday afternoon, so out of three hundred and sixty-five days a year, I have, like, seventy something to myself."

My mom raised her eyebrows. "See, you're good at math!"

I blew my lid, a little. "Mom! School is a full-time job, and I'm supposed to also read, do sports, and have some type of social life at the same time." I could feel my face getting red, but she was really pissing me off, and I'd been in such a good mood. "I don't know what the other parents said, but I'm doing my best here and I hate school and everything about it, so the fact that I even go every day is a miracle of courage and you should really be handing out medals and those silver blankets they give out after marathons. I can't wait to be done, can't wait to have a choice about where I go every morning, like you do."

She looked at me for a minute. Then she said, "You think I have a choice? If I don't go to work every day, we don't eat. I have clients who expect me to show up in court, I have colleagues who expect me to be ready, I have no choices at all. I have responsibilities, I have expectations to meet, not to mention a child who wants the latest phone."

That was unfair. My phone is totally over a year old, but I decided not to mention this, as she was getting that look on her face that means she's actually pissed, not vaguely irritated.

"Plus," she continued, her voice getting louder, "do you think I pay those extortionate school fees so you can waste time? The whole point of going to that school is so you can go to a good college. You work hard because that's how you succeed. That's what life is, hard work and self-improvement."

I stood up, facing her across the bed. "Why do adults talk such shit about mindfulness and living in the moment, and at the same time point us all in the same direction and tell us to run as fast as we can to get ahead? *Do this, you'll be able to level up to a good high school, do this, you'll be able to get into a good college where, if you work hard, you'll be able to get a good job, where you can work harder and get a better job.* When are we supposed to start actually living?" I realized my voice has gotten louder, too, but I don't care. "And if working hard means I get a job like yours, I don't think I want it. You just told me how stressful and hard it is. If that's adult freedom, it sucks. You're going to work until you keel over and die of a stress-related heart attack? What kind of life is that?"

"It's my life. I live this way so you can have choices."

"Well, stop then! You chose to have me. I didn't ask you to work so hard. Maybe I'd rather have a crappier phone and more of you. Will's family has less money than we do, but they're much happier."

Mom was silent for a moment. "You don't know anything about their family."

"No, but I know a lot about ours. It's small, it's unhappy, and I can't wait to get out of it."

And then I went into the bathroom and shut the door, so she couldn't see how much I regretted everything I just said.

JESSICA

I walked out of the hotel, tipping my head back so I didn't start crying. Emily and I had a truly terrible argument, which, I'm ashamed to say, I totally started. I could see the words flying out of my mouth, arcing across the room like arrows, knowing they were wrong, and not able to stop myself. It's like they say, a scared dog is more danger-ous than an angry one.

Dani and Chris were sitting outside the hotel on the edge of a fountain, smoking cigarettes. Wait, no, it was only Dani who's smok-ing and she was vaping; it's not 1995. I walked over and joined them.

"Please tell me I'm not the only one who just said regrettable things to their teenager."

Dani handed me the vape pen. "Have some pot."

"We're not in California anymore, Dani, it's illegal here."

She regarded me pityingly. "Dude, inhale. The New Jersey police have enough to do without busting middle-aged women for inhaling water vapor."

I shook my head. "I get randomly drug tested."

Chris got up and headed into the hotel. "I'll get you a drink," he called over his shoulder. "They don't test for that, which makes no sense."

I sat there in silence until he returned. He handed me a generous scotch on the rocks and spoke. "I'd like to say I'm here because my son is meditating in our hotel room and wanted silence in order to better access his deep and abiding connection to me, but actually he's sulking about some kind of raspberry pie, and I had to leave before I walloped him. I didn't even see it on the menu."

I took a big swig of scotch and felt it burn down my throat. "I think it's a kind of mini-computer, rather than an actual pie."

Chris's face cleared. "Oh. That makes more sense. He kept saying he could keep it in his pocket, and I kept saying his grandmother wouldn't like that, and instead of explaining it to me, he yelled."

Dani exhaled a plume of vapor that twisted and disappeared like the cloud it was. "I asked Alice if she had a good time at dinner, and she bitched at me for ten minutes. The last thing she said was that I have no idea what it's like to be young, because it's been so long since I was." She inhaled again. "She's not wrong, but she doesn't have to be such a cow about it."

I giggled suddenly. "It really is a different world, but they're mean to us in exactly the same way we were to our parents. It's not like they've come up with new, high-tech material."

"*You don't understand me,*" said Chris.

"*All the other mothers said yes,*" said Dani.

"*You're the worst mother in the world.*"

"*You've ruined my life.*"

"*I'm never going to forgive you.*"

"*I hate you.*"

I took another big sip. "And my favorite, *I didn't ask to be born.* Thrown in the face of parents since the dawn of time, and still number one around the globe."

Chris took the vape pen from Dani and inhaled deeply. "They're so fucking immature." He exhaled. "Mind you, we're no better. I say the same shit back to them my mother said to me: *You treat this place like a hotel.*"

"*Would it kill you to say thank you?*"

"*Are you going out dressed like that?*"

"*In my day, music had a melody.*"

"*You shouldn't care what other people think about you.*"

"*You're an ungrateful bitch with pores the size of Poughkeepsie.*"

There was a pause as we both turned to Dani, who took another deep drag and exhaled.

"Only me then?" She shrugged. "Oh well."

EMILY

Mom came back in while I was falling asleep, and we had the other conversation we have a lot.

She says: I'm sorry, sweetie, I shouldn't have lost my temper.

I say: It's okay.

She says: I get really frustrated.

I say: It's okay.

She says: I worry about you, and I know I shouldn't.

I say: It's okay.

Then there is often a pause and she says: You're still mad at me?

I say: No, it's okay. It's fine.

And at that point it goes one of two ways. Either she isn't over it, in which case we fight again, or she is, in which case she'll look at me for a long time, sigh, and go away.

That was how it went just now, and even though she can't actually leave the room, we were lying in bed next to each other, totally alone.

Thursday

New Jersey

8:00 a.m.: Theme breakfast: Passions!

10:00 a.m.: Princeton University

Drive 2 hours and 30 minutes to Rhinebeck, New York, in the
E3 College Coach! *Packed lunch included!*

2:00 p.m.: Check into hotel in Rhinebeck

2:30–6:30 p.m.: Free time!

7:00 p.m.: Dinner at the Beekman Arms—the oldest inn
in the US! (*three courses and two glasses of wine included*)

Overnight in Rhinebeck

17

JESSICA

I woke up this morning determined to do better today. Whatever that might mean. Today would be a day of peace and Zen self-awareness. With hopefully some empty time to google Ostergren's firm and think about his offer. I wasn't interested in the job, but I was interested in the salary. College would be easier to afford, especially if Emily didn't pick one of the many excellent Cal State colleges, as I repeatedly suggested.

I faced myself in the mirror and wondered why I don't look more like my mother. She had been a beautiful woman, though smoking had ruined her complexion before it destroyed her lungs. Not beautiful in the haughty, supermodel way Dani Ackerman is, but in the soft, friendly-eyed, natural way Emily is. Both beautiful and appealing. The kind of face you want to come out of a coma and see . . . I shook my head and started washing my face. I was apparently still more than half-asleep, and I could hear Emily stomping around in the bedroom, getting dressed. She has my mother's stubbornness, too, along with the long lashes that hid it. Everyone thought my dad was the big shiny guy, heading out the door each morning smelling of aftershave and polish, off to do battle with the government or for the government, whichever it was that day. And he was—he was awesome. But my mom was the one who kept it all going, calling out goodbye to him from where she sat in the kitchen, either smoking a cigarette and reading the newspaper, or folding origami and reading the newspaper, depending on when this memory was happening. My dad had opinions, he had knowledge, he had experience in the world. But she had the real strength.

Emily banged on the door. "Hey, Mom, did you fall in?"

"Yes," I replied, "I'm stuck in the toilet and you're going to have to make it through the day without me."

Then I pulled the door open.

"Disappointing," said my daughter, passing me. "That picture would have gone viral in no time."

This being a different hotel, the breakfast was in a different room. Windows, this time, which was an improvement, and a cooked breakfast, which wasn't. I mean, you'd think it would be better, right? Eggs and all that jazz? But we were back in a big circle for some reason, and eating scrambled eggs on a plate on your lap is harder than it looks, and the need to coordinate hands and mouths while also talking and not making fools of ourselves was more than most of us could handle.

Cassidy was unbowed. "Sorry, we're all together this morning, apparently there's a conference of veterinarians monopolizing all the small tables in the hotel." She hesitated. "To eat off, hopefully, rather than examine on." She helped herself to fruit salad, speared each piece expertly in between questions, and generally appeared to be having the time of her life. I sincerely hope that isn't the case, because she can't be more than twenty-four, and life holds more joy than cut fruit in a roomful of customers.

"So, this morning we're going to talk about passions. What motivates you all? What makes you excited to think about the future?" She looked at Casper and smiled. "Apart from geology."

"I like math, too," he volunteered. "And fractals."

"I like sports," said a large kid who'd never spoken before. I mean, he'd probably spoken before, but not to us. See, I've been awake less than an hour and I'm already struggling.

"Any particular sport?" asked Cassidy.

He nodded. "Yeah, football. And baseball, hockey, basketball. And soccer."

"Wow," said Cassidy encouragingly. "And those are all sports you hope to pursue in college?"

The kid was confused. "Well, yes, of course."

"Are you hoping for a scholarship? Which sport is your strongest?" She tipped her head slightly. "You look like a football player to me."

The kid frowned at her. "No, I don't play any of them. I watch them. And, you know, fantasy league."

"Oh."

"So, yeah, I can definitely see myself continuing that in college."

"Right, of course."

The kid grinned, happy to have contributed to the conversation, totally unaware he'd confused our fearless leader. But Cassidy rallied. "Anyone else have a sport they love?"

One kid liked tennis and was hoping for a scholarship.

Another kid said he was thinking of putting rowing on his application because his college counselor said colleges love rowers.

"But do you actually row?" asked Cassidy.

"No, of course not. Where would I row? The LA River?" (Sidenote: The LA River is badly named. The only thing that reliably runs between its banks are homeless people evading the police.)

Cassidy frowned. "So how can you put it on your application?"

"I was going to put it under 'Interests.' I am interested in it."

She gazed at him, opened her mouth to say something, and then closed it again.

Emily put her hand up, which nearly made me spill my coffee.

"This is a dumb subject," she said. "I have no idea what I'm passionate about. When I was eight I was into Pokémon and My Little Pony. I loved that stuff. I collected the toys, I had millions of cards, it was a whole thing. Now there's nothing that really blows my mind, and my ideal day would be grown-ups not asking me questions about my future." She shrugged. "Can you be passionate about not being passionate?"

"There's nothing you can see yourself doing in the future?" Cassidy had put on her serious, encouraging voice.

"Not in the way you all mean." Emily was irritated, which didn't bode well for the rest of my day. "Besides, I don't see a lot of adults following their passion. Most of them work, sure, but they're not super happy about it." She turned to Casper's mom. "Are you following your passion?"

Casper shook his head and spoke before his mom had a chance. "Bad choice, Em, she is literally living her dream life every day."

His mom smiled. "I write code in my sleep then go to work and do it for real. Sorry."

Emily turned to me. "You're not happy at work. You're not following a passion."

I wondered if faking a stroke was an option, as there was nothing I wanted to do less than have this conversation again.

"I like my work," I said. "I get to help people, it's challenging."

"But are you *passionate*?"

I shrugged. "I was passionate about things when I was your age, and working is easier when you love what you do, but even something you love contains hours and days of repetition and grind. It's only on the internet that everything is easy."

Emily looked at Cassidy. "See what I mean? Work is not life. Work is how you pay for food. You should ask us the kind of life we want to live instead." She started counting on her fingers. "I want a job I can forget at the end of the day, where I don't work weekends, where I make enough money to live on my own and have a garden. Wouldn't it be better to start there? There must be hundreds of jobs like that. Work isn't supposed to be your life . . . *Your life* is supposed to be your life." She fell silent. Then she said, "I don't know. Maybe I'm hungry."

She got up and went to get breakfast. All the parents turned to me, and I shrugged. *Teenagers*, my shrug tried to say. *What can you do?* They're vain and self-obsessed, but then they hit on the truth with a hammer so big all you can do is hope the reverberations don't kill you.

EMILY

I made a total idiot of myself at breakfast. This trip was giving me a headache. I wished my mom and I were getting along better; I could have really used a hug.

Princeton is a dream, like something out of Harry Potter. There is no way I'm getting into Princeton, be real. I think a sadist put the tour itinerary together: It's like pulling up to a homeless guy and handing him flyers for luxury open houses. Why not take us to colleges we might actually get into? I've never even seen inside a community college, which is much more my speed.

I was totally getting my period. I wanted to eat chocolate and roll myself in a blanket like a burrito.

Meanwhile, my mom was hanging out with her new best friend, Will's dad, whose name I can't remember, and it's too awkward to ask Will now. They were sitting on a bench, not even pretending to listen to the tour guide, drinking Starbucks and laughing.

Will was being nice to me, though. We were half listening to the tour and half whispering about books we've liked.

One hundred and nineteen people liked my post about Princeton looking like Hogwarts.

JESSICA

Chris and I didn't even attempt to follow the guide around Princeton. Honestly, they should have taken the one or two kids who might possibly attain Princeton, maybe the geology kid, maybe that one girl who literally hasn't spoken all week so far but who always has her nose in a book, and let the rest of us sleep in.

And I was hiding from Emily, who was almost certainly getting her period. I wished we were getting along better; I could have definitely used a hug.

"Did you guys make up last night?" asked Chris. We had come to rest on a bench, sipping coffee and, you know, hanging out.

"Sort of," I replied, "but she's still pissy, as you saw at breakfast."

He shrugged. "Will's not talking at all, which works for me. Sometimes it's easier to say nothing than to keep saying the wrong thing, which appears to be my special gift."

"Mine, too," I said. "I'm particularly good at knowing something is probably the wrong thing to say, biting my tongue for a while until the silence becomes really tense, then blurting it out anyway. The timing is like putting spin on a baseball, it adds an exciting layer of unpredictability."

Chris laughed. It had been a long time since I'd made a man laugh, and I laughed, too, feeling like a regular human being for once, rather than simply my daughter's antagonistic binary star.

He turned and looked at me. His eyes were dark green, and I suddenly realized I found him very attractive. He said, "I also like to ask questions that Will doesn't want to answer, and offer advice he already knows. Do you do that?"

"Of course," I replied, tipping up my Starbucks bag and hoping for crumbs. "I have this fantasy that one day Emily will come up to me and say, *Hey, Mom, the other day I found myself in a situation I hadn't anticipated, and the advice you gave me three years ago suddenly popped into my head. I was able to handle myself perfectly, and I wanted to say thanks. I always feel prepared, thanks to your thoughtful guidance.*"

We both hooted with laughter. I glanced up and saw Emily and Will standing a hundred yards away, staring at us.

"Don't look now," I said, "but they've spotted us."

Chris grinned and waved at his son. "Their expressions suggest concern."

"Only that we might embarrass them."

"We should at least try."

"We should," I said.

Chris pulled out his phone and opened his music app. "Are you ready?" he said, showing me his screen.

"Oh, for sure," I said, getting to my feet.

EMILY

Oh my god, my mother has lost her mind.

She and Will's dad suddenly stood up and started doing this weird dance; they put one arm out in front, then the other, then they put them on their shoulders, then . . . and this was when I started to feel a little light-headed . . . they put them on their hips and started wiggling their butts around.

"What the actual freak are they doing?" I turned to Will, who had his arms folded and his eyes narrowed.

"It's called the Macarena," he said. "My dad loves to embarrass me."

"Is it a thing?"

"It used to be a thing, like, a hundred years ago."

I could hear distant tinny music and realized they had a song playing on a phone. They were still dancing.

We both turned away and started walking.

"Did that just happen?" said Will. "Or did we drop acid at breakfast?"

"I had Cheerios."

"Well, on behalf of my father, I apologize."

"One, my mother was equally as bad, and secondly, no need," I said. "Parents are weird AF."

"They say and do whatever they want."

"Totally selfish."

"Narcissists."

We walked for a bit. Then Will said, "Why didn't we film? It would have been a classic post."

"Like a natural history show where they re-create the mating of the dinosaurs?"

He laughed. I like his laugh, and I like making him laugh. "That's a little harsh. Your mom isn't old." He paused, unsure. "She's still pretty. She looks like you." He paused once more, then: "Wow, I am incredibly suave."

My turn to laugh. "You are."

"I'm like . . . someone suave who I can't think of right now because I'm too busy being suave."

"That cartoon skunk? He's very suave."

Will looked at me. "Pepé Le Pew?"

"Probably," I said, not sure if I ever knew the skunk's name. "The one who always gets paint on a cat and falls in love."

"Yeah." Will turned to keep walking. "He's very suave."

There was silence for a while as we wandered around the campus. It was gorgeous; they should be filming a promotional video *right now*. We walked under a tree that confetti'd us with blossoms, and the light was gorgeous and there was a warm breeze, and I said, "Well, I think you're pretty suave."

Will stopped. "And now that word sounds funny."

"Suave," I said, nodding. "Yup, no longer sounds like a word at all."

Will smiled at me. "You're very pretty." He paused. "I realize I didn't ask for consent there, but I was making a factual observation."

"Can a compliment be a trigger warning?"

Will shrugged. "So many things can be, I lose count." He stepped towards me. "Can I kiss you?"

I said nothing for a moment, because right at the worst moment, I'd lost the power of speech, then he went on. "I'd like to place my hands on your shoulders and lean in and put my mouth gently on your mouth, and then maybe touch your hair, which has been driving me crazy for the last few days."

I nodded. "You're good."

And it was.

18

JESSICA

And it's . . . back on the bus! Chris and I sat next to each other, and I'm not even exaggerating, we had the best conversation I've had with a man in years. I had forgotten how intoxicating it can be, meeting someone you have chemistry with. I felt giddy.

Not that the subject of the conversation was all giggles. At one point we ended up talking about his wife.

"Is she your ex, actually?" I realized that sounded pushy and tried to backtrack. "I mean, you know, legally?"

"Looking for a fee?" Chris said, but he was smiling. "Yes, she's my ex. She got overwhelmed, she had her own thing, you know, she was an actress." He managed to say it without sounding judgmental, which was impressive. "She got offered something good and went off to Vancouver for three months to shoot it. It got picked up, so she stayed in Vancouver for a while and . . ." He stared out the window for a moment, then back at me. "You know the story, everyone does."

"I guess. Are you still friends?"

"Sure, for the kids. They were fourteen, ten, and six when she left. My eldest daughter went and spent time with her mom and got her head turned, unfortunately. She's twenty now, we don't see her all that much." He sighed. "She wants to hang out with her cool parent, right, the one with the parties and the stylists."

"That's tough."

"Sure, but when I was twenty, I didn't hang out with my parents at all, so, you know. She texts. I know more or less what she's doing."

"Is she at college?"

He shook his head. "She takes acting lessons and models and vlogs, or whatever you call that." He nodded over at Alice's mom, Dani, who was sitting a little way ahead of us. "Like her daughter."

"Alice. She's at school with Emily."

"Are they friends?"

"I don't think so, it's hard to tell. Teen girls are like their mothers, friendly in person and vipers in private."

Chris laughed. "Yeah, having had teenagers of both genders, I can confirm the common wisdom that boys are less painful. They're as touchy, and they're bigger, so it's like having a dark version of Big Bird hanging out in the kitchen, staring angrily into the fridge, but there's less high-pitched door slamming."

"Emily never slams her door. She closes it firmly. At least, that's her claim."

My phone rang. It was work. I turned to Chris. "I'm so sorry, I have to take this."

"Of course." He politely turned away, and I answered the call.

"Hi, this is Jessica."

"Jessica, what did you say to Ostergren?" It was John, and it was hard to tell if I'd messed up or won a medal. I felt my stomach drop a little, even though I hadn't really entertained Ostergren's offer.

"I already told you. I suggested he ask for Valentina to be put on his account."

"Well, you clearly made an impression, because he actually asked for you."

"Huh. That's surprising." It wasn't surprising, of course. I lowered my voice. "What a pity I don't work for you anymore. Did you talk to the board?"

"Not yet. But you're not really going to quit."

"Yes, I am."

He laughed. "You're looking at colleges, right? You've done the math, you need this job."

I frowned. "Make Valentina a partner and put her on Ostergren's account, John."

"He wants you."

"I'm not available, John. Unless you don't persuade the board, in which case I can always leave and contact Ostergren from my new job."

"You're too honorable to do that, Jess, it's your Achilles' heel. It's what prevents you from being a truly great lawyer."

I rolled my eyes, a habit I've apparently learned from my daughter. "John, you're not helping yourself here. Don't call me again until you've spoken to the board."

He ignored me. "I've asked Eloise to send you the last five years of business for the account, so you can get up to speed."

I shook my head, not that he could see me. "No, John, send it to Valentina. Even if I stay with you, I'm not taking the account."

He was all charm. "Of course, just take a quick look-see."

"No, John."

"Fine, skim it while you're away, and then we can talk it over next week."

He wasn't going to take no for an answer, so I said, "We'll certainly talk it over next week, after you accept my formal resignation. Goodbye, John."

I hung up and banged my head on the window. I checked my phone and saw a massive file downloading into my email. I guess being a steamroller had helped John get where he was, but it was deeply irritating to be the road. Mind you, it would be good to look over the account, in case I decided to jump ship.

"Problems at work?" Chris asked.

I shook my head. "The usual crap."

He hesitated. "Did I accidentally overhear you quitting your job?"

I looked at him. "Yes, but please forget you heard it."

"Does Emily know?"

I shook my head. "It was a strategic threat." I explained briefly, omitting all personal details.

He looked at me. "No wonder you highly paid lawyers look so stressed. You're fighting the good fight against injustice."

I laughed. "Is that why I'm so tired all the time?"

He shook his head. "No, that's because you have a teenager, and they come in while you're sleeping and suck all the enthusiasm out of you. Like vampires."

"That explains the sleeping all weekend. Poor things."

Chris said, "Will's younger brother James is twelve and hasn't been seen before 2:00 p.m. on the weekends since last August."

"Emily sleeps all morning then gets up, prowls around the kitchen complaining there's nothing to eat, asks to Postmates a chai from Starbucks, gets annoyed when I say no, then spends the rest of the day complaining she's hungry while looking at her phone."

Chris laughed. "They're really very rewarding, teenagers. They give a lot back."

"They're appreciative, that's what makes it worth it."

"Yeah, they notice all the little things you do for them."

"And they're super helpful around the house."

"You never need to nag them."

Suddenly, Will and Emily appeared, swaying in the aisle of the bus.

"I'm not sure you two hanging out is a good idea," said Will. "I have a feeling you're complaining about us."

"Not at all," lied his dad. "Can we help you with something?"

"Yes," said Emily, looking at me. "We have free time this afternoon and we want to go to the aerodrome."

We both goggled at them. "I'm sorry?" I asked. "Is that a club or something?"

Emily looked pointedly at me. "No, Mom, it's an aerodrome."

I frowned at her. "You said that already. What do you mean?"

She flicked a quick glance at Will, then spoke even more slowly. "It's a place where there are planes, Mom, you know, like an airfield."

"Oh . . . an actual aerodrome."

Chris laughed. "Why do you want to do that?"

"There's a museum there, it looks cool."

I gazed at them. "You have the afternoon free and you want to go to an air museum?"

Emily was starting to blush. God, I am so slow.

"Yes, of course, that sounds awesome," I said. "I'll check in for us, and text you the room number. You guys can take off, so to speak, as soon as we get there." I tried to nudge Chris, subtly, but he was way ahead of me and was pulling out his wallet.

"Here, in case." He handed over two twenties.

"We had lunch," protested Emily.

"Yeah, but maybe you'll get coffee or something."

"Or maybe there's a gift shop." I grinned at Will. "Emily loves museum gift shops." I turned back to Emily. Possibly that had been too much information; she was now glaring at me.

"Well, thanks," she said. "I'll text you later."

"Great," I replied, trying to dampen my enthusiasm. God forbid they sense we're happy they're enjoying each other's company; it will put them off immediately. "Don't forget we're having dinner with Helen."

"Great," muttered Emily.

"Great," said Will.

"Great," echoed Chris, and we watched as the two kids move slowly away, clearly convinced we'd lost our minds. I turned to Chris.

"Too enthusiastic?"

"Possibly," he replied. "But I think they've already forgotten we exist, so never mind."

EMILY

My mother is the most embarrassing mother on the planet. *Emily loves museum gift shops.* Oh my GOD. Why not tell Will I kept my Pokémon cards in color-coded binders? Or list my Girl Scout badges, all twenty-five of them? Why not tell him about me getting my period for the first time on a plane back from Grandpa's and having her stand outside the airplane bathroom giving detailed instructions on how to use a pad while the flight attendants stood guard? All I could say was *Mom, I know* over and over again, but it didn't shut her up. That wasn't traumatic at all. I considered blowing the aircraft doors so I didn't have to walk back to my seat.

We sat back down, and I looked out the window. He's going to think I'm such a dork.

"I like museum stores, too," he said instead. "I used to collect those pens that have things that slide up and down inside them, you know?"

"Floaty pens?" I was surprised. "I have like two dozen of those. I love them, too. My mom traveled a lot for work and she would bring them back if she found them. The best ones are made by a Dutch company called Eskesen." Oh crap, I overgeeked it. I might as well go back and sit by my mom.

"Yeah," said Will, "they were the ones who solved the problem of leaking mineral oil."

He outgeeked me. Thank god.

He continued. "My mom left when I was, like, ten, but before that she traveled for work and she would always bring back stuffed animals with the name of where she was, you know?"

I nodded.

"When I was little I thought it was awesome. I put them all together on a shelf, right? But recently I realized it meant she didn't think about me at all until she was about to come home and scrambled to find something at the airport. One time she brought a T-shirt instead, and I said, *They didn't have any bears?* She was confused because she didn't even realize I collected them. She didn't notice much about me at all." He shrugged. "Which sucks differently now than it did when I was nine, but it still sucks."

"Do you see her a lot?"

He shook his head and deflected the question. "Did you collect anything when you were a kid?"

Oh god, this was going to be the end of it. "Uh, Pokémon cards?"

He snorted. "Everyone collects Pokémon cards, that doesn't count."

"In binders? In evolutionary sets? By date of release?"

He laughed. "Okay . . . no, not everyone did that."

"I did." Casper's head popped up over the back of the seat in front. "Did you have any rares?"

I shook my head. "Nothing super rare. Did you?"

He grinned. "My mom collected Pokémon cards back in the nineties, so I have . . ." He lowered his voice. "A shadowless holographic first-edition Mewtwo."

"No way," I said.

"Way."

I laughed and turned to Will. "While we're embarrassing ourselves, I was also a Girl Scout."

"I was a Boy Scout."

"I have badges."

He snorted. "I have *all* the badges."

I frowned at him. "I'm not sure I believe you."

He grinned at me. "When we're back in LA, you can come over and I'll show you."

I raised one eyebrow. "You're inviting me to come over and look at your badges?"

"Yes," he said, "because who can resist that level of suave?" His eyes were warm. I love a callback. We're going to see each other when we get home. Why am I being such a nerd about this? I can feel myself blushing, but he is, too, so it's cool.

"You can come and see my Pokémon cards, too, if you like," said Casper.

"We will definitely do that," said Will. "We both will."

We're seeing each other at least twice. What is wrong with me?

"Yeah," I said, "I'll bring mine, too, we'll make a day of it."

For a minute I think I've gone too far, but Casper's face made it worth it.

Then Sam's head popped up next to Casper's. "Hey, did you guys hear about the scandal at Westminster?" He looked at me. "That's your school, right? Do you know anything about it?"

"No," said Will, "what happened?"

"Like, six kids got expelled for bribing some AP teacher to increase their AP score. They offered . . ." He paused and stumbled over it a bit. "B . . . blow jobs for multiple-choice answers."

"That's not true," I said immediately.

"Aha," said Sam. "So you DO know about it."

I shook my head. "No, I know there were only three kids, and oral sex was not part of it at all. I don't know anything else, because I've been on the tour, right, but it's not that big a deal."

"Because this kind of thing happens all the time at Westminster?" Casper sounded uncharacteristically sarcastic.

I took a slow breath. "No, because it was only three girls. Suspended not expelled. Not actually cheating, just planning to cheat. No sex, oral or otherwise."

"But they're still cheaters."

"Allegedly."

Will made a face at me. "And you said you didn't want to be a lawyer."

19

We've arrived in Rhinebeck, which is nauseatingly picturesque. I could see Emily's face as she got off the bus with the other kids, and could tell she was quietly blown away. This is the thing about West Coast kids, or maybe only mine: They're really amazed by seasons. Literally, the first time we were in DC in the fall, I thought she was going to lose her shit over the leaves. She caught my eye and I grinned at her.

"Pretty, right?"

"Stars Hollow."

I smiled and nodded, although I'm not entirely sure what that is. She narrowed her eyes at me; I was so busted.

"The town in *Gilmore Girls*."

"I know that." I totally didn't know that.

"Folks," said Cassidy loudly, saving me from having to prove it. "Gather around."

We dutifully gathered.

"We're going to check into the Beekman Arms, the oldest hotel in America. Such a treat for you history buffs! It was built in 1704, and George Washington drank here, as did Benedict Arnold. The argument that led to the duel between Aaron Burr and Hamilton started here." She considered the group of disheveled and hungry parents and sped up her patter. "FDR was a frequent guest, as were writers and celebrities of all kinds." She turned and led the way down the street.

I turned to Emily. "Are you heading off? You have your phone?" Stupid question.

She nodded. "I'll text you later."

"We're meeting Helen at seven."

"Here?"

"No, someplace in town."

"Cool, later." She turned to walk away, and I watched her and Will wander down the street, pausing to presumably synchronize phones or whatever. She looked up at him and smiled, and I knew I was literally the last thing on her mind.

Which is as it should be.

EMILY

Rhinebeck is nuts. So cute. We walked for a bit, checking it out, and came across a totally awesome sweet shop.

Two words: Pop Rocks.

And not only Pop Rocks, but also all kinds of candy I'd never even heard of, and it's not like we don't have candy stores in LA, we totally do. It turns out we both love gummy candy, so, you know, there was some spending. Then, feeling mildly sick from gummy sharks, I suggested we go to the aerodrome.

Sitting next to Will in the Lyft, which took, like, twenty minutes to come because apparently Rhinebeck only has three Lyft drivers for the whole town, I prayed he wasn't going to bring up the cheating thing again.

"This is nice," he said, smiling at me, and it was. "The tour is a bit intense, right? I think it's making my dad crazy."

I laughed. "My mom is already crazy, so I can't say I've noticed any difference."

Will shrugged. "My dad worries I'm going to end up like my sister, I guess."

"What's her deal?"

We were arriving at the aerodrome. "She didn't want to go to college, she wants to be an actor."

"Actresses go to college. Emma Watson went to Brown."

"Lupita Nyong'o went to Yale." We got out of the car and started walking across the grass. Will continued, "But my sister went to Vancouver to hang out with our mom and vlog about her experiences."

I laughed. "She's an influencer?"

His face relaxed. "Only mildly."

"Do you want to be an actor?

"Not in a million years."

"You want to be a programmer?"

We had reached the visitors' center, and Will held the door for me. "Programming will mean I always have work, and that's a good thing."

We went in.

"You're very practical."

He let the door swing closed, and shrugged. "I guess."

"What if it doesn't work out that way?"

"Then I'll do something else." He took in the scene. "Wow, this was totally worth the trip."

The building was relatively small, but through the windows we could see plane after plane sitting on the grass, and vintage cars, and as I looked at Will, I could see his eyes gleaming.

I giggled. "You're an even bigger goober than I am."

"Oh, you have no idea," he said, heading to the airfield.

After closely examining a dozen early airplanes, which was super interesting—if for no other reason than when Will was excited about something, it turned out he bounced a bit on the balls of his feet, like my grandfather—we went and sat on the grass and drank soda.

"My mother is deeply against soda," I said. "I never had Coke until I was, like, fourteen." The grass was itchy under my hand, and the breeze was gusty and cold, but I was very happy to be where I was.

We clinked bottles. "To rebellion," Will said. "Speaking of which, do you really think those girls would have cheated at your school?"

I played with the grass. "Probably," I said.

"Why?"

I frowned. "Why else? To get better grades."

"Why? To get into college? They're screwed now, right?"

I nodded. "I guess. Although they didn't get expelled, and they didn't actually cheat, so maybe it will be fine. If they'd cheated on the actual exam, it would have been more serious."

"Totally dumb." Will sounded firm.

I suddenly felt irritated. "It's easy for you to say, you're a smarty-pants. Maybe those girls weren't, maybe they thought there was no other way they were going to make it."

"Make what? Harvard? There are hundreds of colleges. You don't need ridiculous grades for all of them."

"Yeah, but maybe they didn't want to go to a third-tier college. Or maybe they thought their parents would bust their balls. I have a friend whose mother literally grounds her for a month every time she gets less than an A."

Will frowned. "That's lame."

"A hundred percent, but it's her reality. My mom doesn't bust me for Bs, but she does expect me to study all evening, every evening, and to 'give it my best effort.' If I flunk she tries not to show her disappointment, but she's an easy read. All the parents at my school are like that, and the teachers know it and remind us all the time of the 'sacrifices' our parents are making for us to be there. It's not a fun time." I suddenly felt tears in my eyes, which was so embarrassing and unexpected I can't even tell you. "You have no idea what it's like, not finding it easy to do the only thing that seems to matter to anyone."

Will looked away politely. Then, after a pause, he said, "Did you know those girls?"

I continued destroying the grass and nodded.

"Well?"

"Yes."

"Did you know they were planning to cheat?"

I shook my head.

"Would you cheat?"

There was a long pause. Then I shook my head again.

He leaned against me, and touched my chin, turning my face. "That's good," he said, kissing me. "I think you're brilliant."

I could taste a tear on the corner of his lip, but the salt faded quickly. It's amazing what you can ignore when you need to.

20

JESSICA

Helen was my first roommate at college, and we've mostly stayed in touch. She was a philosophy major, and we bonded over our mutual love of argument. She tended to be discursive and curious, whereas I favored facts and irrefutability, which is why she became a professor and I went to law school. I hadn't seen her in over a decade, and even that last sighting had been a brief overnight when she came to UCLA for a conference. However, Helen is easy to spot.

"Wow," said Emily, "that's Helen?"

Helen is six feet two inches tall. At college, she and I developed a drinking game based on how many times men called her an amazon or asked her if she played basketball. (For those of you who have tall friends and want to play, your friend takes a shot for *amazon*, you take a shot for *basketball*; it's a drinking game, not chess.) I thought she was joking at first, but then I saw it in action. It's like they see a woman over five ten and the word *amazon* falls out of their mouth, quickly followed by some reference to dunking. A social scientist would probably have a name for it, but we called it unimaginative.

Helen also has very dark skin and cheekbones you could rest a tea tray on, but I was willing to overlook her beauty and focus on the fact that she inexplicably loved me as much as I loved her. We have that friendship where you see each other once a decade and pick up where you left off.

"Is it possible this is the child Emily?" Helen stood to greet us, extending her hands to Emily and causing a man at a table nearby to drop a cherry tomato. "I understand the laws of both biology and time, but surely you've grown faster than recommended?"

Emily laughed, as dazzled as everyone always is. "It's me, I promise."

Helen clasped her hands for a moment and then smiled at me. "You created a beauty, Jessica Burnstein, no doubt about it." She turned back to Emily. "Please tell me you want to study philosophy."

Emily shook her head. "I don't think so. Sorry."

"Maybe you could major in something else and minor in philosophy?"

Emily smiled. "I really don't know what I want to do."

"Well then, philosophy is perfect!" She turned to me. "The whole point of it is wondering." She grinned. "Although your mother always preferred to be definite, it was her only flaw."

"It still is. She loves to be right."

I glared at them. "Let me head this off right now, this is not a 'let's gang up on Jessica' dinner."

"It's not?" said Emily. "That's disappointing."

We ordered and Helen asked Emily the basic questions all adults

ask teenagers: where she went to school, what was her favorite subject, did she play any sports, what books she enjoyed, and so on. I
realized Emily was right; adults do ask interview questions all the
time. But, this being Helen, she moved on pretty quickly to do you
believe in God, what is the meaning of existence, and what was Emily's point of view on the question of free will.

Then the food arrived.

"So, Jessica, what's the latest with you? Are you running your firm
yet?" Helen was speaking with her mouth full, which was an old
habit I was pleased to see she hadn't grown out of. She needed to say
what she had on her mind, and food in her mouth was no good reason to hold off.

I shook my head. "Not yet, and maybe never." I was obviously not
going to mention the Valentina thing while Emily was there. Or the
Ostergren thing. Or anything, in fact. Emily seemed stressed enough
already. "I love the law part, the managing lawyers part . . . not so
much."

Helen nodded. "And you, Emily? Do you think you'll take a corporate route through life?"

Emily shook her head. "I really doubt it. I don't enjoy thinking in
confinement."

Helen laughed and clapped her hands. "Excellent, a free thinker."
She smiled at me again. "Well done."

I shrugged. "She came out that way. I had nothing to do with it."

"Not true," said Emily surprisingly. "You raised me to question
everything, especially the status quo."

"I did?" I frowned. "No wonder you won't do what I tell you to."

"But that's the point, I am." She grinned. "You told me to never blindly accept authority, so I don't."

"I probably should have thought that one through a little more," I said. "Perhaps all that emphasis on independence and self-determination wasn't the smartest strategy."

"No, it was," said Helen, suddenly more serious. "I'm telling you, I see more kids these days who need to be told their next step all the time, it's incredibly sad. We weren't like that." She looked at Emily. "Your mother was the least compliant person I ever met."

"How do you mean?"

"I mean if someone told her she was supposed to do something, she wouldn't do it, not until she was certain she would have chosen it for herself. It was, I'll be honest, a tiny bit pathological."

I frowned. "That is completely untrue."

"See what I mean? Oppositional."

"I did everything my coach said. I turned in my work on time. I'm really not sure what you're referring to."

"You did what your coach said because you knew it was right, and you turned your work in because you didn't want to flunk classes. However, if one of us said you should cut bangs, or wear a different jacket, or stop sleeping with that terrible guy you had such a thing with, you wouldn't do it."

"Oh my god, not David Millar." Emily was amused. "We saw him the other night, he was creepy."

Helen clapped her hands again. "Yes! I had totally forgotten his name. Your mother was obsessed."

"Oh please, like you didn't have a semester-long fling with a certain . . ."

"Person who will remain nameless." Helen grinned. "We all made mistakes, which is what you're supposed to do in college. I wore Rosie the Riveter overalls all the time also, which was a far bigger crime." She lowered her voice. "Students these days have less fun, and dress like office managers. It's really kind of depressing. And it's not like philosophy majors are going to head off to high-paying philosophy jobs that make it easy for them to pay off their student debt, so when I look out across the lecture hall, it's hard not to feel like I'm part of the problem." She smiled. "Of course, then we get into a spirited debate about the nature of reality, and I see their brains lighting up, and I remember why college was invented in the first place." She shook her head at Emily. "Don't feel like college is the only way to go, life is much bigger than that."

I sputtered an interruption. "Hey, I'm having a hard time selling her on college, please don't make it worse."

Helen looked seriously at me. "Really, Jess, I'm not joking. It's not like it was when we went; it's expensive, it's hard, it's much less lighthearted, kids get shot, get assaulted, get bored, and walk out saddled with a level of debt that means they have to strap on a number and enter the rat race right away." She sighed. "It's enough to make you yearn for revolution." She shook her wrist full of bangles, making several men's heads whip around instinctively.

"So why don't you quit your job?" Emily asked.

"And abandon them completely?" Helen laughed. "I love my students. I love the way they think, the way they approach centuries-old debates with fresh ideas. I know a lot about philosophy, and people say it's a pointless subject, but I swear I see human thought changing in front of my eyes every day. In the two decades I've been teaching, opinions and attitudes have evolved and altered and swung back and forth, and I have a ringside seat." Her eyes were gleaming, and she suddenly reached across the table and took Emily's hand. "Debating the nature of life is part of the human condition, it's the most beautiful thing."

There was a pause, then Emily said, "Well, I can see why you got tenure."

Helen laughed, then said, "Thanks, but don't forget, I'm spectacularly unqualified for anything else."

EMILY

Mom's friend Helen is a trip. I had a teacher like her in elementary school, who made me actually excited at the thought of coming to school every day, who seemed delighted to hear what I had to say. But they're rare.

I drifted off and thought about Will. When I'd gotten back to the hotel room to get ready for dinner, Mom did the most pathetic job of wanting to know all about my afternoon and at the same time not wanting to ask. It was almost painful to watch, and in the end I'd said I had a good time and left it at that. It would be weird to talk about my romantic life with her, especially as she really doesn't have one.

While she was in the shower, I'd finally texted Becca. I'd hesitated for an awkward amount of time; it was time to get over myself.

"Hey," I texted. "Sorry I've been AWOL, I'm on this college thing."

Long pause. Great, she hates me. Wait, three dots, then: "I know. Did you hear?"

"Yeah. What happened?" Pause. "Really. I heard various versions."

"It's simple. Lucy told her mom, her mom told the school."

I frowned. "Did Lucy say that?"

"No, that's my theory. She's not saying anything. Her mom took her out completely. She gone, dude, she never even replies to my texts."

I thought about that for a moment.

"Your parents freak?"

"Totally. Not sure they weren't mostly mad I got caught, they freaked out more when I told them I was failing the class."

I heard the shower turn off.

"Gotta go. Sorry."

"Later."

Now, sitting in the restaurant with this amazing woman who'd done everything right, and my mom, whose entire raison d'être was doing the right thing, I realized there was no way I could ever explain to them what Becca and the others had done. They would never understand. I was completely alone.

But, like I said, Helen was a trip.

JESSICA

After dinner we all headed back to the hotel, and while Emily went up to the room, Helen and I decided to have one more drink in the hotel bar.

Helen gazed around. "It's amazing to think how many people have had a drink with their friends at this place. Hundreds of years of regrettable incidents."

I laughed. "Centuries of false promises and hookups that changed the fate of nations."

"Or led to pox of one sort or another. There were several centuries of drinking here before penicillin was discovered."

"True."

We sat in silence for a moment. Then Helen said, "So, what's really going on with you?"

"How do you mean?"

She tipped her head back and regarded me thoughtfully. "I mean I assume there must be more going on than what you can say in front of your child. If it's all PG, I'm very disappointed."

I shrugged. "I threatened to quit my job in order to ensure sexism-free workplace practices."

"Wow. Way to bury the lede."

"I may not actually have to quit. It wasn't exactly an idle threat, because I will quit, but hopefully not." I explained, not leaving out anything. Helen can be trusted.

"Glad to see your rebellious streak is still alive and well."

I grunted. "No one was more surprised than me."

"Did you tell Valentina?"

I shook my head. "Too much pressure."

"So basically you've only told me?"

"And Chris, this guy on the tour."

Helen raised her eyebrows at me. "Cute?"

I nodded. "Yes, but Emily is interested in his son, and there is no way on God's good earth that I am doing any kind of mother-daughter father-son dating thing. Too weird."

"You're a good mom."

"Because I won't date her boyfriend's dad? Wow, you have a low bar."

The room was cozy, and I was starting to feel a little sleepy. A fire was burning, hundreds of years of dirt dimmed the walls; it smelled of brandy and centuries of smoke.

"I also got offered a job in Maryland."

"Doing what?"

"Windsurfing for charity."

"What?"

"As a lawyer of course, Helen, what else?" I laughed. "After fifteen years at the same job, never even *thinking* about changing, I suddenly threaten to quit and get a job offer in two days. Plus, David Millar hit on me to a nauseating extent, there's a hot dad on the tour, and . . . it's overwhelming." I picked at a napkin. "I am not happy right now."

Helen laughed at me. "Just to increase your confusion, I think you should go back to college. We're always looking for mature students."

I made a face. "I'm a mature student? Ugh." I drank more wine. "No, I have a plan and I'm sticking to it. Quitting notwithstanding."

Helen was skeptical. "Describe your supposed plan."

I leaned back in my chair and counted off on my fingers. "First, get accepted to the California bar, check; move to LA, check; get a good job; put Emily in an excellent elementary school; get a reliable babysitter; work my ass off to pay for the school and the babysitter; get Emily into Westminster; make partner so I can afford Westminster; get Emily through middle and high school without her getting arrested, pregnant, or addicted to methamphetamines; get her into a good college; get promoted so I can afford the good college; keep working my ass off to pay for the whole four years; help her get a good job; then go out into the backyard, dig myself a big hole, and sit in it."

"Wow," said Helen. "That's quite a detailed plan."

"Yup. You know me, I like to achieve my goals."

"When did you come up with that plan?"

"When the second line appeared on the pregnancy test."

"And you haven't deviated from your plan for the last seventeen years?"

I shook my head.

"Jesus, Jess, what happened to you? When we were in college you were stubborn, sure, and yes, you liked a goal, but since when did simply sticking to a plan become the goal?"

I'd possibly had too much to drink for this conversation and said so. "I'm sorry, you'll have to explain, the wine is making me tired."

Helen clicked her tongue. "You wanted to be a Supreme Court justice, remember? We all sat in the student union and watched RBG's confirmation. She was a freaking alum, you were all *I'm going to be the second female Columbia grad to ascend to the Supreme Court, and I'm taking my gold medal with me.* You were so certain."

I laughed. "Well, so much for that, then. No medal, no Supreme Court . . . two for two."

Helen ordered another round of drinks, which was probably ill-advised. "Did you go back to archery? Last time I saw you, in LA that time, you said you were thinking of picking it back up."

"Yeah, still thinking."

"Do you miss it?"

I shrugged. "Sure, but it could only be a hobby. It's not like I can compete anymore."

"So? Would you encourage Emily to only do things she was good at? Isn't it fun to get better at something? Did I tell you I took up cooking last year?"

"No. Really?"

"Yes, really. I'm terrible at it, but I'm learning. I also took up ballroom dancing, but I didn't enjoy it AND I was terrible at it, plus it always resembled a giraffe dancing with her baby." She laughed. "I met a nice guy, though."

"A baby giraffe?"

She nodded. "Yeah. We have fun, nothing serious." She leaned forward. "When did you stop having fun?"

I stared into my drink. "I don't know. Work used to be fun, Emily used to be fun, but lately neither is exactly a barrel of laughs."

"Well, then your current plan clearly sucks. I've got no idea why you're sticking to it so religiously."

My phone pinged, and I turned it over. "It's Emily, she's saying good night." I smiled at Helen. "I've stayed up later than my teenager, that's a first."

"Good. Shake it up." We looked at each other, then she said, "But now, I expect, you're going to bed, too, so you can kiss her good night."

I stood up. "Yup. Way past my bedtime."

Helen stood, too, and we hugged. I wondered if I felt like a baby

253

giraffe and asked her the question I ask every time I see her. "Are you still glad you never had kids of your own?"

She nodded. "I get a new class of kids every year, when on earth would I have had time for my own?" She was serious for a moment. "Besides, actual children grow up and go away, whereas mine arrive fully grown and are much better at staying in touch."

Friday

Rhinebeck, NY, and Poughkeepsie, NY

8:00 a.m.: Theme breakfast: Challenges!

10:00 a.m.: Bard College

Drive 48 minutes to Poughkeepsie

2:00 p.m.: Vassar College

Drive 1 hour and 30 minutes on the E3 College Coach to NYC

5:00 p.m.: Check into hotel in NYC

21

EMILY

When Mom came up last night, she was a little drunk, I won't lie. I could tell because she walked into the closet instead of the bathroom, but also because she threw herself down on the bed and wanted to chat.

Normally I'm down for chatting, but dude, I was tired and I had a lot on my mind. I tried to let her down gently.

"Emily," she'd said into the bedspread. "Do you ever wonder about life?"

"In what sense?" I'd replied cautiously.

She lifted her head and looked at me owlishly. "In the lifeyness sense, like how it keeps going and you sort of go along with it because, you know, it's life and what's the alternative, not anything good, so you meander along and suddenly you're old and then you're dead and what is it all really about?"

I went for something neutral. "Sure."

"Me, too," she said, then laid her head down on the pillow and started snoring. I pulled off her shoes and covered her with a blanket, then climbed back into bed. Then I got out, hunted through my bag for earplugs, and tried again.

Now, this morning, she was clearly hungover and feeling weird. I tried to be kind.

"Do you want me to bring you something up to eat, Mom? You can sleep in."

She shook her head, regretted it, and covered her eyes for a moment. "No, I'm good. What's the theme?"

"It's circus tricks. We're all going to do circus tricks."

She gazed at me in absolute horror.

"I'm joking," I said, "it's challenges."

She narrowed her eyes at me. "Almost as bad, although I am a walking example of overcoming."

She got to her feet, reached out for me to balance herself, and then tottered into the bathroom.

I'm not sure what got into Cassidy's cornflakes, but she was in a Bad Mood. It could be that veterinarians were hogging all the tables again, which meant she had to coordinate one big conversation rather than drinking coffee in peace and quiet.

"People," she said. "This morning we are talking about challenges. You"—she pointed to Alice—"you start. Let's hear what challenges you face, shall we?" Then she went over to the coffee station and poured herself a bucket-sized cup of coffee.

I was next to Will. I leaned over. "What's up with her?"

He turned his head to whisper in my ear, which tickled. "Dinner last night was a disaster. I'll tell you after."

Alice cleared her throat, glanced nervously around the circle, and said, "Um, I guess I'm challenged by the patriarchy."

Casper coughed into his hand, "Bullshit."

I turned and looked at Will, but he closed his eyes and shook his head. *Later*, he mouthed.

"I'm sorry?" Alice didn't look very sorry.

"I said bullshit," said Casper. "You are a girl, yes, and as such you face some institutionalized sexism, but you are about as protected as it's possible for a girl to be. You're white, you're wealthy, you're pretty, you're healthy, and yes, that rhymed, but the point I'm making is you're a special, special princess. The patriarchy will make an exception."

"Hey, I had acne in eighth grade," replied Alice hotly. "It needed lasers."

Casper frowned at her. "And daddy got you lasers, didn't he?"

I looked at my mom, who had taken a cup of tea to her chair and then leaned back far enough so she could fold her arms and rest her chin in her hand. She returned my gaze and shrugged. Then she leaned over and whispered, "I guess we missed the worm-turning convention."

"Hey, where's Alice's mom?" I asked, looking around. Mom shrugged again.

It turned out, I learned later, that dinner at the Beekman Arms had Not Gone Well. Right at the beginning Cassidy had stood up and addressed the table.

"I've had a report from several colleges that a parent on this trip attempted to influence admissions staff by offering bribes." There was a shocked silence. "Literally, cash bribes."

"It wasn't me," said Casper's mom.

"Nor me," said Will's dad. "I don't have a bribe to offer, unless it's offering to install shelves or something." No one was laughing.

Sam's mom asked, "Did they say which parent it was?"

"No," said Cassidy. "As I said before, E3 has a stellar reputation, and they were doing me the courtesy of informing me rather than the FBI. I doubt they'll give us a second chance if it happens again."

Dani Ackerman spat out her drink. "The FBI? Why?"

"Because bribery is a federal offense."

"But they wouldn't take the bribes."

Looooong silence.

"Or so you just said," Dani added weakly.

According to Will, the rest of the dinner had been pretty stony.

Of course, I didn't know that during the breakfast. After Alice and Casper's little spat, it was Will's turn and he, at least, tried to lighten the mood.

"Um, challenges. Let's see. There are the obvious ones, like my relative impoverishment, but to a certain extent those are counterbalanced by my education and incredible personal charm." He coughed. "And my impressive vocabulary."

I laughed, but no one else did. Then it was my turn. Because I didn't know what had happened, I opened my mouth and stuck my foot right in it.

"I guess the biggest challenge is getting into college, right?"

Casper snorted. "Yeah, unless you bribe your way in."

I frowned. "Why would I do that?"

"You might not," he said. "But other people could."

I was confused. "But isn't that sad? All this stress and effort to get into college. How can it possibly be worth it?"

"I don't know," he replied. "At your school they apparently like to cheat on exams and bribe admissions people, so you're the perfect person to explain it to us."

I turned to Will, who didn't say anything at first, but then said, "Casper, Emily didn't cheat or bribe anyone, don't pick on her."

"But maybe she understands why her people think it's okay to game the system, while the rest of us work our butts off."

I opened my mouth to say whoever these people were, they weren't my people, but Mom beat me to it.

Still leaning back, she said, "I'll tell you why. Most parents don't think it's okay to bribe or cheat, but we're constantly told that getting our kids into a good college will be some kind of insurance against the future. Our influence over your lives is coming to an end, and we're desperately trying to do one last thing to help you out." She took a sip of tea. "We've spent the last sixteen years preparing you to be adults, and when we look at the future, it's pretty clear it's a crap-shoot. If a fancy college degree will help you, fair enough, let's obsess about that." She finished her tea and got up to get more, muttering, "It's utterly pointless, of course, because the world could end tomor-row, or you could get hit by a bus, but it's all we've got."

There was a long pause, then I said, "Yeah, what she said, I guess."

Then the door opened and two guys in suits came in. Everyone swiveled to look at them. Cassidy stood up.

"This is a private group," she said. "Can I help you?"

"Are you Cassidy Potter?"

"Your last name is Potter?" said Casper, unable to stop himself.

"Yes," she said, "and you are?"

"I'm Agent Feld, and this is my colleague Agent Larsson. We're from the FBI." He showed his badge; all of us were riveted.

Cassidy went red; this was clearly her worst nightmare. "Is this about the cheating?"

"Yes." Feld nodded. "We're looking for . . ."

"She's not here," said Cassidy. "I guess she's still in her room."

"Emily Burnstein."

Now everyone turned and stared at me.

"Oh," said Cassidy, running out of steam. "Well, she's right over there."

22

JESSICA

This whole thing would be a lot easier if I weren't hungover, I'll be honest.

When Agent What's-His-Nuts said Emily's name, I had a cup of fresh, hot tea in my hand and had to fight the ill-advised impulse to throw it in his face, grab my kid, and head for Mexico.

Then I realized a mistake must have been made somewhere.

"I'm Jessica Burnstein," I said. "I'm Emily's mother. What's going on?" I kept my tone polite, I'm a professional. I glanced at Emily and wasn't reassured by her expression. I'll be honest, she looked guilty. I wasn't sure what of, though, so I smiled at the nice FBI people.

"I'm afraid we need to talk to Emily alone, Mrs. Burnstein."

"She's a minor," I said, "you can't talk to her alone."

"Actually, we can," he replied. "Unless she requests you be present, which she has the right to do."

"Is she being charged with anything?"

The agent was surprised. "No, ma'am, only questions."

Emily spoke, and her voice was pretty firm. "I have the right to an attorney, correct?"

"Yes, of course, but we're not charging you with anything. I said that."

Emily stood up. "Well, even so, I'll happily answer your questions in the presence of my attorney." She walked towards the door.

The FBI agent said, "Who's your attorney, Ms. Burnstein?"

"She is," my daughter replied. "Come on, Mom. Let's do this."

EMILY

In a way it was almost a relief when the agents said my name. I mean, not really, but the whole thing had kind of been hanging over me. I wasn't sure why the FBI was involved, but maybe it was because I was in a different state? I don't know, I'm not a lawyer. That's what Mom's for.

Which is another thing. Until that moment I had never considered the benefits of having a mother who was a lawyer. I hadn't planned on ever needing a lawyer, frankly. We left the breakfast room and walked into the lobby. To my surprise, the agents headed to a coffee place outside, and Mom paused, too.

"Wait, where are we going?"

Agent Feld looked surprised. "To Starbucks."

"You don't want to take her somewhere private?" Mom was getting irritated because she was confused, a state she really doesn't have a lot of experience with.

He shook his head. "Honestly, Mrs. Burnstein, for the third time, she isn't being charged with anything, we just have a few questions."

"It's Ms. Burnstein, and these questions couldn't wait till we got back to Los Angeles?"

He was mildly embarrassed. "Well, we wanted to talk to her in person, as the agents in Los Angeles had handled it up to now."

It was a little awkward at the checkout, because they asked me if I wanted anything to eat and they had those birthday cake pops, which I freaking love, but being questioned by law enforcement while holding a pink cake pop with sprinkles seemed wrong. Such a bummer.

We sat down. I looked at Mom. "I'm sorry, Mom, I didn't want anyone to get in trouble."

She suddenly got it. "Wait, is this about the cheating thing at school?"

I nodded.

She was silent for a moment, which I knew wasn't a good sign. Her eyelid was twitching; she was about to go nuclear.

"Mom . . ." I tried to say.

But it was too late. She blew. "Emily Elizabeth Burnstein, why on earth would you cheat? You know I don't care about your grades. I just want you to do your best."

"I know, Mom . . ."

She interrupted me. "Cheating is never the answer! I thought I raised you better than that! I could have gotten you tutors! My god, what is your father going to say? Or my father? You were a Girl Scout, for crying out loud! Why would you risk your future for a stupid test? You'll never get into college now! I mean"—her voice was loud, and the whole coffee shop was listening to her freak out; I was having zero luck getting a word in—"your record will be sealed once you're eighteen, so I guess we could try . . ."

"Ms. Burnstein," said Agent Feld patiently, but she ignored him.

"Thank goodness I quit," she said suddenly. "We'll leave the country. Or I'll take the job with Ostergren and move to Baltimore." She turned to the agents. "Do you need to Mirandize her? What's the charge? Do you have witnesses?" It turns out there is a middle ground between harassed mother and polished lawyer, and it's harassed lawyer. It was almost adorable, but not quite, on account of the incredible loudness.

"Ms. Burnstein!" Agent Feld put on his big-girl voice. "Ms. Burnstein, Emily didn't do anything wrong. She isn't being accused of cheating."

Mom gazed at him. "She's not?" She stared at me. "You didn't cheat?"

I shook my head and may even have smiled a little bit. "No, Mom, I'm not the cheater." I took a deep breath. "I'm the snitch."

JESSICA

Well, this was unexpected.

It turned out Emily overheard some girls in class talking about a guy who'd approached them online and offered to sell them the exam paper for the upcoming AP Statistics test. One of them was a friend of hers, and when she asked Emily for her opinion, Em said it was a terrible idea. Which of course it was. Em pointed out that (a) they had no way of knowing if the paper was real, the College Board (who administers the APs) is pretty freaking uptight about exam papers; and (b) they were jeopardizing their futures by cheating.

"The thing is," Emily said, leaning across to the FBI agents, one of whom had lemon cake crumbs on his chin, "they were all pretty decent at stats anyway, it wasn't like they were going to fail the AP. But they wanted to do better."

"So you called the cops?" I was sitting there pretty stunned, I'll admit it. After the embarrassment of accusing my innocent child of cheating, I'd kind of kept my mouth shut.

Emily shook her head. "No, I wanted to stop them from cheating, but I didn't want them to get into trouble and have it ruin their transcript or whatever." She shrugged. "All they'd done was talk and think about it, they hadn't even agreed to meet the guy."

"So you told the principal?"

"I wrote a note," said Emily. "I didn't want to get caught snitching, either, although that doesn't seem to have worked out very well." She blushed suddenly. "I had Anna write it, I'm sorry. I knew they would recognize my writing." She tried a small smile. "I told you penmanship wasn't going to pay off."

"Why didn't you tell me?"

She frowned at me. "You're a lawyer. You're a mandated reporter, right? You would have to tell the authorities."

"I guess. But aren't teachers?"

"Yes," said Agent Feld. "The principal dealt with her students as she saw fit, then she contacted the LA field office and told them what the girls had told her about the man offering to sell them the papers.

One of the girls agreed to wear a wire for us and meet the guy, and the LA office managed to catch him and get him to turn on his co-conspirators. It's a much bigger problem than Los Angeles."

"Well, how did you know I wrote the note?" Emily looked worried.

"Your principal made an educated guess, she said. It could only have been someone who knew all the girls, it was reasonable to assume she was also in the Statistics class, and someone who had—her phrase—a strong moral compass."

We all regarded Emily, who was clearly torn between being pleased her principal thought she was a good person and being pissed off she was perceived as a Goody Two-shoes. No teenager wants to be told they have a strong moral compass; they might as well wear a hat with a propeller on it.

Feld continued. "The agents in LA told us they'd heard one of the kids on this tour was going to pick up exam papers from someone in New York, where the College Board is headquartered." He smiled. "You'd think they'd email, but apparently they don't trust the internet."

I wasn't sure what he meant. "Are you suggesting someone at the College Board is selling papers?"

He shook his head. "It's unlikely to be someone who actually works for the College Board, but plenty of people have access."

There was a pause. Then Emily said, "So, why do you need me?"

The agents looked at each other. "We don't, really," said Feld. "We just wanted to ask you if you knew anything useful."

"Useful? No," said my daughter firmly.

"No?" said Agent Feld, crestfallen. "We thought maybe you'd overheard kids chatting about it . . . like you did before?"

Emily raised her eyebrows at him. "Do you think I just creep around, listening in to conversations? Look, it's bad enough you guys just outed me to the entire tour group. So much for confidentiality. There is no way I'm going to do anything else to help you."

"Oh," said Agent Feld, clearly taken aback.

Emily sighed. "Because, no offense, snitching on my friends to the principal was bad enough. The kids in the room you just burst in on basically represent every private high school in Los Angeles, and you can bet they've already texted their friends that Emily Burnstein got arrested by the FBI." She put up her hand. "I know I wasn't arrested, but truth doesn't matter online, you know that."

She turned to me. "Can we go now?"

"Back to the tour?"

"Back to the hotel at least."

"Of course." I stood up. "I'm sorry, gentlemen, my daughter is unable to assist your investigation further."

"Are you sure?" asked Feld. "You handled this whole thing really well, maybe one day you'll work in law enforcement. What are you going to study in college?"

I raised my finger. "My client is done answering questions, Mr. Feld. And besides, she doesn't even know if she wants to go to college."

"Everyone goes to college," protested the other agent, who up until then had said little. "It's fun."

"Goodbye, gentlemen." I turned and took Emily's hand, leading her out of the Starbucks. For once she didn't let go.

Once we got outside, though, she dropped my hand and stopped. "You quit?"

Ah.

EMILY

I think Mom was hoping I hadn't noticed the casual hand grenade she threw out in the coffee shop, but I completely did. Once we left the agents behind I demanded an explanation.

"Well," she said, "my boss was being a dick about promoting a couple of female associates, so I threatened to quit unless he did the right thing."

I gazed at her. "You blackmailed your boss?"

She shook her head and frowned at me. "No, I stood up for something that matters."

"Like I did with the cheating."

"Exactly." She smiled a little bit. "I guess we're more alike than I thought."

I said, "I think we're both just more like Grandma, who was a bit of an ass kicker, in the ways she could be."

"I miss her," Mom said. "I wish I'd spent more time with her."

"She was awesome."

We were walking back to the hotel, and as we drew closer we spotted the group heading out to the bus to go to Bard, the first college of the day. They looked very subdued, but as I was about to call out to Will, Mom tugged me behind a tree.

"Let's play hooky," she said. "I had a massive rush of adrenaline on top of a fairly rocky chemical state, and I'm not sure I can do much more than stare into space."

I was surprised. Mom rarely shows weakness of any kind. "Are you getting sick? Do you want to go back to bed? Are we supposed to check out?"

She peeped around the tree. The group had boarded the bus and it was pulling away. She watched it turn the corner, then headed into the hotel.

"I need a shower, more coffee, and ten minutes to check my email," she said. "Then I suggest we take part in a time-honored cleansing ritual to reset our emotional equilibrium, reconnect our energies, and center ourselves in the spirit of the Feminine Divine."

I hurried to catch up with her. "I'm sorry, are you still drunk? What are we doing?"

Mom's voice floated back. "We're getting our nails done."

Neither Mom nor I are big nail people, which sounds weird. I don't mean we have giant nails; I mean we don't care about the nails we have. I don't seem to have mastered whatever it is you do to stop nail polish from chipping immediately, and Mom once told me that painted nails are a sign of weakness in a male-dominated field. I'm not sure that's true, and I suspect she said it because she has the same polish-retention issues I do. I imagine imperfect nail polish is definitely a liability when you're trying to seem invulnerable.

But there was a period in middle school when I'd been trying to fit in, and she'd taken me to get my nails done half a dozen times or so. I remember being petrified the whole time, because I wasn't sure what to do. Worrying about what to do was a big feature of middle school for me; why does everyone else walk about with complete confidence? Then I met Ruby, and Sienna, and everyone else in my friend group and discovered that (a) no one knows what they're doing, and that (b) girls are awesome.

JESSICA

We got our nails done because I couldn't think of anything I wanted to do less than face the rest of the tour group. Besides, who doesn't appreciate a hand massage?

I was struggling with the revelation that Emily had taken care of a pretty serious situation without any input from me. I'm not sure why it was surprising me; she's been doing her laundry, her homework, and her private life without me for a couple of years. But still, this was a whole different level of independence, and I was a little disappointed to discover I felt left out. I would have helped her.

I also felt bad that I hadn't told her about my work situation right away. She could clearly handle more than I'd given her credit for, and I had that "missed a step in the dark" feeling I really didn't want to get used to.

The nail salon was the best Rhinebeck had to offer, which was actually pretty fancy, and as we sat side by side with our feet in bowls of water with marbles (who came up with the marbles? I mean, yes, I get it, it's fun and distracting, but still, yet another unsung hero), we started chatting like we used to when side by side in the car.

"Do you think you'll actually have to quit?" Emily didn't seem all that fazed by this idea.

"I really hope not."

"Do you like your job that much?"

I played with the marbles. "I like it a lot, actually. I like my clients, the cases are interesting."

"But you'd have clients wherever you went."

"True. But I need a reliable job at least until you're done with college." I sneaked a glance at her, but she was flipping through a magazine. She shrugged.

"I can always not go to college." She looked at me suddenly and caught me staring at her. "I could get a job."

I grinned. "Flipping burgers?"

"Working the stripper pole. Less grease, more tips."

"Good plan," I said, picking up a magazine. "I myself have aged out of that job market."

"Your old boyfriend didn't think so."

I snorted. "He was lonely. In the same way hunger makes food taste better, loneliness makes old girlfriends look younger."

"You're still very attractive."

I looked at my beautiful daughter. "Thanks, babe. Not really something I think about all that much."

She grinned. "I think Will's dad thinks so, too."

"That's just weird," I said, and avoided the subject from then on.

I got bright red nails, by the way. They won't last more than a day, but they're gorgeous.

23

JESSICA

We decided to meet up with the group again at Vassar, but when we got there, Emily lost confidence, and I was still pretty wobbly on my pins. We found a coffee shop and called Helen.

She sailed through the doors thirty minutes later and greeted half the place by name. If you can't slink about unnoticed, I imagine it's better to willingly embrace your local fame.

"Why aren't you two touring my college and being entranced by its beauty?" she said, sitting down. "I'm so disappointed in you both."

I looked a question at Emily, who nodded. I leaned forward. "Can you keep a secret?"

Helen nodded. "I'm a philosopher. I know everything and nothing. What is truth, anyway? What is knowledge?"

I waited until the waiter brought her coffee, which she hadn't even ordered, and lowered my voice. "Emily worked with the FBI to bring an international cheating ring to ground, and she did it all without any help from me."

Emily protested. "That is totally not true." She explained to Helen. "I snitched on some friends who were planning to cheat, because I didn't want them to do something really stupid, and as a totally unintended consequence I assisted the FBI." She was exasperated. "Nobody said anything about international, by the way, that is a complete fiction. Mom loves to summarize and editorialize, it's part of her training."

"It's inexcusable," said Helen.

"Seriously," replied Emily. "I thought being a lawyer was about the sanctity of the truth?"

"No," I said, "it's about the framing and presentation of the truth. Have I taught you nothing?"

"You've taught me everything," she replied. "Including calling BS when I hear it."

"Fair enough," I said. "But anyway, the point is the FBI showed up at breakfast this morning and dropped this bomb on us, and we're still feeling a little delicate." I shrugged at Emily. "At least, they dropped the bomb on me. She knew all about it, obviously."

Helen looked excited. "Are you going to blow off the rest of the tour?"

I shook my head. "No, I think we'll take the train to NYC and join them there."

Helen clapped her hands together. "Don't take the train, I'll drive you, it'll be a blast." She waved at the waiter for the bill and checked her watch. "Road trip!"

EMILY

Say what you like about my mom; once she's made up her mind, she commits. We were packed up, checked out, and clambering into Helen's car within the hour. In this way Mom's more like my grandma, although most of the time she's much more like Grandpa. Grandma was a rare bird, I've said it before, and she didn't feather her nest with regret, that's for sure. I remember standing in the country house garden, watching the smoke from her cigarette curl up in tandem with the smoke from some structure we'd accidentally set fire to and then put in the stream.

"Well," said Grandma. "It wasn't what I would call a successful experiment, but it's sure as shit interesting."

I'd nodded.

"At what point, do you think, will the whole thing fall into the stream and go out?"

I'd shrugged, whereupon it happened.

"Oh well," she said, wading into the stream to fish out the debris (she despised littering), "nothing ventured, nothing gained."

She was full of phrases like that, my favorite being *and the devil take the hindmost*, often said when throwing random ingredients into things, or loading up the grocery cart with marshmallows, or standing next to something flammable with a match. I don't want you to get the impression she was an arsonist, she wasn't, but she wasn't one for hypothesizing. "I don't know," she would say, "let's try it and see." Mom is much more conservative, but every so often, like now, she leaps, and when she does I can see the glimmer of Grandma in her eyes.

Helen's car was as much of a trip as she was. It was one of those old station wagons with the wood on it; I have no idea what they're called.

When Helen pulled up in front of the hotel, my mother burst out laughing.

"You are kidding me. You still have Jezebel?"

Helen leaned her arm on the window and grinned. "Why would I change? She's still running like a champ. I like cars, I take good care of her, and besides, I think my mother would be insulted if I traded in the car she gave me for something new."

Mom laughed. "Even though she gave you Jezebel and went straight out and bought a used, pristine, silver Datsun 280ZX?"

Helen waved a hand. "She felt she'd done her time in the wagon. I was the last to go to college . . . I get it." She jerked her head. "Are you getting in?"

I went to open the back door, but Helen stopped me. "No, I want you to ride shotgun so I can dig into the darkest recesses of your mind and see how you think."

I looked at Mom, but she shrugged and climbed into the back seat. "Don't try to resist, Emily, there's no point."

I wasn't completely convinced this was a good idea. I mean, do these vintage cars even have airbags? Asking seemed rude, so I walked around the car and climbed in.

"Seat belt." Helen was firm. "And then you're in charge of the music." She handed me a shoebox filled with those weird cassette tapes with actual physical brown whatever that is. Tape, I guess. "Play whatever you like."

I rustled through the tapes, and eventually spotted a familiar face.

I will admit that when the opening bars of "Private Eyes" filtered through the surprisingly good sound system, and both women cheered, I felt pretty good about myself.

JESSICA

Talk about a blast from the past. Sitting in Helen's car, listening to Hall and Oates, the breeze from the open window blowing my hair around . . . it was great. Helen and Emily were chatting away in the front, but I couldn't hear them very well, on account of the breeze, and the murmur of their voices was soothing. I hadn't ridden in the back of a car in so long, that feeling of being transported, both literally and figuratively. I'd spent a lot of my childhood in the back of a car much like this one, arguing with my sister over what music to play, getting overruled by my mom.

The back seat of Helen's car was filled with books and papers and smelled like cedar. I looked for a tree-shaped air freshener but instead there was a high-tech diffuser plugged into the cigarette lighter. Do new cars even have cigarette lighters? My mom smoked like a fiend my whole childhood, and I remember her using the cigarette lighter to, you know, light cigarettes. My sister and I would watch from the back, the open windows (*I'm lighting up, ladies, crack a window*) blowing our hair in our faces as it is now, fascinated as Mom waited for the thunk of the lighter, the unlit cigarette pursed tightly, the exciting possibility that as she never paid attention to what she was doing (*Don't take your eyes off the road, those bastards will drive right at you*), she might drop it and set us all on fire. Then she'd suck, her cigarette making the crisp sound of crinkling paper, and shake the lighter as if it were a match. Then, one eye squinting, she'd blindly put it back, occasionally melting the radio buttons instead, then snatch the cigarette from her mouth and exhale a dragon's breath through the window at the drivers who were all getting in her way.

I'd watched my mom a lot; it was a different time, and she didn't share herself the way I try to share myself with Emily. Not that Emily seems interested in what I've got to offer. My mom had lots of habits I enjoyed: a way of wiping the edge of her coffee cup with her thumb before taking every sip; the lining up of socks, top to toe, before rolling them into balls; always saying the dinner needed salt and then getting up to find the saltshaker. There's a famous book by this social scientist called Winnicott, about "good enough" parenting, an idea I really thought I was going to apply to my own life but that I failed to do, not being able to summon the delicious combination of caring and ignoring it required. Mom paid attention to us, but no more than we needed. She fed us, but she sure as hell didn't take dinner orders the way I do. And she'd had no more intention of spending her limited free time playing with her own kids than she would have with anyone else's. On weekends and summers, she'd turned us out of the house in the morning and told us to come back when the streetlights came on. If the weather was bad she'd suggest the movies and maybe drop us off, but she wasn't sitting there watching *The Land Before Time*, I assure you.

I would lose my mind if I caught Emily and her friends doing any of the things my sister and I got up to. Exploring abandoned buildings. Finding stashes of porn magazines and giggling over them, feeling weird but not requiring any kind of therapy over it. The one that really makes my blood run cold is the memory of putting pennies on the train tracks near our house, one summer's favorite activity. A neighbor boy, strange and appealing in equal measure, showed us a gap in the fence and the flattened pennies that were the product of this very limited cottage industry. You could always feel the train before you saw it; a fizzing in the metal that broke into a high-pitched humming, and the train would suddenly thump into passing, close enough to whip our hair back, furiously loud, making us jump and clutch each other and scream.

I turned my head to the side and got comfortable. I was just going to close my eyes for a minute.

EMILY

Mom had fallen asleep in the back. Helen was singing along, enthusiastically warning the world about the man-eater. *Watch out, boy, she'll chew you up* is pretty much the only lyric I know, but I joined in on that one.

Helen looked over at me. "Is your mom asleep?"

I nodded.

"She fell asleep pretty much every time she rode in the back, it was a known thing. She was one of those kids who liked to work late at night, despite the fact that class was early." She smiled at me. "Are you like that?"

I shook my head. "No, I'm a 'get the homework done as soon as possible and early morning' kind of person."

Helen grunted. "How unusual."

"Yeah, well, not all teenagers are the same." I gazed out the window at the other cars on the freeway, wondering what everyone else was talking about. "What was she like, at college?"

Helen flicked on her turn signal, which made an incredibly loud clicking sound, and changed lanes. "She was fun. She was challenging. Argumentative."

I nodded. "She's still like that."

"Is she happy, do you think?"

I shrugged. "I have no idea. She doesn't seem very happy with me."

Helen looked over and frowned. "How do you mean? She's very proud of you, and she loves you to pieces."

I shrugged again and said nothing. Then, "She wants me to go to college and be a career woman like her, and I don't want to."

"Has she said that?"

"She doesn't need to."

"Have you told her you don't want to?"

"No, because the thing I want to do she probably wouldn't like. I'm not even sure about it myself." I sighed. "Can we talk about something else?"

There was a silence, and then Helen said, "What's your position on gene editing and the relationship between for-profit medicine and pure research?"

I coughed. "Uh . . . I'm not sure I have one."

She grinned. "Perfect, let's work it out. Think out loud." She paused. "And turn down the music a bit, I want to hear you wonder."

When we walked into the Manhattan hotel lobby later, many of the kids were sitting there, waiting for me.

Alice was among them, and she saw me first.

"She's free on bail," she called, causing a lot of head turning. "I guess her mom sold a kidney after all." She turned to Casper. "You owe me twenty dollars."

"You're lying," he replied.

Mom squeezed my arm. "I'll go check in," she said. "See you up in the room."

Will stood up and walked over to me, pulling me into a hug. Casper and Sam were right behind him.

"Are you okay? What happened?"

I nodded. "I'm totally fine, it was all a mistake."

That was the story Mom, Helen, and I had decided on, at least publicly.

"Are you going to sue?" Alice hadn't gotten to her feet, but as we drew closer, she did reach up for a hug. I was surprised enough to give it to her.

"No," I replied. "It was a genuine mistake. They apologized." I looked at them. "So, what did I miss?"

Casper answered. "Well, Bard was gorgeous, Vassar was pretty, and the trip to NYC was enlivened by a massive argument between this one"—he jerked his thumb at Alice—"and her mother."

I made a face at Alice. "Sorry to hear that," I said. "About what?"

"You, actually," said Alice. "But now you're here and everything's okay, so I'm going up to my room."

"I'll walk you up," said Casper.

I watched, doing my best to keep my mouth closed, as she smiled up at him and took the hand he offered. They walked off to the elevator bank, and I turned back to Sam and Will.

"I'm off, too," said Sam, looking at his phone. "My mom and I are going to the opera."

"Of course you are," said Will.

Then it was just the two of us.

We sat there and looked at each other for a minute.

"What really happened?" he asked. "If it was a mistake, why did it take all day?"

"It didn't," I replied. "The FBI part was the beginning, then Mom and I played hooky from the tour and got our nails done." I waved my nails at him.

"Why do girls paint their nails? I totally don't get it."

"You're not supposed to, it's not for you."

He frowned at me. "And you're sticking with your FBI story?"

I shook my head. "No, I can tell you the truth, but you have to swear you won't tell anyone, or text it, or put it out on social media in any form."

"Agreed." His eyes were steady. "Unless this is one of those stories that is going to result in my getting chased across four continents by international law enforcement." He tried an uncertain smile. "I've seen *Enemy of the State*, knowledge can be dangerous."

"No promises."

He sighed. "I'll take the risk."

I checked there were no other kids in the lobby, and lowered my voice. "I found out about the girls at school, right, the ones who were going to cheat?"

He nodded.

"I knew it was stupid, and I knew they were risking everything, so I told the school." I shrugged. "That's really all there is to it."

He frowned at me. "Liar. Why did the FBI get involved?"

"I'm not lying. It turns out there's a whole cheating thing, a whole organized conspiracy, and our little part was somehow connected. They wanted to know if I knew anything else." I suddenly found my lap very interesting. "I didn't." I decided not to mention the idea that there was someone on this tour who was involved; we didn't know if it was true, and talking about it was out of the question, even with Will. There was a long silence. I looked up at him. "You hate snitches."

He nodded. "Sure, we all do, right?"

"Yes. But this was different. This wasn't vaping in the bathroom."

"I see that. But . . . it's still snitching. You still went to the teachers and got your friends in trouble."

"Only to save them from getting in even bigger trouble."

"Why didn't you tell them not to do it?"

I felt hurt suddenly. "I tried that, for crying out loud. What, you think I overheard them and scuttled off to the principal's office? They told me about it, asked me what I thought, I told them what I thought, they decided to do it anyway." I clenched my fists in my lap. "I'm not Alice. I'm not a big shiny star at school. I'm just another kid, and they didn't listen to me."

He stood up. "Well, I'm glad everything is okay now."

Then he walked away.

24

JESSICA

I left Emily in the lobby to reunite with her friends, and headed up to the room. I'm not sure why, but for some reason we were given a suite, and I spent a few minutes marveling at how big the bathtub was. Whenever I've stayed in New York before, I've always been surprised by how small they can make a hotel room and have it still count as a room and not a closet. But this time they clearly threw caution to the wind.

I called Frances and told her everything. She was pleasingly horrified, impressed with Emily's bravery, and delighted I'd gotten my nails done.

"About time," she said. "Your hands remind me of the school nurse, all those years ago. Incredibly clean and sensible."

"Isn't that a good thing, in fingernails? I'm not a model, I'm a lawyer. I'm supposed to radiate reliability and competence."

"Well"—her voice was dry—"you certainly do that."

Emily walked in. She did not look good. I made a quick goodbye and hung up. "What's the matter?"

She shook her head. "Will thinks I'm a snitch and now we're not friends anymore."

She started to cry. "I'm always the good kid, the reliable kid, and sometimes that sucks so badly. I want to be the fun kid."

I gathered her into a hug, and she let me. "Baby, you are the fun kid."

"No," she said, wiping her soggy face on my sleeve, making me glad I hadn't changed for dinner yet. "I'm the kid who stands by the side and laughs at the fun kid. I'm not even a toady sidekick, I'm just one of the background kids. I don't get picked first or last, I get picked somewhere in the middle. I'm ordinary. In twenty years when people look at school photos, they're not going to remember my name. I'm going to be that kid who did school paper, or who won the stupid penmanship thing. I'm going to be nameless."

She was working herself up. I decided to let her blow off steam.

"And I've even ruined my safe spot in the crowd by snitching on my friends, so now I'll be remembered as the girl who snitched. Th . . . this is going to be my defining high school moment." She was starting to hyperventilate a little.

"No," I said, "you're going to be the girl who was questioned by the FBI. That's much more fun."

No dice. No laughter setting available. Emily shook her head, sniffed, and stepped back. "No, I told Will the truth and he called me a snitch and walked away."

I watched her turn away, and asked, "Will he tell everyone?"

"No," she said, wise with experience. "But eventually everyone will know, because that's how information works. It leaks to one person, then trickles along to another, then everyone knows." She sat on the desk chair, looking around for the first time. "Why do we have such a big room?"

"Baby, the people who know you will understand . . ."

She was annoyed suddenly, smacking her palm on the desk, deciding anger was more comfortable than sorrow. "Mom, it's not about the people that know me. It's about everyone else, don't you get it?"

"Well, I . . ."

"And what do you know about it, anyway? You barely pay any attention to my life. The only reason you know about this is because the freaking authorities got involved."

"Well, you could have told me." *If she'd wanted to, but she didn't,* said the voice in my head.

"When? In the three minutes you're home every day? I guess I could have sent you an email. Or asked your assistant to pass along a message. Like that time I got her to email a permission slip to school because you were in a meeting." She pulled her leg up under her, curling like a snail.

Her tone was so scornful, I recoiled. "That was one time."

"I'm such a huge disappointment to you."

I was stung, and sad that the comfortable closeness of the nail salon had apparently dissipated. "That is completely untrue. I'm incredibly . . ."

Her face got redder. "I don't want to be a lawyer, I don't have a patent, I don't have a million followers, I don't plan to go to an Ivy League, I don't want to be like you, and you hate me!"

I stood up and reached for her. "Baby, I don't hate you, how can you think that?"

She rolled the chair back, out of reach. "I know it! The other day at dinner with Grandpa you didn't even notice I was gone for, like, twenty minutes."

I frowned. "What?"

"I was in the bathroom and lost track of time and when I got back you were chatting away, probably about your fabulous Valentina." She made a frustrated gesture. "She's the daughter you wish you had, right? A fancy, supersmart, really ambitious woman like you."

"Um, well, first of all, she's too old to be my daughter, and . . ."

"I'm speaking metaphorically!" She stood up again, nearly tipping the chair. "I'm mediocre in every way, compared to Alice, compared to Valentina, compared to you, Mom! I'm a total fuckup, and you're ashamed of me."

"Emily Burnstein, watch your language . . ." This argument was getting completely out of control. "Now sit down and take a deep breath."

Amazingly, she sat, this time on the bed. I went to sit next to her on the bed but thought better of it. I pulled the desk chair around and sat facing her.

"Listen to me. From the moment you were born, you've been the very best thing about my life. Yes, I work hard, because we need to eat and because I love my work. I won't apologize for that. But you come first, you've always come first, and no one and nothing on earth even comes close to how much I love you, and marvel at you, and am blown away by you every single day." I leaned closer. "You're completely your own person, Emily, you're not like anyone else, and I wouldn't want you to be. Least of all like me. I'm boring."

She sniffed. "You're not boring."

"I am. I follow my little path, putting one foot in front of the other."

"You're strong."

"I'm inflexible."

She smiled, a little bit. "You're passionate."

"I'm opinionated."

"You do what's right."

I shook my head. "I do what's expected of me."

"Not lately. You're ready to throw your career away for a principle." There was a silence. She hiccupped a bit. "I'm sorry I swore."

"It's totally fucking fine."

She laughed. "I'm jealous of Valentina."

"I noticed that."

"She sees you more than I do. Everyone in your dumb office sees you more than I do." Her eyes filled with tears again. "What if I leave home and you don't even notice?"

My vision spangled, too. "What if you leave home and don't even miss me?"

She stood suddenly, and sat in my lap. She said, in a strangled voice, "I miss you already, Mom."

I wrapped my arms around her. "I miss you, too, baby."

"I love you, Mom."

"I love you more."

It was at that precise moment my phone rang. I pulled it out of my pocket and looked at it. It was my boss, John. I turned it to show Emily, then powered off the phone and threw it on the bed.

We sat there for ages silently. It was a big, pathetic mess of tears and dripping mascara, but neither of us wanted to be anywhere else at all.

25

JESSICA

Once we'd both calmed down, we got dressed and headed out to dinner at Robert and Amanda's house. I'd suggested to Em we stay in the hotel and order room service, but she wanted to go.

"I love Amanda's place. Besides, I haven't seen Chloe in years."

I closed the hotel room door and headed down the hall. "I'm not sure Chloe will be there, isn't she still in school?"

"It's spring break, remember? She might be there." Emily was visibly pulling herself together. She reminded me of my mother when she did this. My mom was the queen of the quick recovery. She frequently broke things or attempted something she shouldn't have (like replumbing the country house on her own, at seventy) and Things Happened. But she would always survey the damage, wipe whatever needed wiping, and shake her feathers back into place.

Onward and upward, she would say. And onward and upward she would go. I suddenly missed her, that sharp sudden inhalation of cold air, the slice of memory lodging in my throat.

"Well," I said, waiting for the elevator doors to close. "Onward and upward, baby."

She looked at me and smiled. "I was thinking about Grandma, in the shower. That's funny."

"Do you remember her very well?" Emily had been still quite young when my mom had passed away, maybe twelve or so.

Emily nodded. "Of course. She was the best. She had a lathe."

I laughed out loud, having completely forgotten that. "That's right." I frowned suddenly. "She didn't let you use it, did she?"

Emily stepped through the opening doors into the lobby. "Grandma? Let me play on a deadly high-velocity tool? With blades?" She snorted. "Of course not." But then she grinned at me over her shoulder. "How do you think I made you that Mother's Day mug rack?"

I stopped. "You *made* that?"

Emily shrugged and headed to the street.

Amanda and Robert lived, as I have said, in a brownstone they bought at the end of the nineties. I don't know what they paid for it, but let's say they got lucky. Mind you, back then 148th Street between Broadway and Riverside was not a fancy neighborhood. Now it was a stone-cold hipster paradise, and Amanda and Robert would sit on their stoop and tut over how much the neighborhood had gentrified, despite the fact that they were among the first to start the process.

"No, we were here long before it was cool," they would say, and maybe they were right. Anyway, now the house was looking pretty lived in, which is what happens after three kids make their way through both the place and the parents' decorating budget. Chloe was their youngest, but she was still a few years older than Emily. We'd visited every couple of years, usually before or after seeing my parents, and Emily and Chloe had always gotten along. Chloe, being the baby of her family, enjoyed the novel sensation of being an older sister, and Emily enjoyed everything about Chloe. Which explained her squeal of delight when it was, in fact, Chloe who opened the door and welcomed us in.

"Em!"

"Chloe!"

Repeat that a few times in a pitch only dogs and dolphins can hear, and you'll have a perfect re-creation.

Amanda was in the kitchen, as usual, a pen tucked behind her ear, her hair sticking up at the back like always. She looked up as I came in but kept stirring her cooking.

"Hey," she said.

"Hey," I said, sitting down at the counter and dropping my bag on the floor. As always, it was as if we'd seen each other yesterday. We'd lived together the last two years of college, and that kind of intimacy doesn't wear away. Amanda's dog, Harvey, wandered over and blundered into the chair. He was some kind of middle-sized poodle mix, with hair that stuck up like Amanda's. When he was freshly washed he was like a camel-colored dandelion clock, but the rest of the time he was more . . . clumpy.

"Hey, Harvey," I said, scratching his head. His milky eyes gazed up at me, and his tail waved gently back and forth. Everything about Harvey was mellow.

"He can't see a thing anymore," Amanda said, clunking her wooden spoon on the side of the pot, then licking it and sticking it back in. She reached for the salt. "We try not to move the furniture, but sometimes he still walks into it."

"Oh no, poor baby," I said, scratching his head some more.

"I don't think he cares," said Amanda. "He pauses, possibly mumbles an apology, and moves on."

"How old is he now?"

"Fifteen."

"Jeez."

"Right? In dog years he's, like, eighty-three. I found a chart online."

Harvey walked over to his dog bed and spun around three times before lying down and huffing his head onto his paws.

Amanda looked at him. "Every morning I steel myself to find his dead body, and every morning he's standing by the refrigerator door, waiting patiently for it to open." Amanda pretends to be tough, but she isn't fooling anyone. "I thought he was waiting for Chloe to leave for college, but she'll graduate next year and he's still around."

"Maybe he's waiting for you to die first, out of politeness," I suggested, getting up from my stool. "Can I make myself some coffee?"

"Of course, we have one of those pod thingies now, the kids got it for me last Mother's Day."

I dug around in the cupboard and made myself some coffee. "Do you want some?"

Amanda shook her head. "I'm getting too old for coffee in the evenings, it's pathetic." She frowned at me. "Emily's here, right? She doesn't say hello anymore?"

I made a face. "She and Chloe disappeared upstairs immediately. They're probably high as kites already."

Amanda smiled. "As long as they smoke their own stuff, I'm good."

I raised my eyebrows. "You still smoke pot?"

She nodded. "You don't?"

"I'm a lawyer, remember?"

"Isn't it legal in California? I would have thought you would be mildly stoned 24-7."

I shook my head. "Clients like counsel to be fully present and on top of their game. Waving a sheaf of papers at the judge and saying, *Dude, whatever works for you works for me*, would not cut it."

"Yawn," said Amanda, finally stepping away from her cooking and coming over to give me a hug. "Rob will be home soon."

"Where is he?" Robert usually worked from home; he was a free-lance journalist. He had been a less freelance journalist earlier in his career, back when the internet hadn't disrupted the media landscape. He'd had an actual wooden desk, complete with piles of papers and coffee cups, at the *New York Times*, when they decided to cut their workforce and modernize. He said that meant anyone with a jour-nalism degree and a reasonable salary was fired, and anyone younger than thirty with more than a passing familiarity with grammar was hired.

"Is he . . . feeling better?" I trod carefully. Every time I'd seen Robert in the last ten years he was a little more bitter than the time before.

"Much better," Amanda said, pulling a bottle of wine from the fridge. She poured herself a glass and offered one to me. I shook my head. "He's working on a new thing, but I'll let him tell you all about it."

EMILY

It was so incredibly good to see Chloe. It's not like we grew up to-gether, but we saw each other quite a bit, and emailed and stuff. She's like my older sister, or cousin or something. Somehow the kids you've known all your life are less anxiety provoking. They've already seen you cry, even if only over broken Legos.

We headed up to her room, which had changed a lot since the last time I saw it. Then the walls had been covered with photos of her friends, printouts from Pinterest, postcards from everywhere . . . Now the walls were clear, freshly painted in a pale creamy yellow, and featured actual framed pictures.

"Wow," I said. "This looks like a regular grown-up's room." I was making fun of her, and she got it right away.

"Oh please," she said, throwing herself on the bed. "My mom did it while I was away. She said she thought it would be nicer for me to bring friends home to, but I think she was dying to get all the Justin Bieber shit off the walls."

"Who can blame her?" I said. "I think it looks great."

"Really?" She wrinkled her nose. "I feel like I got erased."

"That's heavy," I said, laughing at her.

She tipped her head to one side. "What's up with you? Boy trou-ble?" She paused. "Girl trouble? Nonbinary trouble?"

I shook my head. "Not really. Well, yes, a bit, but mostly the trou-ble is all mine." I lay on my tummy on her rug, as I had done so many times before, bending my legs at the knee and putting my head on my folded arms.

"Nice high-tops," she said. "Spill it."

I told her about everything. The cheating. The snitching. Mom quitting. The tour. Alice and her mom. Will. Even the aerodrome part.

"Huh," she said. "For what it's worth, you totally did the right thing."

"You think?"

She nodded. "Totally. Trust me, if they'd gotten caught actually cheating, you would have felt like crap you didn't say something. Nothing lamer than regret."

"How about social suicide? How lame is that?"

Chloe laughed. "Not super lame. The boy will come around, he's being a jerk. If he doesn't get over it, you're better off without him." She looked at me. "Why didn't you agree to help the FBI?"

I shrugged. "It seemed one step too far."

"Do you think there's someone on the tour who's involved?"

"Maybe. Alice's mom was offering bribes. At least, it seems that way." I told her what Casper and Will had relayed to me about dinner the night before.

Chloe was thoughtful. "It's weird, right, how parents get about college? I thought my mom and dad were pretty laid-back, but they turned into complete monsters when college apps rolled around. And I was the third kid, they'd had two before me and they were even worse with them. Poor Jake, I thought he was going to have a nervous breakdown checking college websites."

"Where did he end up?"

"He got into Brown, went for a semester, then transferred to NYU because he missed his mommy." She laughed. "I'm only semi-joking."

"And now? Is he here?" I'd always had kind of a crush on her older brother, not that I'd ever let on.

"Please don't tell me you still have a crush on him, he's such a loser." Chloe slapped the bed. "You do!" She rolled back, laughing.

I felt myself blushing.

She stopped laughing. "He's still here, he's working at the same start-up as Dad."

"Your dad works at a start-up?" I wrinkled my nose. "I thought he was a journalist."

She nodded. "He is, it's kind of a journalism start-up. I think. He does tell me about it, he's actually adorably excited about it, but I kind of tune out." She smiled at me. "So, apart from turning government informant, what else have you been up to?"

26

JESSICA

"Wait, so it's a start-up? But there are old people like us there?"

Rob laughed, and passed the salad. "Yes, a few of us. It's a start-up because it's new, but it's also kind of a nonprofit. We're funded by the state, the city, grants from philanthropists and such. We generate some income, by running and teaching courses, but largely we're there to help young people." He took the salad back from Chloe and piled it onto his plate.

I glanced at Emily. "And young people listen to you? That's not been my experience." She tossed a piece of bread at me, but I dodged, and Harvey caught it. I turned to Amanda. "How does he catch bread he can't even see?"

"We think he's developed food-specific echolocation."

Rob looked better than I'd seen him in years. His color was good, he'd lost weight, he was wearing a really cool pair of sneakers I secretly coveted. Now he said, "You should quit your job and come work with us. We could definitely use a lawyer."

I rolled my eyes. "Oh my god, everyone wants me to quit my job. How could I possibly afford to live in New York on a start-up salary?"

"You could live here," said Amanda. "We're going to turn the basement into an apartment and rent it out. We'll rent it to you. We won't gouge you too badly, although you will have to pay extra for laundry."

Chloe coughed, and put down her glass. "You are? Since when?"

"Since ages. You guys are all out of the house, it's pretty big for two of us. We'll sell it eventually, but in the meantime we're going to Airbnb or get a tenant or something." Amanda topped up her wineglass. "We're going to rent it to your godmother."

Emily turned to me, her eyes gleaming. "Let's do it! Let's move to New York, it would be so cool."

"You have to finish high school," I said firmly. "Rob, I'm still not getting it. What do you do exactly?"

"Well, lots of things. It was started by a couple of friends of ours, whose kids had grown up and left home, but who were forever calling back with questions, right?"

"I guess," I said. "I thought they all looked things up on the internet."

"Well, sure. But sometimes they had specific questions, or situations they hadn't experienced before, and they called home." He shrugged. "We did that too, right? We didn't even have the internet so much."

I thought about it. "Uh . . . I remember calling my mom in a panic because the toilet was overflowing and she told me how to turn off the water."

"Exactly. And the younger generation is used to being able to get answers to everything, but the internet isn't always enough. The founders started getting calls from their kids' friends, and emails, too. They realized there's lots of practical information young people miss out on or need help with. They had some money, so they started a website and called it AskRabbit, kind of as a joke. You know, like TaskRabbit, but for questions." He shrugged. "It took off, not in a stratospheric, internet unicorn way, but in a steady, meaningful way. They were fielding dozens and then hundreds of questions a day."

"What kinds of questions?" Emily was interested.

Amanda laughed. "Bizarre questions, easy questions, hard questions, everything."

Rob nodded. "But mostly practical questions. How do I settle a dispute with my landlord? How do I quit my job without burning bridges? How do I choose a credit card? How do I get a visa for another country when I don't know my social security number?" He chewed and talked. "They can find this information online, probably, but they want to talk to an actual person."

"And then they also get weird questions . . ." Chloe warned. "Like, how do I get this Malibu Barbie out of my butt?"

"We have never had that question, Chloe." Her father frowned at her, then smiled. "But we do get personal questions, like how do I tell my girlfriend I'm gay, or how do I tell my parents I got arrested . . ." His expression was serious. "Last week we worked with a thirty-one-year-old man who'd found out he had maybe a year to live. We sat down with him and planned out everything he needed to do, legally, personally . . . It was hard. But it was easier for him to do it with us than with his parents, or his wife, all of whom were too devastated to think straight."

"Wow," I said, leaning back in my chair. "That sounds intense."

Rob nodded. "But most days are filled with simple questions and general advice. We also have specialists, like me, who help with work-type questions. It's rewarding. Last week I ran a workshop on developing relationships with whistleblowers, or confidential sources, for young journalists. Most of them had journalism degrees, but this is the kind of practical help you'd normally get on the job."

"And they don't get it there . . . ?"

"No, because there aren't newsrooms in the same way there used to be. Everyone's freelancing, or working remotely, and many bureaus fired a lot of senior people . . ." He looked at Amanda, and then at me. "And here's the thing. The internet is great, and contains billions of bits of information, about pretty much every subject under the sun. But sometimes people want to look at someone, or hear their voice, when they're worried about something. And not everyone has family, sadly." He shook his head. "It's been eye-opening."

Amanda got up from the table. "Who wants dessert?"

EMILY

It would be awesome to live in New York, but I don't think Mom's going for it. Despite this morning's sudden ditching of the tour, she's not usually a quick-change artist. She's . . . methodical. Predictable. Which I actually appreciate, even though sometimes her immovability feels like walls rather than foundations. (Sidenote: Is it a simile or metaphor if you say *like* in one case but not in the other? Ask Mr. Libicki.) To be fair, I'd probably think moving anywhere would be good, because I really want to run away. I'm dreading going back to school next week, because there is no doubt in my mind everyone is going to know who snitched and why. Information is like a bad smell; a little bit is enough to start pointing fingers.

After dinner we all went for a walk along the river, through Riverbank State Park. Chloe was beside me.

I said, "Do you realize how awesome it is, growing up in Manhattan? Living in a brownstone next to the park, going to museums and galleries and being so cool it's almost against the laws of thermodynamics?"

She laughed. Chloe always makes me feel like a more interesting person than I am. That reminds me of Will, because he does that, too. They bring out the smart in me, I guess. In the same way people like Alice bring out the dumb and my mom brings out the . . . I don't know. The confused.

Chloe replied, "I do appreciate it, but at the same time it's what you're used to. I think it must be great growing up in LA, seeing movie stars everywhere and beautiful weather and great food." We paused and let the adults get ahead of us. Chloe leaned on the railing and surveyed the river, the enormous George Washington Bridge to our right. "What do you want to do about college? Why don't you come here? I'm 100 percent confident you could live with us once you're done with dorms."

I sighed. "Everyone's obsessed with college."

She nodded. "I know. I promise you it isn't as vital as people think. I mean, it's great, I'm really enjoying it, but once you're there, it's as good and bad as anything else." She turned her back to the view and leaned on the railing. "You should definitely go, though, it's fun."

"So everyone says." I shrugged. "I'm not good at school. I try, I do okay, but it's such a slog."

"Do something else. Go to art school, or cooking school, or some other thing. Learn what you want to learn." The adults had turned the corner ahead and disappeared. "What are you going to do about Will?"

"Nothing," I said sadly. "There's nothing to be done." My phone buzzed. "Oh my god, it's actually him."

Chloe laughed. "He could feel a disturbance in the force. What's he saying?"

I gazed at my screen in horror, then reached out to grab Chloe's arm.

"Alice has disappeared."

Will and Casper met us outside Lincoln Center, near the hotel. They were polite to Chloe, but they were clearly concerned.

"What happened?" I asked.

Casper shrugged. "She and her mom had that huge fight on the bus, right? I saw her mom with her bags getting into a cab outside the hotel, before dinner, then Alice texted me she wasn't going to come to dinner after all."

I shrugged. "I'm sure she has loads of friends here. She comes here quite a bit, I think."

Casper nodded. "She said that. But after dinner she and Will and I were going to get together to talk about something, but she never showed up."

I frowned. What on earth could Alice have to discuss with Casper and Will? Will was pretty cool, but Casper was the kind of kid Alice made fun of. I decided to let that question pass for now.

I took a big breath. "I have to tell you guys something, but you must promise not to tell anyone else."

They nodded.

"When I met with the FBI, they said someone on the tour was going to pick up AP papers to take back to LA."

They stared at me.

"You know," I added, "in order to cheat . . ."

They kept staring at me.

"And maybe Alice . . ."

Will spoke. "Went to get the papers and got arrested by the FBI?"

I shrugged.

Casper shook his head firmly. "Alice wouldn't cheat. She was furious with her mom, that's what they were fighting about. She said she'd rather fail on her own than succeed with her parents' help." He paused. "It was a whole different side of her." He blushed. "She was amazing."

My turn to stare. I flicked a glance at Will, but he wasn't giving anything away.

"Well," said Chloe, "we still need to find her. I assume you tried texting?"

Casper nodded.

"Did you check her social media?"

Casper frowned. "No."

I rolled my eyes. "Dude, she posts everything."

"Even criminal conspiracy?" Will was scornful. *"Hey, bitches, check me out, getting arrested by the po-po?"*

Casper whooped. "Wait, she added to her story an hour ago." He turned his phone to face us. There was Alice, briefly, then a swinging pan around to a giant stone lion, then back to Alice.

"Public library," said Chloe. She checked her watch. "They've been closed for hours, though."

"Wait, she just posted this." Casper was literally jumping up and down. "It's that clock thing, that round clock thing. She's there right now."

"Grand Central," I said, surprising myself. They looked at me and I shrugged. "I watch movies."

"It's in movies?"

"Casper," I said, "the main hall at Grand Central has been in so many movies."

"Name one."

"Why are we talking about this?" asked Will. "Shouldn't we be heading to Midtown?"

"Come on," said Chloe, "the subway's right here."

"Shouldn't we get a cab?" I asked. "Wouldn't it be quicker?"

She laughed. "Nope, on Friday evening the quickest way to get across town is not a cab." She headed off. "Let's pray there are no subway delays."

27

JESSICA

So, Emily and Chloe went off to do something downtown, leaving me with Amanda and Rob.

"Are they up to something, do you think?" I asked Amanda as we heard the door close downstairs.

"Almost certainly," she replied. "They usually are."

"Well, I didn't think so," I replied, "but Emily surprised the shit out of me this week." I told her about the cheating.

She laughed. "Man, I look back at high school and laugh at how easy we had it, don't you?"

I nodded. "Yup. I don't remember pressure like they have, or even that much interest. Going to high school in the nineties was pretty straightforward."

"I didn't even have a computer until college."

"I didn't have a cell phone until college."

"I didn't have sex until college."

I coughed. "Uh . . ."

She laughed. "Well, you beat me there. But our kids grew up in a literally changed world from us. When they say, *It's not like it was when you were young*, they're actually right. Very irritating."

Rob came in. "Hey, do you guys want to smoke pot and play video games?"

I turned to Amanda. "He's joking."

She shook her head. "Nope. This is the one drawback of him spending all his time around young people. He thinks he is one."

I threw a soft cushion at Rob. "Dude, get a grip."

He laughed. "Age is just a number, Jess. You've followed the rules all your life, why not break down this once?" He waved a little pen-looking thing at me. "It's not smoke, it's vapor. You won't even cough."

I suddenly felt my reservations melt away. "Why not? This has been a challenging week. But I am not playing video games. Whenever I watch Em do it, I get motion sickness."

Amanda grinned and took the vape pen from her husband. "That's fine, you and I can sit here, eat chips, and make fun of him. It's great, I do it a lot these days."

"Okay," I said. "And maybe it will help me work out what the hell I'm going to do with myself after Emily leaves."

"Or even before," said Rob. "If I've learned anything in the last year or so, it's that it's all very well to look before you leap, but you shouldn't look for too long."

"Are you stoned already?" said Amanda, laughing. "You sound like a fortune cookie." She stood up. "Speaking of which . . ." She headed into the kitchen.

I inhaled deeply, proving that smoking is like riding a bicycle;

your body remembers even if you don't. Then I settled back for a quiet, reflective evening of intelligent conversation and emotional clarity. Or eating my body weight in cookies and laughing at everything, whatever.

It's not like I'm going to need to do anything this evening. Emily isn't even here. I pointed at my friends. "You must promise never to tell Emily about this, okay?"

Rob exhaled and nodded. "What happens in Vegas stays in Vegas."

"We're not in Vegas."

"Exactly."

It was after the second round of pot that I suddenly realized I'd never turned my phone back on after I'd turned it off in the hotel room. I probably should have left it off, to be honest, but my stoner brain was very confident.

It started buzzing the minute I turned it on.

"My god," said Amanda, "it's possessed."

"Seven texts from John, four from Valentina, and two from Ostergren." I looked at my friend. "Shall I throw the phone away and tell them I was robbed?"

"Yes." She nodded. "You're thousands of miles away, they'll never know."

The phone rang. I answered it instinctively. "Uh . . . yes?"

"Jessica, it's John."

"Hello," I replied carefully. I heard a noise—Amanda was picking up the vape pen again. I frowned at her.

"Ostergren's acquisition is going through, and he's demanding both you and Valentina on his account."

I thought hard. "Is Valentina a partner yet?"

"No."

I hung up. Then I giggled. "That may have been a mistake on my part."

Amanda stared at me. "Did you just hang up on your boss?"

"Yes. He was asking for it." My phone rang again. John. "Hi, John. Is Valentina a partner now?"

He was sputtering. "Jessica, did you just . . ."

I hung up again.

"You've lost your mind," said Amanda, raising her voice. "Rob, take off that ridiculous headset, Jessica has lost her mind. She's too high, we need to make some coffee."

Rob shook his head. "It won't help, it'll simply add a layer of hyper over the top of the stoned. Can I go back to my game?"

John rang again, and this time he spoke first. "I just sent an email. Valentina is now a partner."

"And Janet?"

"No, it's too . . ."

Click. I started to giggle. "Why didn't I do this earlier?"

Ten minutes later the phone buzzed again. It was a text from Valentina. "I just made partner, and so did Janet, what did you do?"

I called John. "Very impressive, John. I guess your powers of persuasion haven't been underestimated. Now, how can I help you?"

"I need you to come back right away. I need your input on the deal."

"I'm with my daughter. It can wait until Monday. I'll look it over on the plane."

"You've been with her a whole week! What are you even doing?"

I exhaled. "We're catching up. I withdraw my resignation, send me the deal to look over, I'll see you in a few days, don't worry."

I put the phone on the coffee table. "Pass me the headset, Rob. I feel like blowing away some bad guys."

EMILY

There was Wi-Fi on the subway, amazingly. We got out to change trains at Times Square, and Casper checked social media again.

He frowned. "She's going somewhere, I guess. She's not at Grand Central anymore."

"But she's still posting?"

He nodded.

"Well, then she's not arrested. Maybe she didn't meet the contact yet."

"Or maybe she's not meeting them at all." Casper was annoyed with me. Then his face fell. "Oh . . ."

Will peered over his shoulder. "Selfie. Captioned: *Meeting the Man, looking good*."

Casper swallowed. "She's changed from before. She's wearing a dress."

Chloe shook her head. "Why would she dress up to do something illegal? Why on earth would she post about it? I mean, I know you said she's an obsessive poster, but come on. This doesn't sound right to me." She reached for Casper's phone. "Can I?" She squinted at it. "She's inside somewhere in this shot, but I can't tell where."

"Can't you ask her where she is? Text her."

"She's not answering, I've been trying." Casper was upset. "Maybe she's going on a date. You know. With a boy."

Will looked at me but said nothing.

"Wait," said Chloe, "she's at the Met. She posted a picture of the new fashion exhibit." She checked the time. "It closes in an hour, let's go. If we're lucky we'll get a northbound express to Eighty-Sixth."

She started half running through the crowd, Casper close behind her. Will stared at me. "She knows the Met exhibits by heart?"

I shrugged. "She's a New Yorker, maybe it's a requirement, who knows?"

We hurried after her. I couldn't tell if Will was still mad at me, and I really, really wanted to know.

We got lucky and leaped on an express as the doors were closing. The train was crowded, and I had to grab Will's jacket to stay upright. He didn't stop me, and there was a moment when he looked down at me and seemed about to say something. Then the brakes screeched and he turned away again. I have a pretty quiet life, let's face it, and this whole week was starting to be a bit much. I suddenly wished my mom was there, and then felt dumb for wishing it. Why was being sixteen such a challenge for me? Everyone else was cool about their parents; I was such a loser.

The four of us pushed through the crowds at Eighty-Sixth Street and headed south, Chloe leading the way. The steps outside the Met were crowded with people leaving, arriving, and hanging out. It was like a party, and the air was filled with chatter in a dozen languages. I stared around and saw people my age everywhere, school tours like ours, a million backpacks and earbuds and cell phones.

"We'll never see her," said Will. "She might not even still be here."

"There she is," said Casper. And he was right. Eyes like a hawk, that kid.

Alice was standing on the sidewalk, talking to a man I'd never seen before. He was short and well dressed, holding a large yellow envelope and wearing dark glasses, despite the fact that the streetlights were already on.

"Crap," I said, "who's that?" I held up my phone and took a picture. "Wait, I'm going to ask my mom what to do." I sent it.

The man was talking to Alice and she was nodding. She didn't look worried; to be fair, she seemed relaxed and possibly even mildly bored. She reached for the envelope, and the guy jerked it out of reach, clearly explaining something.

"We have to stop her before she takes it," said Casper. "The FBI must be close, they're watching her."

"Oh, so now you believe me?" I wasn't happy about it. Part of me wanted to be right, but a bigger part of me was sad Alice was the cheater. She was many things, none of them super admirable, but this was going to really suck for her.

Suddenly, a car pulled up and a man in a dark suit got out.

"Shit," said Will, "it's the feds."

Casper started running towards Alice, and the three of us weren't far behind.

Casper was yelling as he went, and the FBI guy, Alice, and Envelope Man turned quickly. As Casper got close, the agent stepped in front of Alice and Envelope Man and held up his hands.

"Hold on, kid," we heard him say, and then Casper sidestepped him and knocked the envelope out of Alice's hands.

"Don't do it, Alice," he said, "you're so much better than this."

Which was when the guy in the suit jumped on him.

JESSICA

If it's possible to feel guilty when receiving a text, I felt guilty. *Sheepish* might be a better word, and it's certainly a funnier word.

I looked at my phone and frowned. I was wearing a tall stripy hat, pulled from an old dress-up box somewhere, and Amanda was sitting next to me, wearing a pair of aviator goggles. It had made sense at one point.

"Emily texted me," I said. "Look."

I angled the phone so Amanda could see it. "Huh," she said. "They're at the Met, how boringly educational of them."

"Kids these days," I said. "They've got no sense of adventure."

"But who's that?" asked Amanda. "Is that a friend of Emily's?"

I examined the photo more carefully. "Yeah," I said, "although I'm surprised they're hanging out, they're not very close. That's Alice."

"Alice the bitch?"

"Yeah." It's possible I had maligned Alice a little, in talking about the trip.

"Who's that with her?"

I peered at the photo and smiled.

"Oh, that's sweet," I said. "It's her dad."

28

EMILY

Well, that was awkward.

It turned out that Alice was meeting her father. He was in town for work, and the big yellow envelope had contained cash for shopping and an upgraded first-class airline ticket. Alice was in the process of saying she'd rather sit in coach with the rest of us when Casper had crashed into them. Once the confusion of who was who was sorted out, and Alice's dad's driver had apologized to Casper, we all had a moderately good laugh about it. Of course, Alice had slowly turned to look at me when Casper explained I'd thought maybe she was involved in the cheating plot, which probably meant total social destruction when I got back to school. But hey, you might as well go out with a bang.

I got a text from my mom just as we were all sorting ourselves out.

"That's her dad," she said. "How nice. Are you having fun?"

"Yes," I replied, then put my phone in my backpack and decided to ignore it completely.

Alice seemed particularly touched that Casper had been willing to tackle a potential criminal in order to save her reputation, and her dad invited us to dinner with them. Casper seemed pleased and went, despite having already eaten dinner, but Chloe had somewhere else to be. That left Will and me, and I was about to make my apologies and head back to the Upper West Side, when Will spoke.

"It's very nice of you, sir, but Emily and I already have plans." He stepped back and shut the car door, and we both watched it glide away.

"We do?" I asked. "What are our plans?"

He pulled me close and kissed me. "I'm going to apologize for being kind of a dick about this whole thing, and then we're going to get the subway downtown to Union Square and get the best hot chocolate in the city."

"I do like hot chocolate."

"There you go," he said. "I'm sure your mom won't mind if you're a little late."

I shook my head. "I'll text her. She worries."

"Good idea," he said, then we turned and started walking back to the subway, side by side. I'd have to wait to text; I couldn't do it with one hand.

JESSICA

I had already sobered up quite a bit when I got another text from Emily, saying she was fine, she was with Will, and she was going to be a bit late. I told her I would see her at the hotel and turned to Amanda.

"That's nice," I said, "she's hanging out with the boy she likes."

"The one who gave her the chocolate?"

I nodded.

She smiled. "Well, hopefully they'll get up to all kinds of mischief and have a wonderful time."

"That would be good," I said, looking around for my handbag. "Kids are so serious these days."

Amanda walked me to the door. "You've given Emily the best seventeen years of your life, you've done everything for her. She's beginning to live her own life, and you can live yours, too."

I shrugged. "I am living my own life. Sometimes I felt I was working to take care of Emily, but maybe that was just a convenient excuse. I work because I love it, and I'm good at it. I'm not sure I wouldn't have been a crappy mother if I'd put my own needs second. Maybe I'm going to be the best mother ever of a young adult. Maybe little kids aren't my forte."

"Who knows?" said Amanda, opening the door. "Emily seems to have turned out totally awesome, regardless of your influence."

"Yeah." I stepped through the door and turned to face my friend. "Sometimes limits are their own form of freedom."

"You're stoned," she said. "Text me when you get to the hotel."

She shut the door and I hailed a cab. It was only when I got back to the hotel and went to the bathroom that I realized she'd totally let me leave the house with the stripy top hat still on my head.

She's probably still laughing about it.

........................▶

———

New York City

8:00 a.m.: Breakfast: Review of the tour

10:00 a.m.: Columbia University

12:00 a.m.: Lunch at famous Upper West Side institution
Tom's Restaurant

2:00 p.m.: NYU

◀........................

29

EMILY

Breakfast was surprisingly entertaining this morning. Will and I sat next to each other, as did Alice and Casper, who were clearly now an item. I prayed she wouldn't be a total bitch and dump him as soon as we all got back to LA. He wasn't her usual type (she tended to date older, cooler, scornful guys) but then again, Alice's superpower was her ability to transcend the trend. Her dad was sitting on her other side, trying to hide the fact he was full-on working, and failing completely.

I was kind of hoping the adventures of the night before would stay secret, but Alice opened breakfast with the story of Casper tackling her chauffeur, and everybody thought it was hilarious.

Well, everyone except Cassidy. She glared at me accusingly.

"Wait, the FBI told you someone on this trip was a potential cheater and you didn't tell me?"

I shook my head. "I didn't think it was true." This was a lie; I'd thought it was probably Alice or her mom, but I didn't need to underscore that again.

Cassidy clicked her tongue. "What if it had been true? What if the reputation of E3 was ruined forever on my watch? The embarrassing calls from admissions people was bad enough, but if this gets to my bosses, I'm done." She was clearly annoyed.

"I'm sorry," I said. "The FBI told me not to tell anyone." Then I made an egregious error. "Besides, what if it had been you?"

"Me?"

I paused, taking in the sudden glint in her eye, and shook my head. "No, of course not." I swallowed. "It couldn't possibly have been you."

"Me?" Cassidy stared around the ring of people, then completely blew her stack. "Me? Do any of you realize how hard the other side works? All of you are obsessed with your college applications, taking classes, hiring coaches, bribing people . . ."

She glowered accusingly at Alice, who turned up her palms.

"Not me, dude," she said. "Talk to my crazy-ass mother."

"Allegedly," chimed in her dad, ever the professional.

But Cassidy was past caring. "And none of you—NONE of you—ever think about the hours and days and weeks of work that go into the college process from the other side. The colleges have people working around the clock trying to fill each class with the best and most deserving kids, sorting through every single application, trying to make sure nothing gets missed and no one is unfairly treated, all the while being inundated with thousands upon thousands of essays and transcripts and personal statements and references and all of them are children with parents who pressure the shit out of them to be the best and then all of a sudden you don't get into your first choice, or your second choice, or your safety, and you end up going to community college and discovering that doesn't really make any difference!" She stared at us wildly. "It's what you do with it that matters! *It's all the goddamn same!!*"

She'd gotten up during this speech, presumably in order to get more lung capacity. "And the parents? The parents are the worst! They completely lose their minds, like academic bridezillas, focused on getting their precious mini-me into college and never for a minute thinking about what happens when the poor bastards actually get there, not to mention when they get out! God forbid they learn to fend for themselves or trust their own judgment or fail and struggle and succeed on their own terms. No! Everything has to be smoothed out and landscaped for Tiffany and Kody and Jasmine and Joshua, and if regular people get run over in the process, then that's how the cookie crumbles!" She threw her sheaf of papers into the air. "I've had it with you people!" She stormed out of the room, pulling her phone from her pocket as she went. The door slammed behind her and we all sat there in silence.

Alice's dad scrambled to his feet. "She's amazing. I'm going to hire her." He headed after Cassidy, and the rest of us sat there taking a moment to let our blood pressure settle.

Casper said, "Well, I've had a great week. And I have a confession: I already know I'm going to Caltech for earth sciences." He sounded sheepish. "I got in last year, but my parents thought I should finish high school like any other kid."

"Why did you come on the tour then?" asked Alice.

"Because my mom thought it would be a good social experience."

He smiled at his mom and suddenly hugged her. "And she was totally right."

Will spoke up. "Casper and I are starting a company together."

Casper nodded. "I filed articles of incorporation the other night."

"We're doing a monthly geology crate. It's going to be fantastic." Will looked around. "We're calling it Rock Gods."

"I'm helping them," added Alice. "I'm doing their social media."

I stared at her. "Since when do you like geology?"

"Since diamonds."

JESSICA

After a somewhat exhausting breakfast, most of us headed up to Columbia anyway. Cassidy was never heard from again, but I like to keep her number in my phone as a memorial to a fallen college admissions soldier.

Emily and I seem to have established a new . . . something. *Relationship* is putting it too strongly, as I managed to irritate her twice already this morning by asking her if she was hungry, but somehow the tension between us has lessened. She made some friends, she had an adventure, and I feel like maybe I didn't ruin her life by working all the time, which is a relief. I mean, maybe it wasn't ideal parenting, but you know what? After spending a week with a dozen other parents, I realize there is no such thing. Cheesy, maybe, but true nonetheless. We're all doing the best we can, for ourselves, for our kids, for the whole shebang.

Walking around the Columbia campus, I suddenly realized

Helen was right: I could go back to school myself. Why not? The point was, one phase of my life was coming to an end, but only that one bit. The rest was still my oyster. I could stay in my current job, I could move to Baltimore, I could move to New York, I could go be a sheepherder in Ulaanbaatar, if Ulaanbaatar is an actual place. (I googled it: It's the capital of Mongolia. You probably knew that.)

It's time for a new plan. Or maybe no plan at all.

EMILY

Columbia was a lovely campus, and I could see Mom was enjoying showing me everything. I feel like I know her better after this trip: the young woman she used to be (thanks to the weird ex-boyfriend), the friend and student (thanks, Helen), the young adult (Amanda and Robert), and I already knew what a good mom she was. She might have been at work all the time, but she was happy, busy, and I never thought she wouldn't put me first if she had to. And I learned to handle myself, so, you know, that's good. I guess this part is coming to an end, the kid part, but it's not the end of everything.

"Mom," I said, swallowing nervously. "Can we sit down a minute?"

"Sure," she said, heading over to sit on the edge of the fountain in the center of the main quad. "What's up?"

I took a deep breath. "Mom, I don't think I want to go to college at all."

She looked at me and tried out a smile. "What do you want to do instead?"

"I've been thinking about technical school."

She frowned. "Is that community college?"

I sighed. "No, Mom, it's a two-year college that teaches actual skills. I want to be a cabinetmaker."

"A what now?"

I smoothed my hands on my jeans. "Mom, do you remember Grandma's lathe?"

She nodded.

"I loved that lathe. I loved the smell of sawdust. I loved making things. Grandma taught me everything she knew about building stuff, because she loved it, too. But when she was my age, a woman couldn't really become a carpenter, or a welder, or a plumber, or whatever. It wasn't done. Now it is." I squeezed her hand. "You taught me I can be anything I want to be. You have work that you love, that makes you happy. I want that, too. I want to make things."

She didn't say anything for a moment.

I spoke again. "Mom, if I'm qualified in a skilled technical field, I will always have work. I was talking to Will's dad about this, he has a friend who's a steamfitter . . ."

"When did you have this conversation?"

"After breakfast the other day. Why is that important?"

"It doesn't matter. What's a steamfitter?"

"Someone who installs the heating and venting systems in large buildings, working with the architect, you know? His friend has a company that makes millions of dollars a year. He always has plenty of clients. And he still has a life."

She didn't look convinced.

"Mom, I know this is something people like us don't usually do, but it really appeals to me."

She was still quiet. Mulling it over, maybe. Or panicking.

"Are you worried what your friends will say?" I asked, feeling sick suddenly. She was ashamed of me. "I realize it's not very fancy, it's not something you can show off about . . ."

Finally, she spoke. "Emily Elizabeth Burnstein, do you think I give a single shit about what other parents think?"

"Uh . . ."

"Well, maybe I have at times, but you know what? I want you to find a life that works for you, and the fact that you've worked out what that might be is the best news I've heard all year." She pointed at me. "Emily, you are awesome, and I look forward to ordering a dining table, or whatever it is you end up making."

Will and his dad walked up, and my mom said, "Hey, Emily wants to be a cabinetmaker."

"Cool," said Will's dad. "Will wants to go to Caltech."

Will looked sheepish. "I want to stay close to home, and also, you know, Casper and I are starting our business."

"West Coast is the best coast," I said.

"True story," said Mom. "Do you guys want to blow off NYU and go to the Natural History Museum instead?"

"For sure," I said.

She seemed pretty stoked. She loves a museum shop, my mother.

Epilogue

From the *Larchmont Chronicle*:

LOCAL ARCHER SWEEPS STATE FINALS

Larchmont resident and mom Jessica Burnstein recently topped the senior category in the California State Archery Championships, in both compound and recurve contests. Burnstein plans to go on to the nationals, which will take place in the fall.

Acknowledgments

The careful and detailed itinerary of Jessica and Emily's college tour was created by Dr. Michelle Nitka, who is a Los Angeles–based expert on schools and education. She is also, sadly for her, my neighbor and very good friend. Any errors of timing or order are my fault completely.

Parenting teenagers is something of a shit show. I wouldn't be able to get through the day, let alone write, were it not for the friendship of Charlotte Millar, who's known me and my kids since we were all so much younger, and whose gentle counsel and fierce loyalty make her the very best of best friends.

I WAS TOLD IT WOULD GET EASIER

Abbi Waxman

Questions for Discussion

1. At the beginning of the book, Jessica and Emily don't have a very good connection, not because they don't love each other but because they've slowly grown apart. What's the difference between experiencing that kind of relationship damage compared to, say, a sudden breakup?

2. Jessica is a single parent by choice and a working mother. What cultural assumptions are made about both of those groups, and how do those assumptions affect Jessica's opinion of herself?

3. Jessica talks about the differences between parenting younger children and teenagers. Do her experiences match up with your own?

4. Emily is a very independent young woman. What impact do you think Jessica's parenting had on Emily?

5. Emily often compares herself to other young people and finds herself wanting. What strengths do you see in her character that she may not be able to see in herself?

6. Emily talks about the pressure on young people to be perfect in every way. How has that pressure changed over time, and why does it feel particularly hard to be young these days?

7. Jessica talks about the pressure on parents to be seen as "good at" parenting, as reflected in their children's success. Is this something new, or has it always been an issue?

8. As the tour progresses, both Jessica and Emily learn new things about each other. How does travel impact the way we see other people?

9. Towards the end of the novel, Jessica reflects that maybe she'll be a better parent once Emily is older. How has your relationship with your parents changed over time and, if you have children, once you yourself became a parent?

10. Ultimately Emily and Jessica are both changed by this trip. Have you ever taken a trip that had an unexpected personal outcome?

Ready to find
your next great read?

Let us help.

Visit prh.com/nextread